The Long Road Home

A Lucky Shores Novel

by

Kerry J Donovan

Edited by Nicole O'Brien.

The city of Lucky Shores is a figment of the author's imagination.

This book is written in US English and follows US grammar and punctuation conventions.

Dedication:

To my Meg, who brings a smile to my life and sense and peace to my world.

Chapter 1

A Wyoming Pit Stop

The curvy waitress in the tight uniform held up the carafe and leaned over the stainless steel counter, making sure Chet Walker didn't miss her guaranteed-to-increase-her-tips assets.

"Top off that coffee for you, honey?"

Her smile appeared genuine, and the bright setting sun through the plate glass windows brought a sparkle to her dark blue eyes.

Despite the location—a diner attached to a gas station—and the lateness of the hour, she looked fresher than she had any right to be. A homespun, woman-next-door type with a clear complexion to match the freshness of all outdoors and easy on the makeup. If the woman's welcoming smile said anything, Wyoming had to be a great place to set down some roots.

After spending the better part of two days driving through a dust-dry Midwest, tasting nothing but rest stop food and road grit, Walker appreciated both the change of scenery and the aroma.

Through the diner's recently polished windows, the nearby foothills of the Rockies promised his journey's end.

He could not wait.

"Thank you, ma'am. Can't remember the last time I refused a decent cup of java."

He pushed his near-empty cup forward.

She poured and ran a red-polished nail over the name embroidered on the pocket of her apron. "People hereabouts call me Shirley."

Shirley had a good, warm smile, too. It improved his mood, and no doubt the mood of all her patrons. Walker returned it with as much interest as a road-weary traveler could muster.

"Well, Shirley. You do make a fine cup."

Although not quite the best he'd ever tasted, her coffee *was* pretty good. If he kept a personal Billboard Coffee Hot 100, it might even have made his top ten. It would definitely make the top twenty.

The top dog, number one status in the coffee charts, belonged to an altogether different diner. If things panned out as expected, it would be the place he'd take his next breakfast. A diner owned by the most beautiful woman on the planet—bar none—and looking out on perhaps the third prettiest view in the world. Not that Walker was at all biased in its favor, of course. Oh no. Not a bit of it. His decision happened to be scientific in its scope and permanent in its nature.

Without doubt, the proximity of the *Lucky Shores Diner* had everything to do with Walker's current state of being—his growing excitement and optimism. Dang it, his happiness.

Inwardly, Walker smiled, but made sure to keep it from his face. Smiling too much in a public place might draw too much attention.

Yep.

He'd make Lucky Shores by morning even if he had to drive through the night to do it. Hence the additional cup of coffee.

Before leaving *Shirley's Place*—the name hanging in lights over the rest stop eatery—he'd get her to fill his two-pint thermos, and the emergency reserve would see him through the final leg of his journey. After that, he'd pick his way along narrow back roads and make it safely home.

Home.

It sounded so good in his head.

Although he'd only lived there for a few months of his life—winter months at that—Lucky Shores *was* his home. Home, both spiritually and emotionally. It was where his heart lay. His Josie.

While nursing his drink, Walker continued to stare through the window at the gently rising foothills of the Colorado Rockies. They started a few dozen miles out back of the gas station and cast an imposing shadow over the diner.

The thought of seeing his Josie again, this time without a ticking clock to mark the end of her brief holiday visits, made his spirits soar. The three-year wait would soon be over. The years had flown by in a whirl of antiseptic white walls, purple scrubs, and medical textbooks. But it had also dragged past in agonizing, super slow motion—especially the times when he crawled, exhausted, into his lonely bed. No one to hug. No one to hold. No one to share his life with. At least not in person.

Video calls could never make up for them being apart so long.

Walker cast his mind back to that early spring morning. The morning he broke the news and damn near broke his own heart in the process. He'd made his decision weeks earlier, but had chickened out of telling her, growing more anxious with each passing day. Eventually, he found his opportunity when they made their first pilgrimage to the destroyed cabin on the shores of Little Lake.

#

The log fire popped and fizzed in the grate, but it gave out more light than heat. Walker sat on a folding chair inside the ruins of Josie's mountain hideaway, huddled close to the flames. He waited for the sun to climb over Tooth Mountain and give life to a sparling new day.

Josie's justified desire to scatter Mickey's ashes over the quiet waters of Little Lake was as good an excuse as any and an early spring thaw the third weekend in March gave them the opening. Walker had an added reason to make the trip. He needed Josie alone.

Josie's recovery from the bullet wound had been nothing short of spectacular. As spectacular as the scenery surrounding him. She'd been on her feet after a week and had returned to the diner within fourteen days of leaving the hospital. Although Jean said she wouldn't be able to work at the saloon until Christmas, Josie made it back behind the bar by Thanksgiving.

The ornery creature could never take no for an answer.

Walker's run as the saloon's resident singer had gone pretty good. He wrote a bunch of new songs and debuted each one to a supportive if hugely biased audience.

His relationship with Josie flowered into something really special, forged in the fires of adversity. They worked hard, played harder, and adopted Millie—Doc Matthews's orphaned dog—by default. No one else in town wanted to offer a new home to the high-maintenance pooch.

Deep down, though, Walker knew it couldn't last. He couldn't live out the rest of his life as a busboy and occasional singer, tied to the apron strings of the beautiful woman who happened to be one of the richest people in the county. It didn't sit right with him.

Not one bit of it.

The trip from Lucky Shores to Riley's Cove—normally around six hours using the direct route via the river—had taken them ten. To Josie's huge annoyance, Walker had insisted they take fifteen-minute rest stops every hour to avoid risking her recovery, and they eventually reached Riley's Cove in a late evening drizzle. They scattered Mickey's ashes over the icy black water, pitched the tent, and turned in after a hurried supper of cocoa and fruit cake—a tribute to their first breakfast at Vantage Point.

Despite the warmth and relative comfort of the tent, Walker had spent a restless night listening to Josie's gentle breathing and remembering the first time they'd visited the cove. The memory of her bleeding to death in his arms put paid to all hope of sleep.

At 4:50 a.m., Walker gave up on rest. He rebuilt the fire, sat in a camp chair, and fought the cold, with a rifle lying across his lap—just in case. Animals weren't the only dangerous critters in the mountains.

Millie replaced Walker in the tent, and lay beside Josie, snoring and chasing butterflies in her dreams.

Despite his increasing nerves, Walker smiled.

Dumb dog.

The stars blinked out one by one, a gray light leached into the eastern sky, and the birdsong built into a rousing dawn chorus.

The moment the sun said a bright and cheery hello to the day, the tent flap moved, and Josie popped her head through the opening.

"Morning, sleepy head," he said and pointed to the pot suspended on a stake over the fire. "Coffee?"

"I'd love one."

She crawled from the tent and stood, back arched, and threw her arms overhead in a glorious yawning stretch. Her thermal undershirt lifted to expose the Z-shaped scar, still red, but fading by the week. She shivered and ducked back into the tent for her fleece.

Walker handed her a large mug of coffee—black, no sugar. Still standing, she blew over the top before taking a sip. "Couldn't sleep?"

"Things on my mind. We need to talk." He patted the seat of the spare camping chair.

She threw a hand to her breast. "Oh my God, that sounds ominous. You're not pregnant are you?"

He laughed. "Idiot. Come sit down. You need to hear this."

"Can it wait 'til I've watered the shrubbery? I'm bursting."

Five minutes later, she returned and took her seat. "What's up, Chet? You're worrying me."

She took a hankie from the pocket of her jeans, soaked it in water from a canteen, and wiped her hands and face.

"You know I can't stay in Lucky Shores forever, don't you? It's not working for me. I hate being a kept man. Everything I own can fit in a backpack and guitar case. You deserve so much more than that."

The speech he had planned in his head for so long didn't come out right. He reached out to hold her, but she slapped his hands away, jumped up, and marched to the water's edge. Millie growled, leaped from the tent, and raced to Josie's side, yapping like the demented mutt she really was at heart.

"Go then," Josie shouted, arms crossed, back toward him.

"Damn it, Josie. Please don't be like that. You know I can't live as your kept man, your pet. It wouldn't work. We'd end up resenting each other. I need to bring something more to our relationship than a few unrecorded songs. I need to earn a proper living, and ..."

She turned slowly, eyes brimming. "And?"

The word came out so quietly, he could barely make it out.

"... and ... that's why I'm leaving town next month."

The tears spilled and rolled down her cheeks. "You're going back on the road, to search for that elusive song?" Her words shot out in a plea. "If so, can I come too?"

He closed the gap between them. He'd screwed things up completely. She had it all wrong.

"No, that's not possible."

"Why not? I can sell the diner. Buyers are queuing up now the holiday resort's definitely going ahead. We can live off the money and use it to rebuild the cabin and put in a recording studio. Ship in a generator for power. You're a wonderful singer, Chet. Everyone loves you. And your songs ... they're brilliant."

Walker sighed. "No. Don't you see, it would be the same thing. You'd be keeping me fed and watered like Millie. I need to ..."

He stopped talking for a moment. His whole carefully choreographed plan had gone hideously wrong. Josie's tears tore him up inside.

"No, Josie, I'm sorry. I'm not explaining myself very well. Listen. I'm never gonna make it as a singer. There's too much luck involved, and I'm not really good enough. I know that now. Okay, I can hold a note and write a half-decent song, but there are tens of thousands of singer-songwriters in America who'll never make it big, and I'm one of them. We've both got to face that."

"I thought we were good together." She stepped back. The water splashed at her ankles. "I thought you loved me."

He grabbed her upper arms. She resisted his pull.

"Silly girl, I do love you. I love you more than anyone ... anything I've ever loved in my entire life. I want to spend the rest of my days with you. And that's why I have to go back east. It's all down to what I did in the mine."

"The mine?" Her face creased in confusion.

9

"Yes, the operation. When my hands stopped shaking it was sort of a revelation. They … the AMA, I mean, said I can carry over my original credits, but still need to sit all the exams again. One year. That's all it'll take. One year, and two more years of residency. After that, I can take my board certification."

Josie looked up at him, frowning. "You've lost me, Chet. What on earth are you talking about?"

"You know my mom's a surgeon, right? Well, she's pulled some strings at Johns Hopkins, and I'm going to retake my final year." He broke out a huge smile. "I'm going to become a doctor, Josie. And I plan to hang my shingle in Lucky Shores, if the town will have me. I'm also going to marry you. Again, if you'll have me."

Josie's brows knitted tighter together.

"I … I …"

Walker feigned shock. "Wow, now that's a first."

"What is?"

"Josie Donoghue, stuck for words."

She shook her head as though she was having trouble taking in all he'd said. Then she stopped and looked up at him, anger blazing in her dark brown eyes. She punched him hard in the chest.

"Ow," he said although it didn't hurt that much.

"Chet Walker, don't you ever do that to me again."

"Do what?"

"Frighten me like that."

"I'm so sorry. Been planning what I was going to say for weeks, but screwed it all up. Forgive me?"

"Yes, to both questions."

"Sorry?"

"Yes, I forgive you. Just this once, mind. And yes, I *will* marry you." She tilted her head up for a kiss. As usual, he complied, and he took plenty of time doing it.

After a long, long hug, they returned to the remnants of the cabin, arm in arm.

"Now that's all settled," he said, smiling wide, "how about you making good on your promise to cook me breakfast for letting you come up here?"

She faced him square on, hands planted firmly on hips.

"You *let* me come up here? Listen up, Chester Walker. Nobody *lets* me do anything. I do what I want and when I want. Get me?"

"Yes, Josie," he said, trying to look suitably downcast. "But you were under doctor's orders, remember."

"You aren't a doctor yet."

"True enough, but I will be soon."

"Hmm."

"So, what about some grub?"

"If I make breakfast, what do I get in return?"

He pointed to the guitar case. "I'll provide the background music."

She grinned. "It's a deal, so long as you help with the dishes. I'm not doing all the housework in this marriage."

"*Marriage*," he said. "Yep, I like the sound of that."

While she prepared breakfast, trying to fend Millie away from the food, Walker freed Suzy, his handmade, six-string, semi-acoustic guitar from her case and flexed some life into his cold fingers. He picked the opening to his latest tune, *On Lucky Shores*, and sang it to Josie for the first time.

Judging by her reaction, the song met with her approval.

Chapter 2

Another Diner in Another World

Still gazing though the diner's window, sipping the last of his second refill, Walker relaxed and allowed the smile to form. Reminiscing was good, but it didn't get the miles rolling under his wheels.

Josephine Donoghue, his pint-sized, feisty, mountain goat, dream of a woman—his muse, his love, and his fiancée—waited for him. He patted the outline of the jewelry box in his jacket pocket, inside which sat a modestly expensive diamond ring. Although they'd been engaged for nearly four years, he'd never done the "down on one knee" thing, nor had he presented her with a proper ring. He planned to correct the omission the minute he got her alone.

God, he'd missed her so damn much.

Walker blew gently across the top of his drink, sipped, and smacked his lips.

"Excellent."

Shirley straightened and pulled her assets away from his face, an act for which Walker was truly grateful as he needed the added breathing space. He'd seen and admired plenty of full-bodied women in a former life spent on the road, and back then, it was fine. But his head had been turned and his heart won by an elfin creature with a slim frame, a stunning smile, and the fighting spirit of an Irish banshee.

Shirley tilted her head in appraisal. "You look kinda beat, honey. Been on the road long?"

Walker scratched his two-day stubble and hid a yawn behind his hand. "Six years, give or take, but only a couple of days for this particular trip. It shows, huh?"

"A little." She nodded. The blonde fringe fell into her blue eyes, and she scraped it away with the little finger of her left hand. The wedding band on her ring finger glowed under the light of the setting sun.

"You a New Yorker?"

He narrowed his eyes. "Didn't think my accent was that obvious."

"It ain't, but the Empire State tags on your Ford gave you away."

Walker took another pull of coffee before responding.

"So, as well as grilling one heck of a burger and producing this fine coffee, you're a detective in your spare time?"

"Not particularly. Just observant. Helps to pass the long hours. We don't get too many out of state visitors in these parts. This here's not what you'd call a tourist destination. Where you heading?"

Walker took a second before answering. Apart from the two of them, the diner stood empty. No truckers fueling up for an overnight trip, no cops on a clichéd donut run, just Shirley and Walker in a quiet little tête-à-tête. Despite the apparently come-hither welcome, she gave the vibe of wanting nothing more than to pass the time with some innocent conversation, which was fine by Walker. He'd give her as long as it took to finish his drink and use the facilities.

A few minutes chatting to a lonely waitress at the end of her working day wouldn't hurt. He stretched his back and rolled the crick from his neck before resting his elbows on the counter, hands cradling the coffee cup.

"I left Syracuse at nine thirty yesterday morning, and I'm aiming to reach home in time for breakfast tomorrow."

Shirley climbed onto a stool next to the till, keeping a respectable distance between them, and poured herself a cup of the brown stuff. She added creamer and three sugars, demonstrating how she maintained her comfortable figure. Walker wondered what her cholesterol count might read.

Quit that, Chet. You're off duty.

13

Shirley pursed her lips and took a delicate sip. "Where exactly do you call home?"

"Tiny place in the high Colorado Rockies you'll never have heard of."

"Try me," she asked, looking over the top of her coffee, eyes bright, full lips still stretched in a pleasant smile.

"Lucky Shores."

She sat up straight. "You're kidding, right? The city on a lake where they're building that massive ski resort?"

Walker couldn't prevent his brows arching to his hairline. "You *have* heard of it."

"Shoot, honey. Everyone in this part of the state's heard of Lucky Shores. That city's finally living up to its name, huh?"

Walker resumed his default expression—noncommittal—and added a shrug for good measure. "Lucky Shores hardly rates the title 'city.' A few dozen streets, a fishing dock, a small harbor, and that's about all."

Shirley frowned. Confusion painted her mobile face. "Hell no. You got that wrong. The place is booming. Biggest development site in the whole of Colorado. Hadn't you heard? Thought it was your home?"

Walker nodded. "It is. If you'll excuse the cliché, home is where the heart rests. I've been away a little over three years."

The waitress dipped her head and took another sip, regarding him from over the top of her cup. "Long time. You'll notice one hell of a difference, honey. That's for sure."

He nodded. "Guess so."

During her all-too-sporadic and flying visits, Josie had deliberately avoided discussing the changes to her home town. Truth was, they had other, more pressing things on their minds. For his part, Walker didn't have the spare capacity or the inclination to search the internet for news of his future home. But he had felt Josie's tension as the years passed. Wouldn't be long now before he found out exactly what had happened to Lucky Shores in his absence.

He couldn't wait.

"Dwight, my husband, is a civil engineer," Shirley said. "Been working up there ever since they started construction on the ski lifts. I ain't never seen the place, but Dwight says we'll take winter breaks up there soon as it's finished. Don't think that'll happen any time soon, though"—she waved her free hand at the pristine little eatery—"this place takes up most of my time. Anyhow, the way Dwight tells it, Lucky Shores is a peach of a town."

Walker couldn't disagree. "Most beautiful place I ever saw, and I've seen quite a few places in my time."

She cupped her mug in her hands and stared into the dispersing foam. "Dwight says when the construction's done and the resort's open, Lucky Shores is gonna rival Breckenridge. Maybe even Aspen." She sipped some more coffee and added a heavy sigh. "Don't help me none, though. Hardly see Dwight for weeks on end, and when he does come home, he spends most of his time asleep. Long-distance relationships can put a strain on the strongest marriages."

Tell me about it.

Her head snapped up and her eyes met his, wariness dulled their shine. "Darn, didn't mean that to come out the way it did. Me and Dwight are solid. It wasn't no pickup line."

Walker raised a hand and patted it in the air between them.

"That's okay, Shirley. I didn't take it that way, and I'm already spoken for. My fiancée and I've been living apart for more than three years, but I'm happy to say that all stops tomorrow morning."

He took another drink and stared through the window once more. The sun shot orange flames into the pale sky and looked to be trying to melt the snow from the lofty peaks.

"Your fiancée lives in Lucky Shores?"

Walker paused before nodding. He really wanted to get moving. "Sure does. Owns a diner not unlike this one."

Not unlike, although the view in the Lucky Shores Diner— both behind the counter and through the windows—happened to be a million times better. No offence to the comely Shirley.

15

"You kidding. Ms. Donoghue's your fiancée?"

Walker took his turn to sit up straighter. "You know Josie?"

Shirley shook her head. "'Course not. I ain't never set foot in Lucky Shores, not yet. But Dwight says the townsfolk call her Joey."

"Josie's my name for her. Rest of the town knows her as Joey. It's short for Josephine."

Shirley arched an eyebrow and dipped her head in a nod. "Understood. Dwight says she's the brightest woman living in that town. Fair tweaked my jealous bone when he first started talking 'bout her, but he said I didn't have no cause to fret on account of her being in love with some trainee doctor from way back east. He says the guy's going to take over the town's hospital the moment he gets himself qualified. I'm guessing that'd be you, huh?"

He tilted his head to the side in a self-deprecatory shrug. "Guilty as charged."

She pushed out a water-reddened hand. "Pleased to make your acquaintance, Doctor …"

Heat rose to Walker's face. His brand new title still had the power to make his stomach flip and his face flush warm.

"Walker, Chet Walker. Likewise, Shirley."

They shook hands formally.

"According to Dwight, just about everyone in Lucky Shores speaks highly of you. They say you and Ms. Donoghue saved the town from bankruptcy."

Again, Walker shrugged. "That was all down to Josie. I didn't do much more than cling to her shirttails."

She scoffed.

"Mr. Google and the local news media tell it different."

"Don't believe everything you read in the papers or see on the newsfeeds. Nothing but hype and bull-jerky."

She gave him a look that said she didn't believe him but was happy to let it pass.

"Seems there's a picture of you behind the counter in the Lucky Shores diner and another behind the bar in the saloon. You

16

don't look like the way Dwight describes you from the photo, mind you. What happened to the long hair and the beard?"

Walker rubbed the back of his head and grimaced at the barely-familiar cropped style. "The attendant on my last rotation frowned on residents who turned up on the unit looking like members of a rock group."

"Shame. I reckon you'd look pretty cool with long hair and whiskers. 'Specially with those silver streaks flashing at your temples. Not that it's any business of mine, y'understand."

As though to emphasize her point, she stood and loaded her cup into the dishwasher. Then she grabbed a tray and started bussing the tables. It wouldn't take her long. It was a small place with only eight tables, six of which were already spotless.

Walker let out a breath. Shirley's words brought some relief. Although he didn't consider himself God's gift to the opposite sex, he'd been sidestepping the amorous advances of women ever since his voice changed. For some reason, things had gotten worse during his years of residency. He never could figure out why certain folks found doctors a romantic challenge when most hospital residents spent their time out on their feet through overwork. Most days he flopped into bed, asleep before he'd face-planted into the pillow, and awoke five hours later with all the energy and charm of a ten-day-old cadaver.

Since passing his medical boards and becoming a fully qualified medical practitioner—six days earlier—Walker had done nothing but stay at his parents' house, sleeping, wrapping up his affairs, packing his meager possessions into his new car, and preparing for his brand new life.

While Shirley cleared the final table and Walker finished his coffee, the last arc of the sun slipped behind the razor-tipped mountains and the western sky changed from pale orange to blood red. Over the hills lay a new home and a new life. He'd left the old one behind with excitement for the future, but sadness in the leaving.

Looking back from the perspective of a two-day road trip, the parting scene with his parents held an almost comical stiffness.

As expected, Walker's dad, Brigadier-General Atlee Dean Walker, took his son's departure in his default, stiff-backed, hide-all-emotion manner. An time-served professional soldier, he refused to let his emotions show. Mom, the harried and exhausted chief of surgery at St. Joseph's Hospital, Syracuse, had been shiny-eyed from the moment Walker returned home and started packing. On the morning of his final day, she fell to pieces, and her tears ran in streams down her cheeks.

When he'd left for his musical odyssey nearly six years earlier, Walker disappeared without warning, and she'd missed out on the exquisitely painful, teary departure. Walker couldn't do the same thing to her for a second time. She'd earned her sad parting, and he was determined to let her wallow in its painful glory. His throat had tightened in sympathy.

"Lucky Shores isn't the other side of the world, Mom," he told the top of her head as they hugged beside his car for the final time.

"That's true enough," Dad said, his face still deadpan, "but we'd be able to reach Sydney, Australia in half the time it takes to make it to Hicksville, Colorado." He counted off the journey on his fingers. "Drive from here to Hancock National. Take the red eye to Denver International. Cool our heels for seven hours waiting for the connecting flight into Aspen or Grand Junction, whichever's open. And that depends on the time of year and the weather conditions. After that, we need to hire a car and drive the rest of the way to the Boonies on two-lane blacktops that are barely passable during the winter months. Two days minimum if the connections all work. Did I get that about right, son?" His gruff voice contradicted the barely hidden emotion behind the words.

Walker gazed at his old man, trying to swallow past the boulder in his throat. "Jeez, Dad. Who taught you how to power up the laptop and use Trip Advisor?"

Dad tucked in his chin. "Yeah, well. You don't expect your mom and me to drive across the country for the wedding, do you?"

Walker shuffled his feet. "Don't go getting your hopes up, Dad. I haven't really asked her formally, and we still haven't set a date."

The retired soldier snorted and drilled Walker with a look that would have had his former subordinates melting into a puddle of military flop sweat.

"What planet do you think we live on, boy?" he said and rubbed his grizzled gray flattop. "Just 'cause your mom and I are a couple of old codgers doesn't mean we walk around with our eyes closed. That girl's a keeper, and—"

Mom waved her hand to silence him. "You speak for yourself, old man. There's only one pensioner in this here conversation."

Dad scrunched his face into a mock scowl and deferred to the only person on the planet he'd allow to interrupt him short of POTUS himself. "Well, we've seen the way you look at each other. Josie and your mother have been video calling and planning the shindig for months."

Walker turned to his mom. "You've been doing what?"

She smiled through the drying tears. "Never you mind, Chester Walker. Just be careful driving all those miles. Take plenty of time and rest up along the way. Josie won't be happy if you have an accident on the route."

"Neither will I, Mom." He smiled.

She kissed his cheek, wiped off the lipstick with a snick of her thumb, and hugged tight to Dad's arm while Walker slid behind the Ford's steering wheel and reversed out the drive onto the road.

He blinked back a tear of his own as his parents grew smaller in the rearview mirror and disappeared when he rounded the first corner.

#

Walker smiled at the happy reminiscence and refused Shirley's offer of a third and final top off. Instead, she filled his thermos to the brim, and he sealed the lid ahead of the final leg of the trip. After a quick visit to the rest room, he sidled up to the counter. "I'll be on my way now. What do I owe you?"

Shirley rang up the ticket and handed it across. He paid in cash.

"Lucky Shores is a good six hours from here," she said, looking into the darkness. "You planning on driving through the night?"

"Yep." He nodded. "Been away more than long enough."

"Take it slow on the switchbacks when you reach the high mountains. I guess your Ford has all-wheel drive?"

"Yes, ma'am. It's the main reason I nearly bankrupted myself buying the beast last week. I've seen what happens to drivers who take liberties on those mountain roads, especially in winter."

He shivered at the memory of his first arrival at the outskirts of Lucky Shores and the accident that had indirectly led to Mickey Donoghue's death. On a positive side, the tragedy had ultimately resulted in his meeting Josie, and for that miracle he would be eternally grateful. He tipped his hat to Shirley and made ready to leave.

The roar of a high-revving diesel engine destroyed the quiet of the evening. Shirley stared past Walker's shoulder through the huge window.

"What on God's green earth is he doing?"

A beat-up old station wagon—a late '70s GMC—screeched to a bumping, sliding halt inches behind Walker's car, throwing up a cloud of dust and grit. A diagonal crack ran across the mud-spattered windshield. Body panels were half-eaten by rust. The thick layer of red mud probably held the old wreck together. Blue-black exhaust gasses shrouded the parking lot.

The driver's door wrenched open. Hinges squealed. A young man—no more than a kid—jumped out. Scrawny, wide-eyed, bathed in sweat. Blood spotted his grubby shirtfront.

He staggered into the diner and leaned against the counter, holding tight to the edge as if to keep himself upright. Desperate bloodshot eyes ignored Walker and latched onto Shirley.

"H-Help … p-please help!" he cried between gasps. "I-I n-needs me a … a … am-bul-ance."

Chapter 3

Baby Blues

Shirley reached into the front pocket on her apron, fished out a cell phone, and dialed.

Walker closed on the lad, who had collapsed in a panting, eye-rolling heap the moment he delivered his message. He sat on the floor, leaning against the counter. Knees up, arms wrapped around bent legs, the kid started rocking. Tears flowed down hollow cheeks ingrained with dirt. Silent sobs wracked his gaunt frame.

Walker squatted in front of him, but kept at arm's distance, not wanting to crowd the distraught kid.

"Are you hurt?" he asked quietly, noting the blood-spattered shirt, but seeing no obvious injury.

"S-She started wailing. Cut herself b-bad. Real bad. B-Blood spurting ever'where. I tell't her. I tell't her not to do it. But ... but she wouldn't listen."

The lad stared at the floor tiles between his feet, seemingly oblivious to Walker's question.

"All that b-blood and water. I c-couldn't do ... c-couldn't do nothing for her. Then she up and went to sleep."

Tears continued to flow from vacant eyes.

Walker touched the boy's forearm. He flinched. His head jerked up, and he seemed to notice Walker for the first time.

"C-Couldn't do n-nothing. N-Nothing for her. Honest. Phone's been cut off years ... an' I had to leave her." The boy unclasped his hands and grabbed Walker's arm. "I t-tried. I d-did. But couldn't carry her none. Had to leave her there. Oh, Lord A'mighty. She be dead by now. Must be."

Walker tore free of the kid's grasp and took him by the shoulders. "What happened? Who are you talking about, your wife?"

"N-No, no." The kid shook his head. Sweat flew from the tips of his straggly hair and landed on Walker's sleeve. "My s-sister. She ... she growed big. You know. Big belly. Like dogs as are having pups. Can't walk ... and I c-can't ... c-can't carry her none. You gonna go help her, mister? Won't ya? W-Won't ya?"

"I'll try, son. What's your name?"

The boy's expression changed from fear to confusion. He blinked twice before lowering his head.

"Help her, mister. Please, h-help her. Couldn't carry her. So much b-blood, an' all. She were screaming so loud. Then she stopped an' f-fell asleep. I had to get out. Get help. Papa's gone. Went up mountain and he ain't, ain't ..." He lifted his head and stared at Walker again, eyes pleading. "Can you help her, mister?"

"I'll do what I can, son."

Walker patted the kid's shoulder and stood.

With her back turned toward him and the boy, Shirley spoke quietly into her cell phone. Walker could see her in the mirrored wall above the sink. The color had drained from her face. Her eyes met his in the reflection. She said something else, hit the screen to end the call, and turned to face him.

"Ambulance can't get there for at least forty-five minutes. Police will make it in about thirty."

"Get there? You know this boy? You know where he lives?"

Shirley nodded, still frowning. "That there's Little Billy Hatfield. Didn't know he could drive. He's a little"—she tapped a finger against her temple and lowered her voice—"slow-witted, you know?"

Walker nodded. That much had been obvious.

Shirley continued. "The Hatfields have a farmstead of sorts, three miles up Chain Cut Road. Mind you, farmstead's too grand a term for it. Far as I know, they scratch out a bare living rearing a few pigs and hunting, but ..."

"Billy said something about his Papa being gone. 'Up mountain.' Might mean the youngsters have been left on their own."

Shirley nodded slowly. "Haven't seen old Fulton Hatfield for an age. Months maybe. Wondered what had happened to them all. Strange man, Fulton. Full of fire and brimstone, y'know? Bible spouter. Keeps his family isolated."

Walker spared a glance at Billy, who had returned to his earlier position, arms folded around bent legs, swaying to an internal rhythm, still shivering.

"Can you spare the boy some water?"

"Of course. What was I thinking?" She shook her head, reached for a glass, and filled it from a siphon.

"Said he has a big sister," Walker said, looking down at the kid.

Shirley shook her head. "No, that ain't right. There's Mary Anne, but she's only thirteen. Some six years younger than Billy. Haven't seen her for months, neither. Why?"

"I think that's her blood on his shirt."

Shirley threw a hand to cover her mouth.

Walker had put the information together and didn't like the implications. Shirley seemed to be drawing the same conclusions.

"The Hatfield place, how easy is it to find?"

Shirley tilted her head to one side.

"Easy enough. Turn left out back, drive two miles south, and take the first right. That's called Chain Cut Road, but it's more a dirt track really. Take it slow or you'll likely bust an axle. Keep going until it peters out. You'll find the place no problem. Ramshackle clapboard house held together with spit and prayers."

Walker took a couple of seconds to ground himself, trying to think what emergency equipment he carried in the car and balance that against what he might find at the farm. His medical bag contained the basics. Probably all he needed to deliver a baby, but clean linen and hot water?

"Do you have any towels?"

"What?"

24

"Billy's confused. I think he's misunderstanding the symptoms. From what he tells me, his sister's in labor. She might have already delivered the baby."

"Pregnant? But she's only thirt—"

"We don't have time for that now. Do you have any spare towels?"

"Yeah, sure. Just a minute." She ran to a door along from the serving counter and disappeared inside. "How many do you need?"

"As many as can you spare."

Seconds later she reappeared with a pile of folded towels in her arms and a heavy-duty flashlight.

"Thought you might need this. I'm not sure what the Hatfields have in the way of power."

Walker took the offerings and rushed out the door shouting, "Take care of Billy and point the ambulance in my direction the moment it gets here. No telling what I'll find when I get there."

"'Course I will. You look after—"

The door closing behind him blocked out the rest of her warning.

#

Whoever christened Chain Cut Road must have been either a liar or a comedian. The deeply rutted track didn't deserve to be called a road. Walker's SUV, in four-wheel drive mode, barely made the incline as the trail, hacked out of the virgin forest, snaked its way up the side of a mountain so steep he wondered how the Ford managed to stay upright through the turns. He used low drive and took it as slow as he dared.

How Billy had coaxed the ancient GMC down the hill and made it to the service station in one piece, Walker couldn't imagine. Luck and a fair wind must have played a part.

After three miles that felt like thirty, the track widened into a turning spot and opened into a small clearing. The Ford's headlights raked the farmstead and picked out the faded, hand-painted letters on a warped sign.

Hatfield Livestock Co.
Private Property. Keep Out.
Trespassers will be shot.

Such a warm welcome.
Wonder where they hang the bunting?
Behind a sagging five-bar gate, a big shack—too dilapidated to be called anything else—stood between a cruddy barn and a bunch of single-story outhouses. If the buildings had seen better days, they'd have seen them before the Great Depression.

He parked in front of the gate, killed the engine, and switched to his parking lights. He cracked open his door and listened.

With little wind to rustle the canopy, an oppressive quiet boomed around him. Tall pines loomed overhead. No owls screeched, and no critters scurried through the bushes or disturbed the undergrowth. Only the clicking of the cooling engine broke the threatening stillness.

The sweet smell of the mountains had bypassed the Hatfield farm, beaten into submission by mildew, rot, and pigswill. Of the animals, there was no sight or sound.

The area's only illumination came from the Ford's parking lights.

Brooding, ominous silence.

Walker shivered, grabbed the flashlight from the pile of towels on the passenger seat, and played the wide beam over the front of the main house—a two-story wooden monstrosity with more than half the windows boarded over. The roof sagged as badly as the gate, and missing shingles promised wet rooms when it rained.

"Mary Anne?" he called. "I'm Dr. Walker. Billy sent me. Don't be scared. I'm here to help."

Walker tugged the lever to operate the Ford's tailgate. It sighed open. He collected his medical bag and the towels, and headed for the house.

He climbed the three steps leading up to a wraparound porch. The treads sagged and creaked under his weight, and he half expected each one to give way and drop him to the ground below. The front door stood partially ajar and opened into a front room. He shouldered the door fully open, crossed the threshold, and stood on bare floorboards that creaked worse than the steps. The whole place smelled of mold and decay. The flashlight's beam cut a brilliant white cone through the gloom.

"Mary Anne? I'm coming to help you. Are you upstairs?"

He paused and listened but heard nothing other than silence.

A threadbare carpet covered a part of the floor once designated a living area, and a kitchen of sorts lined the far wall. As a sign of defiance to the grim interior, someone had cleaned and stacked pots and flatware neatly on the drainer. A posy of cut flowers, dead and drooping, stood in an old-fashioned milk bottle on the kitchen windowsill. The tall yellow ones with the red eye in the center were blanket flowers—Josie's favorite.

Someone had tried to give the place a homey feel. They'd failed miserably, but at least they'd made the effort. A rusted oil lamp hung from the center of the room. It was cold to the touch. Walker shook it. Empty.

On the left, an open staircase—bare treads and no risers—led up to a rectangular black hole.

"Mary Anne. Where are you?"

A whimpering above his head had Walker racing up the rickety staircase. He kept to the sides where the treads would likely be the strongest. At the top of the stairs, he followed the sound, turned left, and entered a small, unlit bedroom.

An iron-rich tang suffused the air. Blood mixed with urine and human feces.

A tiny, pale-skinned girl, no more than a child, lay on a mattress on the floor, still and lifeless. A dark patch discolored the nightdress between her legs.

Walker shone the light on a scene of darkness and squalor.

Movement!

Movement beneath the nightdress was accompanied by the barely discernible mewling of a newborn.

A moan escaped the girl's cracked lips.

Thank God. She's still alive.

Walker rushed forward and knelt beside the makeshift bed. The woman-child's eyes flickered open. Fear showed in the cornflower blues.

"My baby …"

"Don't worry, Mary Anne. I'm a doctor. You're safe now."

"Billy? Where's Billy?"

"At the gas station. He raised the alarm. He's scared, but he'll be looked after."

"Papa?"

Walker didn't really know who she was referring to, but made the obvious connection.

"I told you, Billy's safe," he said, trying to keep the anger from his voice. "Let's worry about everything else later. I need to check this little one over and cut the cord."

Walker lifted the sodden cotton to expose what he expected to be carnage, but the hour-old baby—a full-term girl who looked perfect in every way—rested safely between her mother's thighs, sucking her thumb and apparently quite content with her lot.

The placenta had been expelled and post-partum bleeding had all but stopped. Relief flooded though Walker and he couldn't help smiling in wonder at the tenacity of life. Although he knew all the terms and processes leading to childbirth, the power of nature never ceased to amaze him.

After pulling on a pair of surgical gloves, he picked up the newborn and checked her vitals. Walker wiped her face with a sterile cloth from his bag, and lay her on her mother's stomach, wrapped in one of Shirley's clean and fluffy towels. He helped Mary Anne sit up, opened a bottle of water, and drip fed it to the new mother. The water revived her in another of nature's wondrous miracles.

She threw him a weak smile. "Thank you, Doctor."

"Just relax for a sec. I need to cut the cord."

Walker closed his eyes and cast his mind back twelve months to his pediatric rotation. He didn't have the exact kit in his bag and would have to improvise.

After confirming the umbilical cord had no pulse, he tied suture thread as makeshift clamps, and made the cut with a pair of sterile scissors. Blood oozed from the severed ends of the cord, but stopped within seconds as the tube emptied.

The infant gurgled happily in her mother's arms, apparently none the worse for her ordeal.

"Baby will be getting hungry soon. Do you know how to feed her?"

Mary Anne's lower lip quivered and she shook her head.

"Don't worry. You did the difficult part all on your own. Feeding her will be easy."

As if on cue, the baby wriggled and started crying. Walker showed the girl what to do, and the baby took over. The little mite latched on and started sucking. Mary Anne's contented smile brought a lump to Walker's throat. It brought anger too. How could this sort of thing happen in the richest country in the world? Two kids, one of them with special needs, left to fend for themselves in the back woods of Wyoming, less than ten miles from the Interstate.

How did they survive?

Where were their parents? Their father?

No matter. Mother and baby were doing well. Social Services would have to handle the fallout. Walker's official responsibility ended when the ambulance and paramedics arrived. Since he was just passing through the area, he couldn't offer Mary Anne anything more than stop-gap medical treatment.

Behind him, the bedroom door crashed open. A thin man—full black beard, wild eyes, lank salt and pepper hair hanging down to his shoulders—stood framed in the doorway. His angular shape matched that of Billy Hatfield, only taller and older.

Legs apart and braced, he carried a big black hunting rifle. Its muzzle pointed squarely at Walker's chest.

Chapter 4

Standoff

T he wild man's eyes glazed in the torchlight.

"Who the Devil are you and what you doing with my daughter?" The man's voice boomed through the small room. Mary Anne whimpered. The baby lost her hold on the nipple and started crying.

Walker raised his hands.

"Mr. Hatfield?"

"Who's asking?"

"I'm Dr. Walker. I ran into Billy at the gas station. He pointed me here."

The way the wild man's eyes roamed over his daughter's exposed body turned Walker's stomach. Enlightenment struck, and he made a mental promise to apologize to Billy for thinking the worst of him. Mary Anne's questioned "Papa?" became clear, too. Anger boiled through Walker, but he took care not to show it.

"How's the baby?" Hatfield asked, his voice an emotionless grunt. He lowered the rifle a couple inches but kept his finger curled around the trigger.

"She seems fine, sir."

"The Good Lord be praised."

The Good Lord has nothing to do with this, buddy.

"The afterbirth looks healthy and complete," Walker continued, "but the doctors will want to give them both a full examination at the clinic. The ambulance will be here soon."

Hatfield dragged feverish eyes from his daughter's breasts and turned them on Walker. His upper lip curled into a sneer. "Ain't no ambulance gonna make it up that drive, boy. And ain't nobody gonna take my family from me but the Good Lord hisself."

The way Hatfield spoke, with triumph in his eyes and a challenge in his voice, turned Walker's blood to ice. The rifle's huge muzzle remained pointed at his belly. Hatfield's trigger finger tightened. It wouldn't take much added pressure for things to end badly. Walker swallowed hard.

Take it easy, Walker. Keep cool.

"Mind if I stand? Getting a crick in my neck looking up at you."

Hatfield jerked up his bearded chin. "If'n you have to, son. But do it slow. Real slow."

"Thank you, sir."

Walker pushed himself to his feet and raised his hands again, an act of supplication. The rifle's muzzle rose with him to maintain its target. Walker took half a step to the side. Any shot fired at him would miss mother and daughter.

Walker licked his lips. Tasted Shirley's coffee.

Hell.

It dawned on him. If he'd refused that second refill, he'd have been on his way to Lucky Shores, and well out of this domestic quagmire. But then again, Mary Anne and the baby might not have survived.

You've done a good thing here, Walker. See it through.

Hatfield leaned against the door jamb. Walker followed the rifle's movement.

"The police will be here soon," he said. "They'll help me transfer Mary Anne and her baby to the ambulance."

Hatfield's eyes burned, he pushed away from the door, and took half a step forward. His fingers tightened on the stock.

"I told, ya. Ain't no one taking my family from me. Sheriff Hoover knows better'n to send any of her men onto my property, if'n they value their hides."

"Mr. Hatfield," Walker said, keeping his voice low, controlled, "no one's taking your family away. It's just that the baby needs to be checked over, registered, and given her shots. And Mary Anne's suffered a little tearing. She'll need stitches and antibiotics to guard against infection."

"Tearing?" Hatfield's brows creased in confusion. "What?"

"Yes, Mr. Hatfield. It happened during the delivery. Quite normal, but a gynecologist needs to patch her up before …"

"Papa?" Mary Anne's trembling voice floated up from the floor.

Hatfield turned toward the sound.

Now!

Walker shoulder-charged and pinned the smaller man against the doorframe. He grabbed the muzzle, pushing it up and away from the girls.

The weapon exploded, deafening in the confined space. Heat from the shot scorched Walker's hand.

Hatfield roared and turned, trying to yank the rifle from Walker's iron grip. The slightly built man proved stronger than he looked. Walker found himself locked in a power struggle he couldn't lose.

Hatfield's shoulder muscles bulged and the sinews in his neck corded. He was winning.

The wild man used the rifle's length to gain leverage, concentrating on the weapon, not his opponent. It gave Walker the opening he needed.

He released his grip on the rifle. Hatfield yanked hard, twisted, and fell backwards, cracking the back of his head against the sharp edge of the open door. He grunted.

Walker threw a stiff-knuckled punch to Hatfield's exposed kidney. The pig farmer squealed and crumpled to the floor, ending up in a gasping, groaning heap. Walker wrenched the rifle from the man's hands and stepped back out of reach.

The baby squealed, Mary Anne cried, and Hatfield stared up at Walker through pain-filled, teary eyes.

"Whatcha go and do that for? I weren't gonna hurt ya none. Them's my babies, and I'm only protecting what's mine. As the Good Lord is my Holy witness."

"Your babies? You mean your daughter and your grandchild, don't you?"

Hatfield hesitated before nodding so hard his lank hair flopped into his eyes. He swiped the strands away.

"Yeah. That's 'xactly what I meant. Daughter and granddaughter. That's right. As the Good Lord is my Holy witness."

Yeah, you already said that.

"And you're going to try to convince me Billy's the father?"

"Billy? 'Course it's Billy," Hatfield said, hugging the floorboards and refusing to meet Walker's eye. "No one else it could be. Ain't no one visits this place for months on end. 'Course, it could be of them boys from Grafton Falls when we went to town for provisions. Mary Anne's turned out to be a whore, just like her momma. The mark of the fornicatin' Beast is upon her. If'n that's the case ain't no telling who's the child's daddy."

He slid his gaze from the rifle to Mary Anne and back again.

Walker worked the rifle's bolt, ejected the spent shell, and slid a fresh bullet into the chamber. Hatfield's rambling words and strengthening voice told him two things. The pig farmer would throw the blame for Mary Anne's condition anywhere it would stick. Anywhere but onto himself. It also told him that the man was recovering from the bruised kidney quicker than he should have done.

"Keep on the floor and shuffle yourself over into that corner below the window. Sit cross legged. Hands under your butt, palms up."

"Huh?" Hatfield frowned. "What's that you say?"

Walker raised the rifle and took aim somewhere close to the pig farmer's groin. "You heard me. I don't like to repeat myself, nor do I have much patience for pedophiles."

Hatfield's jaw dropped and his eyes bugged wide. "What the Hell! I … I ain't no pedo—"

"Save it for the judge. I'm not listening."

Walker jerked the rifle, pointing it at the corner. Still frowning and grumbling, Hatfield shuffled sideways. He worked his way into the corner and crossed his legs.

"Sit on your hands, palms up."

"Huh?"

"Palms up, I said. Turn those hands over."

Walker had seen the trick in a film. Making a prisoner sit with the palms up removed the ability to use his hands for leverage. Thank heavens for Saturday morning reruns of old black and white movies.

"Whatcha planning, boy?" Hatfield said, his eyes darting around the room, assessing his options.

"Well, I thought we'd just rest here nice and friendly and wait for the police. Won't be long now. But you know what?"

"What?"

Walker aimed the rifle at Hatfield's groin. "What I really want is the excuse to shoot you in the crotch. People who hurt kids are the lowest form of life on the planet, and when those kids happen to be their own children ...." Walker threw him an evil smile. "Well, you'll understand when I ask you to please, please try to get your gun back."

Walker cast his mind back a week or so to when he recited the Hippocratic Oath in front of a gathering of his peers. At this precise moment, in this filthy bedroom, he had no use for the words, "First do no harm."

Would he really shoot the man who raped his own teenage daughter and tried to lay the blame on a son with cognitive dysfunction? Walker didn't have to wait long for the answer.

Hell yes.

The baby's crying stilled. Walker risked a quick glance to the mattress. Mary Anne had reattached her child to the breast and stared down at the baby. A content smile softened her shockingly young face. Despite everything she'd suffered, a mother's love for her child shone through bright and strong. There was hope for the two, but only if he could get them away from their abusive father and keep them away.

Walker reached into his back pocket for his mobile, but, as expected, it showed no signal. Billy had already told him the phone line was down. Should he risk carrying mother and child to his car and drive them down the mountain or wait for the cops?

If he could find a way to restrain Hatfield, the first option might be better.

"Mary Anne, is there a storage room with a lock?"

Her mouth opened, but snapped shut when she looked at her father.

"Don't say nothing to him, child," Hatfield whispered. "He's the Devil's own slave. The Good Lord is watching over you and the baby."

Walker squeezed the trigger. The rifle exploded and a hole appeared in the outer wall, two inches above Hatfield's head. Hatfield cowered, Mary Anne jerked and screamed, but the baby kept suckling.

Walker reloaded in a blur of movement and shook his head.

"Say another word and it'll be your last."

A damp patch spread in the crotch of Hatfield's faded denims. Tears flowed, his eyes closed, and his face crumpled. He quivered. Tears rolled down his sallow, bearded cheeks, and he started mumbling. The mumbles sounded like prayers.

"Mary Anne, listen to me. He's never going to hurt you again. Is there a place I can lock him up?"

She nodded, still unable to tear her eyes from the man who'd probably tormented her all her life. Fixing the psychological damage would take counselling and time, but for now, she needed safety.

"Pigsty's got a lock and it's real sturdy." She spoke with confidence, but her voice was still weak and dry.

"Take some more water. You need to rehydrate … you shouldn't let yourself get thirsty when you're feeding your baby," he added when confusion played on her childlike face.

Used to obeying the only man she likely knew, she drained the bottle and wiped her mouth with the back of her hand. She had so much to learn, but without the malevolent creature in her life, she might still have a chance to thrive. Billy too.

"Okay Hatfield, time to go visit with your livestock."

"No, please … no. You can't put me in with them pigs, it ain't human. Ain't fed them for a couple days and they'll be hungry. They'll tear me apart." Genuine fear showed in the beseeching eyes and the squeaky voice. His shoulders curled and he turned into a shaking, cowering ball.

"Can't stand small spaces, neither. Shoot me if'n you want, but don't put me in the cage with them pigs. Please, mister."

Unmoved by the monster's weasel words, Walker surveyed the small room with its pitiful occupants, both the victims and the offender.

"That's 'Doctor' to you, Hatfield. Now stand!"

A gurgling wail struggled out of the pig farmer's throat. He shook his head. Lank strands of hair flopped around his shoulders. Walker thought about grabbing the mop and yanking Hatfield to his feet, but that was probably the man's intention. Walker wasn't falling for it.

At an impasse, he had to incapacitate Hatfield somehow, but didn't take to the idea of shooting an unarmed man, not even a pedophile. What the hell was he going to do?

As if in answer to his question, the rumble of two powerful diesel engines cut through the outside silence. White headlights and flashing red and blue lights backlit the bedroom walls. Walker smiled. It wasn't often he welcomed the arrival of small town officers of the law, but this time, he was happy to make an exception.

Glory be!

Keeping the gun trained on Hatfield's belly but well out of the man's reach, Walker backtracked toward the cracked, fly-spattered window. Two police SUVs bounced into view up the hill and pulled to a stop alongside his Ford. Four officers climbed out and took cover on the far side of their vehicles. Four white cowboy hats stood out clear in the backwash from the headlights.

Walker raised the rifle's muzzle, pointing it at the pig farmer's head. "Lie flat on your face."

"No way I's doing that, boy. I's real comfortable right here."

Hatfield sneered, clearly seeing a way to turn the tables. While the cops remained outside and Hatfield knew the lay of the land, he had a chance to escape. He wasn't going to give up that faint hope easily.

"If'n you shoot me, the cops is gonna open up with everything they's got and likely everyone in here's gonna catch a whole load of lead. And I know you don't want that."

Walker ground his teeth.

Given the chance, Hatfield would happily use his own children as shields.

Walker's cool left him to be replaced by a cold fury. He stormed across the room, said, "Thought that's what you were going to say," and jabbed the muzzle into Hatfield's right eye.

The pig farmer squealed. He freed his hands from his butt cheeks, and threw them up to protect his face.

Walker took a handful of greasy hair and tugged hard.

Hatfield fell forward onto his face. Walker kept pulling until the man lay flat, face down on the bare boards beneath the window. Only then did he released his hold. He shook away the clumps of hair clinging to his gloved hand, wiped his hand on his jeans, and planted a foot on the back of Hatfield's neck, pinning his head in the angle of where floor met wall.

"Mary Anne," Walker said, seeing the tears in the child's eyes, "concentrate on your baby. Don't look at what's going on over here. Everything's going to be fine. I promise."

The girl nodded and lowered her head closer to her baby.

Hatfield's foul language could have stripped wallpaper—if the room had any wallpaper. The pedophile's fingers scrabbled at Walker's boot, trying to free himself. Walker added a couple of pounds more pressure. Hatfield screeched, stopped squirming, and dropped his hands to the floor.

"Keep still or I'll crack your head open with the butt of your own gun, you piece of filth. Got it?"

Walker made sure to keep out of sight of the cops, hidden by the frame of the window and the corner of the room. Trigger-happy police officers had made the news plenty of times in recent

37

months, and the last thing he wanted was to end up as yet another statistic.

Walker split his attention between Hatfield and the events taking place outside. One of the white hats dipped into the SUV and popped back out again a second later, its owner's face partially obscured behind a bullhorn.

A second cop played a spotlight over the front of the house, training it on the ground floor. Walker kept quiet. He had no idea how excitable the local LEOs might be and was in no hurry to find out.

A six-month rotation in the emergency room had taught him all he needed to know about law enforcement tactics in modern-day America. He'd patched up enough Baltimore gangbangers to know what to do when the law came a-calling, so he kept quiet and let them make all the moves. The wood and clapboard walls of the Hatfield farm would offer precious little protection against bullets fired from a police assault rifle.

The bullhorn crackled and emitted a high-pitched feedback wail before falling silent.

"Dr. Walker?" A woman's voice, calm and authoritative.

Hatfield had mentioned a Sheriff Hoover earlier. It seemed that the pig farmer's confidence had been misplaced. She most certainly wasn't too scared to encroach on his miserable little patch of the Wyoming backwoods.

"Dr. Walker, are you in there?"

"Upper floor," he called. "Bedroom window on the left. It's my hand you see waving."

The spotlight found the window, lit up his waggling fingers.

"Everything okay?"

"Yep. You need to know I have a rifle pointed at Mr. Hatfield. He didn't appreciate my trying to help his daughters."

"Daughters?" Hoover asked. "There's only one daughter, Mary Anne."

Not anymore.

"Sheriff, please tell your men to take it easy coming up the stairs. There are two innocent children up here. I'd hate to see them hurt in an accidental crossfire."

"Okay. We're coming up, weapons drawn, but safeties on. You hear that, deputies?"

Three white hats bobbed in agreement.

Hatfield squirmed under Walker's boot, trying to escape before the cops arrived and ended all chance of freedom. Walker added a little more weight to his heel. The pig farmer's nose splintered an instant before he let out another scream.

Walker held the rifle by the barrel and the stock, kept his fingers well away from the trigger, and leaned forward, resting both hands against the window frame. He watched the top of the staircase through the reflection in the window.

Hatfield's struggles increased and his curses grew more vile, while police-issue boots clomped over the veranda, crashed through the front door, and entered the house.

Chapter 5

Sheriff Hoover Comes to the Party

Walker held his breath. Sweat ran down the middle of his back. Hatfield lay still beneath Walker's pressing foot, cussing in Old Testament prose. The baby suckled noisily, Mary Anne hummed a gentle lullaby, and the footfalls grew louder.

Flashlight beams searched the darkness, found the stairwell, and lit it up.

"You still up there, Doc?" the sheriff called, her voice deep and throaty.

Where the hell else would I be?

"Still here, Sheriff. Can you hurry this along? This rifle's getting heavy."

"Can you put it down?"

"Not safely. Hatfield's desperate. Liable to try something stupid. I'd hate to have to shoot him."

"We're coming up the stairs now. No sudden moves, y'hear?"

"I'm playing statues, Sheriff, but my arms are getting tired."

As is the heel of my foot.

Reflected in the glass, the flashlight beams steadied, drew closer to the head of the stairs, and stopped when they reached it.

"We're outside the door now, Dr. Walker. Coming in slow."

Four police officers, led by the slim and diminutive Sheriff Hoover, edged into the crowded room. She had one of her men relieve Walker of the rifle. He gave it up gladly and leaned against the wall to stop himself collapsing in a quivering, relieved heap.

The shaking started slow at first, but built into the shivers. The aftereffects of an adrenaline rush. He took three deep, steadying breaths and waited for his head to clear and his stomach to stop roiling. A second deputy helped restrain a wildly uncooperative Hatfield, who called down the vengeance of the Old Testament and promised fire and pestilence on all their houses.

Save us from pedophile Bible bashers.

"Can I turn and lower my hands please?" he asked the sheriff.

"Sure, but do it slowly."

Walker followed her instructions precisely. The danger still hadn't passed. Sheriff Hoover appeared calm, but her deputies looked jittery and panted louder than if they'd just completed a marathon—underwater.

It took two deputies to subdue Hatfield. One held his arms, the other closed the handcuffs around his wrists, and still the man kept fighting and yelling oaths.

"Take him out to the truck, boys. We'll give him plenty of time to settle before Mirandizing him and asking a few questions."

"You arresting me?" Hatfield yelled. "Darn it, Sheriff, I'm the *victim* here. I caught this man interfering with Mary Anne. Then he up and hit me with my own gun."

Hatfield tried to tear loose from the lawmen and launch himself at Walker, but they held firm, and Walker kept silent. Time enough to say his piece without the ranting of a madman drowning out his words.

As the three men descended the stairs, the sheriff looked up and sideways at Walker from beneath her wide-brimmed cowboy hat. She studied him closely, needing to stretch her neck muscles to do it.

The woman had to be the smallest law officer Walker had ever seen, but what she lacked in stature, she more than made up for in quiet authority and steely determination. She'd shown that in her handling of what could have been a tense situation. If she'd misread the signs or had burst into the Hatfield house the moment she'd arrived, things could have turned out differently.

Still, if you carried a firearm on your hip and had the full weight of US law at your back, you didn't need to be six four and two hundred pounds to speak with authority. A slim-built, five foot four inch woman weighing one hundred twenty pounds fully clothed, she could have been Josie's older and slightly taller sister.

Unlike Josie though, the sheriff's brown eyes didn't have the same power to quicken Walker's heart and turn his insides into goo. Similar color maybe, but they held none of Josie's magic pixie dust.

Quit that, Walker. Things are serious.

She raised the brim of her hat with a forefinger and nodded.

"Sheriff Geraldine Hoover, but everyone calls me Gerrie." She pushed out a gloved hand.

Walker removed his torn and filthy surgical gloves and tossed them into the corner of the room before taking hold of her hand. They shook. Her hand felt tiny in his, but her grip was firm enough.

"Seems like the county owes you a debt of gratitude, Dr Walker."

Walker shook his head. "I didn't do much. The baby was already delivered by the time I arrived. Had a little trouble with Hatfield though, as you can see."

Walker pointed to the bullet hole in the ceiling above the mattress close to where the new mother had finished feeding her baby, and had looked up at them through wide open, but tear-filled and terrified eyes.

Sheriff Hoover blanched. "Good Lord. That was close."

"Tell me about it."

Walker brushed dust from the knees of his jeans and straightened out the twist in his jacket.

The sheriff stepped into the hall and signaled for Walker to follow.

"Is Mary Anne okay?" she asked, keeping her voice low, almost a whisper.

"Far as I can tell. Haven't had the chance to examine her or the baby fully, but things look promising. They'll both need a proper assessment for … Well, I think we can leave the details to the obstetrician. The baby's going to need a heel stick test too, for whatever it is you screen for in Wyoming. Any idea how long the ambulance is going to be? The sooner the girls are under proper medical care, the happier I'll be."

"The baby's a girl?"

Walker nodded.

"I told the paramedics to park at the gas station and await our arrival. They'll never make it up Chain Cut Road."

"So Hatfield was telling the truth, in part?"

"You spoke to him?"

"Briefly, and then things got a little out of hand, for a while."

Walker's left calf cramped. He winced and straightened his foot to stretch out the muscle.

"You okay?"

"Old injury. Plays up now and again, especially if I overexert myself. I'll be good soon as I've had a chance to rest it. A hot shower would help, too."

"Good ... good. We'll need to bring the girls down to the ambulance. Is it safe to move them?"

Walker raked his fingers through his hair, dislodging grit and dust in the process.

"We'll have to take things slowly, but they'll be better off being cared for in a medical facility than in this germ factory. If you carry the baby, I'll take Mary Anne. Poor kid's malnourished. Doesn't look like she'll take much lifting."

"I can spare one of my men if your leg's not up to it."

"It's not a problem, Sheriff. I can manage."

They returned to the bedroom and Walker squatted beside the filthy mattress. "Mary Anne?"

The child looked up at him. A timid smile formed. "Dr. ... Walker?"

"Well remembered, lass. We need to take care of you and the baby—"

"Can I call her Barbie like my dolly?"

Barbie? Oh dear.

"You can call her whatever you like. She's your baby. For now though, we need to take you both to the hospital for a check-up. Is that okay with you?"

Her lower lip trembled, dimpling her dirty chin.

"Papa says hospitals is full of germs and run by the Servants of Satan. Barbie and me don't want our souls took by the Devil."

Hatfield had clearly been feeding the girl such garbage all her life, probably to keep her and Billy ignorant and subservient. Inwardly, Walker damned the man's black heart.

Mary Anne's eyes filled again and she sniffled. The baby picked up on her mother's fear and started griping. Tiny fingers clutched at the towel that acted as swaddling.

"Your Papa's wrong, Mary Anne. You and the little one, Barbie, will be in good hands. I promise. Will you trust me?"

Big blue eyes opened wide and stabbed like a dagger into Walker's chest. How could anyone hurt such a helpless child? Again, he ground his teeth. At that moment, he wanted nothing more than five minutes alone in a soundproofed room with "Papa" Hatfield. He wouldn't need the rifle either.

"Sheriff Hoover's going to carry your baby, but don't worry, she'll be okay. You can watch her all the way. And I'll stay with you until you're both safe, okay?"

Mary Anne nodded, but her attention never left her newborn.

Sheriff Hoover took the baby and waited for Walker to wrap the featherweight new mom in a sheet and pick her up. The smell of blood, stale sweat, and excrement wafting up from Mary Anne would once have turned Walker's stomach, but if a six-month ER rotation didn't immunize a trainee doctor against bad human odors, they would never be strong enough to qualify.

Mary Anne threw her frail arms around his neck, and the sheriff led the way. They made it down the stairs and into the fresh air without incident, Walker whispering calming words to his charge all the way down to the first floor and out of the hell hole.

The second they stepped through the doorway, Hatfield—secure in the back of the lead wagon—started up again with his oaths and his Old Testament threats. Mary Anne whimpered and hugged Walker tighter.

"It's okay, Mary Anne. He's never going to hurt you again."

Not if I have anything to do with it.

Sheriff Hoover waved the SUV away and they watched it until the flashing lights were nothing but a ghostly blur against the trees as it wound its way down the mountain.

Mary Anne pulled closer and whispered in his ear. "I-I's scared. Where's Billy?"

"Billy's fine. A little confused maybe, but he sent me here to find you."

"Billy's a real good brother. Protected me from Papa best he could. At least he tried to. Took plenty of beatings for me. Wouldn't run when he coulda."

Walker turned to the sheriff. "Did you hear that?"

She frowned and shook her head.

"She wants to know where her brother is."

Sheriff Hoover's expression hardened. "We have him safe and sound. She's got no need to fear."

Hell, she doesn't know? Hasn't worked it out?

Fear for the boy's safety and anger forced Walker's next move. Still holding tight to Mary Anne, he stepped in front of the sheriff and the baby and refused to let her pass.

"What do you mean, 'he's safe?' What've you done with him?"

"Whoa, there. Pull in your horns, Doc. We don't make war on the slow witted in Husqvarna County. When I say the boy's safe I mean it. He's still at the gas station. One of my volunteer deputies is watching him. He ain't under arrest just yet, although I could take him in for driving on the highway without a license."

"What? Are you serious?"

Sheriff Hoover's loosed a smile that surprised Walker both in its pleasantness and in the way it took years from her face.

"Kidding, Doc. Shirley said she'd keep the diner open and would feed him when he's cleaned up. They have a rest room and some coveralls he can change into."

45

Walker stood down. "Sorry, Sheriff. My temper's a little frayed after … after what's just happened."

She nodded. "Understandable. But don't say any more until we're back in my office, and I've read you your Miranda rights."

This time, she winked and smiled before he could take offence. No doubt about it, Sheriff Hoover did things her own way. Walker found it a refreshing change, if a little confusing.

"I know my rights, Sheriff Hoover."

"Sure you do, Doc. Sure you do."

Walker lowered Mary Anne into the back of the sheriff's SUV and helped fasten her seatbelt. Sheriff Hoover handed over the baby and the new mom smiled and cooed to her child. In the middle of all this horror and desolation, a mother's love for her baby could still shine through.

Walker blinked away his blurring vision, and he struggled to swallow. Must have had something to do with all the excitement and the fact he had the thirst of a man in the middle of a three-day trek through the desert. He cleared his parched throat.

"Don't have any water, I suppose? I'm thirsty and no doubt Mary Anne could use another drink."

Sheriff Hoover took a blanket from the back shelf of the SUV and covered the girls against the chilly night air. Mary Anne smiled her timid thanks and returned her attention to the baby. After making sure her charges were comfortable and secure, Sheriff Hoover signaled to a deputy, an older man with drooping eyelids and a matching gray moustache.

"Horace," she said, "these folks are thirsty. Can you help them out?"

Loose-limbed and taking his own sweet time, Horace strolled to the trunk of the SUV and returned carrying two plastic bottles of water. He tossed one to Walker and handed the other to Mary Anne. Walker downed half its contents in three long, enjoyable pulls.

"Excellent. Thanks, Deputy …"

"Shawcross, but Horace will do, Doc. No need for formalities around here less'n you've broke the law."

"I haven't."

"Remains to be seen, don't it?" Horace said, his voice a rasping whisper, and his delivery pure Clint Eastwood out of *High Plains Drifter*.

Craggy faced, lean, stooped at the shoulder, every inch the wizened cowpoke. Superficially, not a whole lot different from Caspar Boyd, the longtime sheriff of Lucky Shores.

Sheriff Hoover flicked a hand at her elderly deputy. "Now, now, Horace. No need to be so hostile. Doc Walker's a stranger in our county. We don't want him thinking badly of us."

"If'n you say so, Sheriff."

Horace gave Walker a mirthless grin, tipped his hat, and rested his hand on the gun in his holster. For some reason, the veteran law officer seemed unable to drag his eyes from Walker, and being on the receiving end of the older man's glare wasn't a pleasant experience.

The sheriff headed for the driver's seat and called over her shoulder.

"Doc Walker, you'd best get in. Horace can drive your car back to the gas station. You look dead on your feet."

"Thanks, Sheriff, but,"—he showed her his hands—"I need to get my medical bag and clean up. Can you give me a minute?"

Walker turned toward the cabin, but Horace stepped out to bar his way.

"Sorry, *sir*," Horace said, making the "sir" sound like an insult, "but that there's a crime scene. We can't let you back in."

"But my DNA and fingerprints are all over the place anyway, and I'll need my bag."

Horace refused to back away. Walker stared hard at the deputy. The harsh light from the car headlights and the mobile spotlights threw the older man into sharp relief. His grizzled face could have passed for a topographical map of the nearby Rockies.

"Again, I'm sorry, but there's a stand pipe outside the main barn, yonder. You can clean up over there, if you have to."

Walker followed the direction Horace was looking. The corrugated iron building looked as though it had been standing since before Abe Lincoln took office.

"You've been here before?"

"Once or twice. Last time was two years ago." The aged deputy scratched his chin, the rasping of fingernails on day-old whiskers matched the chirruping of cicadas and the rustle of pine needles blown by the breeze. "Me and Deputy Cooper"—he pointed to the officer on the veranda sealing off the crime scene with police tape—"served him a writ for keeping his kids out of school."

"What happened?"

"Sorry?"

"What happened when you served the writ? Did Hatfield kick off?"

"He weren't home. The woman from child services we had with us was a mite put out by missing Fulton and the kids."

"Did you ever follow up on it?"

Horace shrugged. "Not my place. I just do as I'm told."

Walker stared him down.

"Pity."

The deputy fixed Walker with a death glower. "What you mean by that?"

"I mean, if you'd followed up on the writ, maybe that poor girl would be happily attending junior high rather than giving birth to her own sister."

"What's that?" Horace stepped closer, chin jutting out, jaw clenched. "You sayin' what I think you're sayin'?"

Walker raised a hand to calm the man. He'd said too much already. Best to save it for the official statement. He forced the tension out of his shoulders, took a breath, and counted to ten.

"Where did you say that stand pipe was?"

"Corner of the barn, behind that there water barrel," Horace answered, still holding himself tense.

Walker stomped toward the barn, treading over weeds and years of fallen pine needles, the beam from his flashlight leading

48

the way. The tightness in his left calf shot a lance of pain up his leg. A reminder of the old injury he'd rarely felt since curtailing his life as a hitchhiker walking the quiet roads in search of the muse for a wonder song and a new life. He missed the freedom, but he didn't miss the bayonet hacking at his damaged leg at the end of each day's walk.

Still, the exercise had done him good and reminded him how much his life had changed since meeting Josie.

The rusted iron faucet let out a reluctant dribble of ice cold water. Walker scrubbed his hands as best he could and dried them on his mud and blood spattered jeans. He finished by splashing water on his face and neck—the shock of the near-freezing liquid sent electric sparks through his head and worked better to chase away fatigue than coffee could ever do.

Walker returned to the sheriff's SUV refreshed, but only slightly cleaner.

"Ready now?"

He shook his head. "What happens if there's an emergency on the way back to the gas station? I'll need my medical bag."

Sheriff Hoover studied Walker for a moment, before shaking her head. "Sorry, Doc. As Horace said. That's a crime scene and shouldn't be disturbed."

Time to play hardball.

Without his very expensive medical kit, he'd be stuck in this area until the sheriff decided to let him go. The only other thing of importance in the car was Suzy, his six-string acoustic. He didn't want to budge until he had both safely in his possession. The rest of his stuff was replaceable—the Ford included. He crossed his arms and settled onto his heels.

"Sheriff Hoover. I'm going nowhere without my bag. You're going to have to arrest me, and think how that'll play in the national media. I can see the headlines now, 'Hero doctor arrested after playing good Samaritan. Young mother he tried to save dies of prolapsed uterus on the way to the ambulance after being bounced around in the back of a police wagon for half an hour.' Not too snappy, but I'm sure the headline writers will come up

49

with something I can take to the courts when I sue you and your county for wrongful arrest. Am I making my point clear enough?"

Sheriff Hoover sighed. "There's no need for all this animosity, Doc."

"Yep. I know there isn't." Walker hiked a thumb in Horace's direction. "But he started it. And we're wasting time. Mary Anne and the baby need medical attention, and I need my medical kit."

"Coop?" Sheriff Hoover called to the deputy standing guard at the shack. "Get the doctor his bag, but take plenty of photos with your cell phone before you move anything."

Walker uncrossed his hands, lowered his arms to his sides, said, "Thanks, Sheriff," and called to Deputy Cooper. "You can leave the used swabs and the suture pack, just close up the bag as it stands."

Walker stayed where he was until Cooper returned with his kit.

"Well now, Doc. Seems you chose the wrong profession," Hoover said, matter-of-fact.

"Really?"

"Yep. With that attitude, you should have been a lawyer."

Unable to find an answer that wasn't sarcastic, Walker kept his mouth shut and yanked open the passenger door. The courtesy light glowed bright, but the sheriff's smile did little to soothe his anger. He slid into the back of the SUV and checked on his patients.

"Feel any better, Doc?"

"Not a whole lot."

Sheriff Hoover eyed him through the rearview mirror. "Can we go now?" she asked.

"Horace going to follow us in my car?"

With Suzy and the rest of my gear?

"What's so important about your car?"

He waved his hands over his stained and grimy clothes. "No doubt you'll be wanting to take these rags away for evidence?"

"Depending on what you tell me in your statement, I prob'ly will."

"In which case, I'll need fresh clothes to change into. That's why I was so keen not to leave my Ford here. Everything I own in the world is in that Explorer."

"Horace is gonna follow us in your car. Your things will be safe. You have my word."

"Good enough for me. Let's go, Sheriff."

She fired up the engine, made the multi-point turn, and headed down the hill. She took the curves a lot slower than Walker had done when he climbed into danger, but if not for the safety restraints, the big vehicle would still have thrown them around in the back like pebbles in a tumble dryer. He helped Mary Anne steady the baby with one hand, while he held onto the grab strap with the other and tried to prevent his head cracking against the window.

Despite the journey a theme park rollercoaster would have been proud of, the baby slept soundly the whole way down. Clearly made of strong stuff.

Walker didn't go in for rollercoasters, never saw the joy of standing in line and paying for the right to hold back on the vomit. He took deep breaths all the way down in an effort to fight the growing sense of motion sickness.

By the time they reached the blacktop, sweat had popped on his brow and soaked his back, his palms had sprung a leak, and his guts had churned. He wanted to hurl, but held it together until Sheriff Hoover pulled into the gas station parking lot and stopped in the same space Walker had used what seemed like half a lifetime earlier.

The moment the wheels stopped moving, he jumped from the SUV and rushed ten paces to a patch of scrub behind the diner before doubling over and upchucking most of his dinner.

With an empty stomach and breathing deeply through an open mouth, he stood, bent over, hands on knees, waiting for the nausea and dizziness to pass.

Wrapped up in his own discomfort, Walker missed much of the joyous reunion between the siblings, but Billy's delighted and yelled, "Y-You ain't d-dead. You ain't d-dead!" improved Walker's mood more than a little.

Still bent over, he studied the siblings.

Billy leaned through the open window of the police SUV and stared in slack-jawed wonder at the baby. For her part, an exhausted Mary Anne looked up at her brother, a tired smile playing on her sweet little face.

Walker accessed his memory of the disheveled boy who'd crashed into his life in the diner.

Billy, tall and gangly with prominent brow ridges and a lantern jaw, couldn't have been described as anything other than plain. Speaking strictly scientifically, Mary Anne, at around four foot nine but perfectly proportioned, might be classed as a homunculus. As a slender beauty she stood apart from her brother. Her coloring, fair compared with Billy's dark, suggested her mother and Billy's weren't the same woman—assuming Hatfield had fathered them both.

Although siblings, they were so physiologically different, there was a chance the baby, Barbie, had sufficient genetic separation for her not to be in danger.

Walker smiled at the touching family scene in the SUV, but the sights and sounds of the fight with their father came back in a flip-scene frenzy. How close had he been to death? How close had he been to missing out on a lifetime of loving and living with Josie? Kids, grandkids maybe. It all could have been taken by a child-abusing, Bible-thumping madman with a hunting rifle and the desire to use it.

With a good woman at his side and a medical degree hanging on his office wall, Walker should be settling down, building a medical practice, not dodging bullets in crumbling farms in the middle of Husqvarna County, Wyoming.

At least something positive had come out of it. He'd saved a child and her baby from a monster. Them and Billy would likely be cared for by the state. Walker had that to hold onto.

As he straightened, another bolus of vomit rumbled up from his stomach, clawed into his esophagus, and tried to reach his mouth. He battled its expulsion.

Sheriff Hoover approached, stood close. "You okay, Doc?"

Walker raised an arm to fend her off, spun, and puked into the grass once again. His discomfort ended with a loud, burbling, embarrassing belch.

Damn it.

"Sorry, Sheriff. Didn't want to dirty those nice shiny boots of yours."

He stood up straight and looked at his hands. They trembled worse than an addict on the first day of the detox program.

Sheriff Hoover held out a fresh bottle of water. "Thought you might need this."

"Thanks." He turned his back on the mess he'd made. Hopefully it would rain soon and wash away the crud. "Don't know what just happened."

"Shock affects different people in different ways. You held it together until you knew the girls were safe. Says a lot, Doc. I'm impressed. Really impressed."

Walker took a mouthful, rinsed, and spat before swallowing the rest of the water. He crushed the empty bottle flat, replaced the top, and tossed it into a wire trash can. Two paramedics, a man and a woman, had already found their way to the back of the sheriff's truck.

"I should give them a case history before they take the girls away. Be right back." He looked at the sheriff's sympathetic face. "And if you can scare up a cup of coffee, I might just nominate you for sainthood."

"How d'you take it?"

"Black, no sugar. Shirley probably remembers."

A female deputy dragged a reluctant Billy back into the diner while the female paramedic helped Mary Anne and the baby onto a gurney.

Walker introduced himself to the male paramedic.

"Jacques Flambeau," the man replied, pointing to the nametag on his uniform. "And my better-looking partner's Eva Sherry."

"Pleased to meet you, Jacques. Mother and baby appear healthy, but the mother's undernourished ..."

He offered Flambeau as comprehensive a history as he could, and the paramedic asked all the right questions. It gave Walker confidence that the sheriff wasn't the only one in Husqvarna County who knew their jobs. He checked his watch. 12:23 p.m.

Holy crap.

Had it really been five hours since Billy had crashed into his life? Five hours? No wonder he was so utterly exhausted. Fighting off a murderous attack would do that to a timid, city doctor.

He ran the math and spoke again to the man with the notepad. "Billy turned up here a little before eight o'clock, and I must have taken twenty-five, maybe thirty minutes to reach the Hatfield farm. The placenta had already been ejected, so that puts the baby at six or seven hours old. She's already breastfeeding and everything appears normal."

Flambeau nodded. "Thanks, Doctor. We'll take it from here."

"Okay, but also make sure they run a full blood panel on both patients and check the mother for malnutrition. She's far too small for her age, although reasonably healthy or she wouldn't have carried to full term." He leaned closer to Flambeau and lowered his voice. "The baby looks healthy and has all her fingers and toes, but make sure the OB-GYN checks her vision, hearing, and run a test for neonatal diabetes ... You understand what I'm saying here, Jacques?"

Flambeau frowned as the meaning of Walker's words struck home.

"Yes, Dr. Walker. I get your drift." He glanced at Mary Anne and shook his head. "Poor kid. Don't worry, we'll take good care of her." Flambeau gripped his ballpoint so hard, Walker felt sure it would break apart in his hand. "It's a forty-minute run to the hospital and that baby needs a wash and a bed. You coming with us, or can we scoot?"

"Assuming Sheriff Hoover okays it, yes please. The sooner they get to the hospital the better."

Sheriff Hoover exited through the diner's doors, a carry-out cup in each hand. She waved the paramedics away and Walker beckoned her over.

"Sheriff, you need a statement from me right now?"

"If you're not needed with Mary Anne, I'd like to get it done tonight. Then you can be on your way to wherever you're headed. You'll need to make yourself available for the trial, though. Assuming there is one."

The ambulance, blue lights flashing, but the sirens off, pulled away from the gas station, heading north and travelling slowly.

"Where are they headed?"

Sheriff Hoover handed him a coffee, which tasted even better than he remembered.

"Laramie Mercy Hospital. It's got one of the best neo-natal facilities in the state. Chief OB-GYN is Dr. Samuels. She's a damn fine doctor—delivered my sister's preemie twins. Don't worry, Doc. Mary Anne and the baby will receive first-class care."

Walker stared at his hands. They still shook with the after-effects of adrenaline. He hadn't faced so much danger since the last time he'd been in this neck of the woods. Hadn't even entered a fight ring since resuming his medical studies. During his studies, he'd hardly had the time or the energy to visit the gym. Only managed a few miles a week of road work. The wrestle with old man Hatfield proved how slow and weak he'd become since his time in the mountains.

Nearly four years older and a little wiser, the adrenaline comedown pained him more than it used to in his younger days on the wrestling mat. Walker had hung up his wrestling jersey fifteen years back, but the fighting skills hadn't fully deserted him—thanks to whatever deity happened to be in vogue at the moment.

Sheriff Hoover took a sip and grimaced. "Darn it. Forgot the sweetener. Mind if we take this inside? I'll need to talk to Billy.

Tell him what to expect next, assuming he's bright enough to understand what I'm saying."

"He drove all this way in that beat up station wagon to save his sister. Trust me, Sheriff. He's bright enough."

She tilted her head, her expression noncommittal.

Walker turned in the direction of the Hatfield farm. "What do you think happened back there, Sheriff?"

"Obvious, isn't it? Poor little girl. Never thought Billy had it in him to father a child. And with his half-sister, too."

"That's what you think, is it?"

She shot Walker a strange look he couldn't interpret.

"Well, the facts fit. Billy took advantage of his half-sister, and then he panicked after seeing all that blood. I guess you've probably already worked out he's at least one bottle short of a six pack."

Walker kept his counsel. It wouldn't do Billy any good for them to hash out the case in public court. For all he knew, Sheriff Hoover could be the sort of law officer who stood on a soapbox and made public announcements that led to lynch mobs roaming the streets of hick towns in cowboy country.

Nope, he'd keep his cards covered for the moment. In Billy's best interests.

Chapter 6

The Short Arm of the Local Law

Two abreast, Walker and Sheriff Hoover strode toward the diner. The brim of her cowboy hat barely reached the height of his shoulder.

"What were you saying to the paramedic? Looked conspiratorial."

"Not sure that doesn't come under doctor-patient privilege—"

She threw an arm out and stopped dead. "Are you planning to play that close-mouthed confidentiality bullcrap here, Doc?"

The firm set to her jaw and the narrowing of her eyes showed a layer of steel beneath her feather-light exterior. Walker nodded at her. The woman probably didn't win her election by baking cookies and organizing yard sales. And the way she handled her team back at the pig farm showed she had a certain level of moxie.

"But," he said, dipping his head and meeting her angry glare, "before you interrupted me, I was going to say, given I'm not really Mary Anne's doctor, I guess you need to know—for the record."

"Glad you see it that way, Dr. Walker. I'll be needing that formal statement."

"I know. Can we do it here? It's a long way back to Laramie and I'm headed in the opposite direction."

Sheriff Hoover creased up her face and tilted her head back to look at him. The white cowboy hat took on a life of its own and waggled left and right.

Hell. Here it comes.

Walker could see the hours stretching out ahead of them. Questions and answers, statements, more questions, and more answers. The chances of him ending his journey tonight and reaching Lucky Shores in time for breakfast had just taken a nosedive into the Wyoming dust.

"Sorry, Doc, but we have to do this formally. Wouldn't want your actions today to come back and bite you on your butt, now would we? Cute butt though it is."

"Excuse me?"

"Don't worry, Doc, you're safe from this old law officer. I'm old enough to be your … big sister. Don't mean to say I can't appreciate a well-filled-out pair of denims, though."

Heck. Talk about mixed messages.

"Oh, right. Sorry, my humor tank's running on empty, but to answer your question, no I wouldn't want my actions to come back and cause me any discomfort." Walker pulled open the door and allowed the sheriff through first. He took the opportunity to arch his back and ease the cramping muscles in his lumbar spine. Scrambling about on the floor wrestling Hatfield after two days of sitting behind the wheel of his SUV hadn't done him any favors. "Is that likely to happen?"

"Might do. Way I heard it, Fulton Hatfield is claiming assault and trespass. Said you turned up at his house and tried to interfere with his daughter. Then lashed out at him without provocation. Now, *you* know that's a crock, and *I* know that's a crock, but in a court of law …."

She let the statement, and the possible threat, dangle, but Walker wasn't about to bite. The sheriff would get her statement, but before that, he had two other things to do.

"Mind if I check on Billy first? He's had a real shock tonight. I probably need to refer him for a psych evaluation."

"How long's that gonna take?"

It was his turn to stare at the sheriff. "I'll tell you that when you tell me how long's this piece of string." He held up nothing between his pinched index fingers and thumbs.

She snorted. "Point taken, Doc. I was only thinking of you and your onward journey."

Yeah, sure you were.

58

"Thanks, Sheriff. I appreciate that. Now, I'd like a little time alone with my ... with Billy, please." He narrowly avoided calling Billy his patient.

The youngster sat in a corner booth, digging into a vanilla and chocolate ice cream sundae, with the full works including sprinkles and raspberry sauce. A look of furtive guilt scrunched up his freshly scrubbed face. His eyes scanned the others in the room, and he covered the tulip-shaped glass with one arm as though terrified one of the deputies would steal his dessert, or yell at him for eating it.

Walker approached, but stopped a few paces away.

"Hi Billy, that looks nice. Enjoying it?"

He nodded quickly but didn't speak.

"Prefer strawberry ice cream, myself. Is that coffee or chocolate?"

Billy swallowed before answering.

"S-Shirley s-says this is chocolate. Chocolate's the b-best."

He pronounced every syllable in the word "chocolate" as though he was trying it out for the first time, and the way he savored every mouthful suggested the same thing.

"Mind if I sit with you? My legs are sore."

Billy nodded slowly, chin jutting, and dug his spoon into the juices at the bottom of the glass.

"S'all right."

"Thanks, son." Walker eased onto the bench opposite and sighed as the padded cushion took the strain off of his legs. "That's better. You know what? That sundae looks so nice, I'm going to have one myself, only I'm not a huge fan of chocolate. Like I said, I prefer—"

"St-Straw-berry," Billy said, pushing his glass out and licking his spoon clean. He held it in a hammer, rather than a precision grip.

"That's right. Shirley," he called, "don't suppose I could have a strawberry sundae over here, could I? And what about another for you, Billy?"

59

The kid's eyes lit up for a moment and then dulled. "Don't have no money."

"It's okay, son. The county's paying because you were so brave earlier when you saved Mary Anne."

"Y-You mean I-I ain't in t-trouble?"

"Not as far as I'm concerned, Billy. Why would you think you're in trouble?"

"Don't have no l-license for to drive on the r-real r-roads. Is t-the sheriff gonna 'rest me?" Tears welled, and his voice cracked.

From the corner of his eye, Walker saw Sheriff Hoover shake her head.

"No Billy, Sheriff Hoover might just be wanting to give you a certificate of bravery for what you did tonight."

"Really? I-I ain't never had no … cert-if-cate." His frown deepened. "S-So. Mary Anne had a baby, huh? She weren't dead? But all that b-blood." He shuddered and shook his head.

"No, Billy, she's fine, and the baby's doing well—"

Billy continued as though Walker hadn't interrupted. "I was sure she were dead and Papa'd b-blame me for it. Papa, b-blames me f-for everything as g-goes wrong on the farm." Again the tears threatened to flow.

Walker added more mental notes to aid his tentative diagnosis. Billy had a functioning short-term memory, as demonstrated by remembering Walker preferred strawberry ice cream. The grip on the spoon suggested either impaired fine motor skills, or he'd never been taught to hold it properly. Add to that, Billy also understood abstract concepts like right and wrong and of legal ramifications, at least in broad terms.

Shirley arrived with two fresh sundaes and the kid looked up at her and smiled. "T-Thank you k-kindly, Miss Sh-Shirley."

"You're welcome, sweetie. Enjoy." She smiled at him and extended it to Walker as she turned. She added a nod of encouragement.

"Billy, listen to me," Walker said before the kid could attack his second sundae. "There's no need to be afraid of your father anymore. He'll be going away for a long time."

"Y-Yeah?" He dry swallowed and disbelief showed in his raised eyebrows.

"Yes. He's not a good man, Billy. In fact, he's a really bad man. Now, enjoy your ice cream before it melts."

The youngster didn't need a second invitation and immediately started digging in. Walker took a couple of mouthfuls for show and pushed his glass away—he never had developed much of a taste for ice cream. Josie's homemade donuts and her lemon drizzle cakes, now they were something else.

He left Billy to his digging and joined the sheriff and Shirley at the counter.

"Don't care for my sundae, Doc?"

He looked sideways at Sheriff Hoover before patting his belly and saying, "No offence, but my stomach's a little delicate right now. Maybe a piece of toast and butter will help settle it down a little."

"Toast and butter coming right up." Shirley poured him another coffee and turned to her task, leaving Walker and Sheriff Hoover alone at the end of the bar, monitoring Billy's progress.

"What's your professional opinion?" Sheriff Hoover asked, pointing to Billy.

"Like I said, he needs a detailed developmental assessment. He's definitely well below the normal IQ range, but higher functioning than people might give him credit for. With special needs teaching he'll do well. The way he looked out for Mary Anne took strength of character. He's a really fine brother."

Sheriff Hoover listened in silence to his diagnosis and waited until he finished before saying, "You're talking as though he's the innocent one in this?"

"He is, Sheriff Hoover. That, he most definitely is."

"Care to explain yourself?"

"When I make my statement. This isn't the place. Meanwhile, what happens to him now?"

"I'll get Horace to take him to Mercy Hospital, put him in the psychiatric wing for an assessment. That sound reasonable to you?"

Walker stiffened and turned to face her.

"No, Sheriff. No, it doesn't. What sort of child services infrastructure do you have in the county?"

"One that's stretched to breaking, same as everywhere else. In any event, Billy's nineteen. He doesn't fall under their purview."

"I'd say his mental age is closer to ten than twenty."

"Still doesn't qualify him for child services. I really do think Mercy's psychiatric ward's likely the best place for him. At least overnight. It's a place of safety. He'll receive the best of care. I can assure you of that."

"He won't be under arrest?"

"No arrest, no charges. At least not for the moment. Just care and treatment for shock and whatever else he needs."

Walker paused long enough to glance at Billy and assess the sheriff's words. He couldn't really see any alternative for the lad.

"Good enough. Will I be able to visit him in the morning? Professionally, I mean."

"If that's what you want. But I'll need to take your statement first. I'd prefer to get things squared away soon as possible. The state police will likely take an interest in this situation."

"Really?"

"Surely will. Hatfield Farm straddles the border between Wyoming and Colorado. There's a jurisdictional issue and a complaint's been made against you. However ridiculous that complaint might be, we'll have to investigate it."

Despite his queasy stomach, the smell of bread toasting under the grill made him feel better. The threat of legal action against him didn't worry him too much. He had plenty of powerful medical ammunition to bring to his defense. Walker had every intention of using the heavy artillery the moment he and the pint-sized sheriff were alone.

Shirley placed a plate on the bar with two thick slices of rye bread slathered with butter so thick and yellow, Walker could feel his arteries hardening just by looking at it.

Naughty, but what the hell.

"Can I eat this now while it's hot, or do I need to ask Shirley to wrap it up to go?"

The sheriff snorted. "You enjoy it while its hot. I'll make sure Horace gets Billy tucked up safe for the night."

She moved away and started talking with the grizzled lawman.

Shirley appeared in front of him, smiling, but looking exhausted. "Want me to put some bacon on that for you, Doc? Grill's still hot. Won't take but a minute."

"No thanks, Shirley. This is perfect. So's the coffee. Hopefully we'll be out of your hair soon. How much do I owe you for everything, including whatever Billy's had?"

She shook her head emphatically. "Nothing, Doc. That's on me. Poor kid looks as though he hasn't had a square meal in weeks. Mary Anne looked in a bad way, too. What little I could see of her."

In the mirror, Horace and Sheriff Hoover crowded over Billy who looked about ready to bolt. He threw a piteous glance at Walker.

"D-Dr. W-Walker? What—"

Walker raised his hands in a calming gesture.

"It'll be okay, Billy. Go with the Sheriff and Deputy Horace. I'll come see you in the morning after you've had a shower and a good sleep. You'll be able to see Mary Anne and the baby, too."

Slowly, he relaxed and he broke out a tentative smile.

"Okay. Th-That'll be g-good."

Billy allowed them to lead him to the door, meek and mild, but at the same time, scared and confused.

By the time Walker finished his toast and coffee, and settled his stomach, Sheriff Hoover had returned.

"Ready to come with me now, Doc?"

"Do I get a phone call first?"

The sheriff tucked in her chin, a move that reminded him of Josie in full defense mode. "You think you need a lawyer?"

Walker grinned and shook his head.

"Nope. I want to call my fiancée and tell her I've been delayed. She'll be waiting up for me and will be fretting for my safety."

"Mind if we do that in my office? You can leave your car here. I'll have one of my men drive it into town ready for you in the morning. Don't want you behind the wheel after the night you've had. Wouldn't forgive myself if you got into an accident."

Walker guessed the ulterior motive. Sheriff Hoover wouldn't want him crossing the border into Colorado and leaving her jurisdiction, either.

"After that food and water, I'm fit to drive, Sheriff Hoover."

"Why take that chance, Doc? Your car's gonna be safe, I promise. And why not call me Gerrie? Sheriff Hoover makes me seem so old."

Walker bypassed her request. He could never see himself calling any sheriff by their given name. Although he'd developed a deep friendship with the Ghost of Lucky Shores, he would never dream of calling the man "Caspar". Not even in his head. He would always be "Boyd" to Walker.

Reluctantly, he accepted Hoover's "generous offer" of a lift into town. They took their leave of Shirley and he followed the sheriff from the diner.

"Are we headed for Laramie?" he asked as Hoover showed him into the front passenger seat of her SUV, which in itself was a positive sign. If she'd considered him a danger or any sort of suspect, she would surely have locked him in the cage in back and maybe would have fitted him with a complimentary set of steel bracelets for his troubles. It wasn't as though Walker were a stranger to the back seat of a police vehicle.

He clicked the seat belt into place and relaxed into the comfy front seat.

"Nope. As you said, Laramie's too far. We're heading to my office in Fort Wycombe. It's up the road a short ways, and we'll be much more comfortable there than in the diner."

She smiled, fired up the diesel engine, and threw the wagon into drive. As they pulled away from the gas station, Walker was relieved to see one of the sheriff's men slide into the driver's seat of his Ford. Its headlights burst into bright life and the car followed them along an empty and unlit WY-230.

After ten miles on the odometer, Sheriff Hoover turned off the state road onto a two-lane black top which wound uphill through a tree-lined valley. They continued for another fifteen miles, and the lethargic rumble of tires on poorly maintained asphalt soon had Walker's lids drooping.

Sheriff Hoover feathered the throttle as the SUV hit a rutted piece of road that threatened a loss of traction, and then floored it again when the surface improved.

"See those lights up ahead?" she asked.

Walker jerked awake and rubbed the sleep from his eyes.

"Excuse me?"

"The lights over yonder," she repeated, pointing through the windshield, her lips drawn thin, eyes narrowed. "That there's Fort Wycombe. One of the safest, quietest towns in Wyoming. It's been a pure joy to police this town. Until this evening."

Chapter 7

Chet Walker, Phone Home

Sheriff Hoover made a sharp left and the SUV's headlights lit up a sign that proudly proclaimed:

You are entering
Fort Wycombe, Husqvarna County, Wyoming.
POP. 23,573 (c.2010).
Welcome. Please drive carefully.

A ridiculous question flashed through Walker's fatigued mind. Was that population a figure for the town or the whole county? He might have asked the sheriff, but there were other things on her mind and he didn't want to interrupt.

She pulled to a stop outside an angular, brick building. Walker climbed out of the SUV and, despite the darkness, had the impression of a heavy weight of rocks pressing in all around them. The mountains closing in, making their mark, imposing their will on the town. The familiar smell of pine and fresh air made him fill his lungs and smile. Lucky Shores carried a similar fragrance, but with the added freshwater tang of Big Lake.

Walker smiled to himself. Strange how often he compared his surroundings to that small town hidden in the high Colorado Rockies.

Somewhere off to his left, water roared over rocks. Fort Wycombe clearly boasted a fast-moving river.

He followed Sheriff Hoover up four stone steps into a two-story building. A lamp hanging above the stout oak door illuminated a shingle nailed to the wall. It bore a wood-burned notice:

Fort Wycombe Police Department.

"How many police officers do you run in the county?" he asked, as much to break the silence as to increase his understanding of the FWPD.

Sheriff Hoover ignored his question, continued to the far corner of an office hotter than a greenhouse, and tore off her uniform jacket. She draped it over the back of a chair, set her dusty white hat on the desk, and stepped across to a water cooler.

"Need a drink? I can offer you water, coffee, or green tea."

Green tea? Not a chance.

Walker tugged off his jacket and read the time off the wall clock hanging over the sheriff's desk. He could tell it was the sheriff's desk from the nameplate sitting on its surface and the bottle of perfume next to the computer monitor. He very much doubted that Horace or Coop would use Yves St Laurent's *Black Opium*.

"Green tea?" he scoffed. "At two thirty in the morning you offer a full-grown man green tea?"

She smiled. It was a good smile, an pleasant smile, and Walker didn't believe it for one second. Something passed behind her eyes he couldn't read and wasn't sure he wanted to. All he wanted was to answer the petite law officer's questions, sign his statement, jump in his Ford, and skedaddle out of town. Not that it would happen that way. Not now he had other commitments.

His chances of having breakfast at the Lucky Shores diner that morning had disappeared the moment he took on the care of a mother and her newborn.

Sheriff Hoover left the water cooler and stepped a couple of paces to her left. "Guess that's a 'no' for the tea and a 'yes' for the coffee?"

"Yes for the coffee." Walker nodded. "Can I sit anywhere, or are you taking me to an interview room?"

Back turned to him, but making sure she could still see his reflection in the window, Sheriff Hoover snorted.

"We don't run a separate interview room, Doc. There's no call for anything like that out here." She pointed to a chair on the visitor's side of her desk. "Help yourself. And to answer your earlier question, we have a full-time staff of four and you saw them all tonight. In an emergency, I can call on half a dozen volunteer deputies. One of them's Arlene Carter. She's the one who looked after Billy at the diner."

"So, with Cooper and the other guy back at the Hatfield farm, it's just you, me, and Horace?"

"After settling Billy in Laramie, Horace will head straight home. He doesn't like to miss out on sleep too much at his age—which is seventy-three, in case you were wondering."

"Seventy-three and he's still a cop?"

"Just 'cause I said he was full-time, doesn't mean we pay him anything. Deputy Horace McCloud is part of the furniture hereabouts. Draws his state pension and helps out as and when he can. Claims it's to keep his gun hand loose and his brain active, but I know it's mostly to do with the fact Martha McCloud can't stand to have him under her feet all day."

Who could blame her?

Walker nodded. "Looks good for his age. Wouldn't have put him at a day over sixty. Must be the clean mountain air."

Sheriff Hoover turned and held out a large mug of black coffee. Hers contained hot water. A teabag floated on its clear surface, the string dangling from the side of the mug. "Help yourself to cream and sugar if you need it."

"Black's fine for me, thanks." He took a sip and nodded in appreciation. "That's a pretty decent coffee."

"Made with fresh mountain spring water."

Walker covered a wide yawn with a loose fist. "Mind if I make my call now, Sheriff? I tried in the car, but couldn't scare up a signal."

"The mountains catch us all out. You can use my landline unless you're calling someone in the UK?"

Here it comes.

"Why would I want to do that?"

"With that accent, you have to be a Brit, right?"

"Nope. I did most of my schooling in England, but I was born in New York State. I'm as American as you and New York bagels."

If his revelation surprised her, she hid it well enough with a nod of acceptance. She took hold of the string and bobbed the teabag in the water, but the action did little to add color to the steaming liquid. Walker was more than happy he chose the coffee.

"Is there a room anywhere I can talk in private? The call's kind of personal."

She shook her head. "'Fraid not, but I can walk this outside"— she held up the mug—"if you don't take all night. It's pretty cold out there."

"Thanks, Sheriff. I appreciate that."

He waited for the door to close before dialing. Josie took a while to answer.

"Chet?"

Her sleep-fudged voice lifted his spirits in a way that nothing else in the world could manage. Unable to sit still at the sound of her voice, he paced the floor throughout the call.

"Yes, it's me. Sorry to wake you."

"I wasn't asleep. Been waiting up for your call."

Her loud yawn gave the game away.

"Liar." He chuckled.

"Yeah, well, it's been a long day."

"Tell me about it."

"You're late. Where are you?"

"Before I say anything else, can I let you in on a little secret, Josephine Donoghue?"

She let loose another long, comfortable yawn. He pictured her stretching out her arms and pointing her toes while lying in her— soon to be *their*—double bed. "If you insist."

"I love you more than the stars in the night sky, and all the rainbow trout in Little Lake."

69

She made a choking sound as though putting her fingers down her throat to induce a vomit.

"Cut the poetry crap, Walker. Where the heck are you?" Despite her stern words, the smile in her voice lifted his mood another few notches.

"Ever heard of a place called Fort Wycombe? It's in Wyoming close to the Colorado border."

"Nope. What are you still doing in Wyoming, and why didn't you call earlier?"

"Got a little sidetracked and my cell phone can't raise a signal around here."

"So, you're on a landline?"

"Yes, well guessed. You should be a cop with those detection skills."

"Sarcasm won't get you into my bed, Walker."

Despite his fatigue, he couldn't help smiling. God, it was good to hear her voice.

"I do love you, Josie Donoghue."

"Hmm."

"That all you have to say?"

"Keep going, you're on the right track."

"Josie, will you marry me?"

"Better, but you've already asked, and I've already said yes. On the other hand, hearing you beg is good."

"Not begging, asking. But if you really want me to beg …."

"No need. I love you, too, you big lump. So, c'mon, why the stopover in Fort Wick-ham?"

"No, Wycombe." He spelled it out for her. "Look it up on the internet. It's about three hundred miles northeast of you."

"It's late Chet, I'm not looking anything up on anything. Are you fresh enough to drive the mountains at night? You sound tired."

"Aw, honey. You do care."

"Of course I care, you big dumb ox."

"Good, that's a relief. And you're right. I am exhausted. I plan to get some sleep and stay here until sunup. But …"

"But?"

"I might still be … delayed a little in the morning."

"Chet, I hear that tone in your voice again, the one as tells me you've gotten yourself in some sort of trouble. You're scaring me." A rustling on the other end of the line suggested she was sitting up in bed. A small part of his mind—the dumb caveman part—tried to picture what she was, or wasn't, wearing.

Don't go there, Walker. Not the time or the place.

"Now take it easy, Josie. It's nothing to worry about, so don't start frett—"

"Chet, tell me now!"

The story he told included most everything in great detail, but left out the rifle, the fight, and the police standoff. No reason to scare her any more than he had already. She listened in relative silence until he wrapped up with, "So, I have to make a statement and can't leave in the morning until I've checked out Billy and the girls. You understand? It's my medical duty."

"I do. You're a good man, Dr. Walker. Knew there was something about you to love besides your firm butt and your six-pack."

"Josie … that reminds me, darn it. I've got a terrible confession to make."

"What's that?"

"Not sure I should tell you right now. Perhaps it can keep until we meet tomorrow."

"Chester Atlee Walker III, you tell me right now."

"Sorry, darling, but I've packed on a whole load of blubber since you last saw me. Long hours in the ER without the chance to hit the gym coupled with an newfound addiction to blueberry cheesecake has taken its toll. Before I left Johns Hopkins, the nurses and medics took to calling me … Tubby." He pretended to blub. "So darned hurtful."

"Yeah, right. If that's true, Chet Walker, I have two things to say."

"Yes?"

71

"First, you really hide it well during our video calls. Wouldn't have guessed."

"I was careful to make sure you saw headshots only. And the second thing?"

"It doesn't matter a damn to me what you look like. I love you any which way you are."

"Now that, Josie Donoghue, is the nicest thing you've ever said to me."

"Is it?"

"Not really, but just about."

"Either way, the minute you reach Lucky Shores, I'm putting you on a strict low-carb, high-fiber diet, and I'm gonna run you up and down Tooth Mountain until you're my lithe athlete again."

"That's my girl."

"I am, and don't you forget it." She paused for breath before adding, "Being serious for a minute, this Sheriff Hoover, what's he like? Trustworthy?"

"Far as I can tell, Gerrie Hoover's a straight shooter, and—by the way— Gerrie's short for Geraldine. Good looking too. In fact, she could pass for your big sister, but with a little less sass and a little more, I don't know, respect for members of the medical profession."

"That's it. I'm on my way right now."

"Josie, no. I don't want you on the roads this time of night. It's too dangerous. I'm being serious now. Please wait until morning. I'll call you first thing. Promise me you won't come tonight."

Silence thundered down the line.

"Josie? Promise me."

A sigh.

"Sheesh. Okay, I won't drive there tonight. I promise. But …."

"But?"

"But we've been apart for so long, I don't want you taking a fancy to this Sheriff Gerrie Hotpoint and deciding to hang your medical shingle in Fort Wycombe."

"No way that's going to happen, my little firebrand. So, you'll wait for my call? Please?"

72

"Okay, but I won't get a wink of sleep until I hear from you."

"In that case, you'll do what you always do."

"What's that?"

"Open the diner early and go do some baking."

She scoffed. "Think you know me so well, don't you?"

"Not as well as I will after fifty years of marriage."

"Aw, now that's lovely. You're such an old romantic."

"At least you didn't say fat old romantic."

She laughed and he could imagine her shaking her head.

"Call me the moment you have any news, you hear?"

"I will. Promise."

"I'm gonna hold you to that."

Hanging up on Josie was always among the hardest things he ever did, but they eventually ended the call, and he replaced the handset with an anvil-heavy heart.

"Sheriff Hoover?" he called. "I'm done now."

Chapter 8

Another Night in the Mountains

Sheriff Hoover threw open the door and closed it gently behind her. She set her empty cup onto the side table and rubbed her hands together over the pot-bellied stove.

"Darned cold out there. Fall's coming early this year."

She pointed him into the visitor's chair again and took her seat on the other side of the desk, her back to the brick wall. Walker sat and managed to avoid groaning as his legs, especially the damaged calf, signaled their appreciation of the rest.

She opened a drawer and took out a small black voice recorder, a notepad, and a pen. "I'll be recording this for Nancy to transcribe later. She starts her day shift at nine a.m. Sorry 'bout this, but you'll be here at least most of the morning."

"I kind of figured that already, Sheriff. I've just cleared the decks with my boss."

"Oh, I thought you were talking to your fiancée."

"I was." He showed her a slight grin.

She shook her head and added a facepalm.

"So," she said after hitting the record button, "let's start with the basics. Name, date of birth, address."

Walker sighed. The minute he decided to make the trip by road instead of air, he should have considered typing out his résumé. He'd been through the "quiet interview with the local police" a number of times in the past, but not since he'd given up his life as an itinerant songsmith and returned to med school. He really thought his new, short-haired, clean-shaven status as an upstanding member of the medical profession would have given him a hall pass for such an interrogation.

Not a chance in hell.

Walker answered her questions and showed her his driver's permit. "For the benefit of the recording, this is a New York State driver's license, Class D."

She stared hard at the photo and held it up level with his face. "Doesn't look much like you. Long hair and a full beard in this picture, and there you sit all professionally barbered."

"I keep meaning to update the photo, but I've been busy recently and need to get a Colorado license anyway, so I let it slide. My passport photo's up-to-date, though." He fished around inside his medical bag, found the little blue booklet, and passed it over. "This better?"

"Certainly is. A perfect likeness. Mind if I make a copy?"

Without waiting for his answer, she stood and made busy with a huge and archaic copier. It sat on a table in what he took to be Nancy's admin corner. The machine took an age to cycle through its startup routine and splurge out the image, but Walker was in no hurry. He was in for the long haul, and sunup wasn't due for at least another four hours. The fact that the sheriff kept her office warm enough to grow orchids made it a comfortable enough place to soak in the heat and wait out the night. He'd spent the occasional night in colder and far less comfortable accommodations.

Sheriff Hoover returned to her desk and eased into the chair. It squeaked as she leaned forward.

"So, Dr. Chester Atlee Walker, let's start with what brings you to Husqvarna County."

"Nothing. Just passing through on my way to somewhere else."

"And where's that?"

"Place called Lucky Shores, Colorado. A few hours south of here."

She noted the name on her pad, but unlike Shirley, didn't admit to recognizing it.

"From Syracuse to Colorado by way of Laramie?"

"How do you know I came through Laramie?"

"You were on the WY-230 heading south. Nowhere else you could have come through. Not unless you travelled the back roads."

"Well worked out. Do you double as the town's detective?" Again, he grinned to avoid giving offence.

"When I have to." She shot him another of her guarded smiles. "So, tell me. Syracuse to here doesn't seem like the most direct route. I'd have thought you'd take the I-70."

Walker blinked hard, trying to ward off the vision-blurring effects of fatigue and the stultifying office heat. "I've travelled the I-70 a couple of times and fancied something different. I'm one of those guys who doesn't like to retrace his steps if he can avoid it."

She tapped her pen on the pad.

"What's in Lucky Shores?"

Walker breathed out long and hard and pointed at the phone on the sheriff's desk. "The most beautiful woman on this here planet."

If he expected the woman in the law office to show softness, Walker was disappointed. Sheriff Hoover rode straight past his comment. "So, luck brought you to my county?"

He nodded. "That's right. Pure dumb luck. Good or bad, I haven't decided yet. Billy and his sisters might consider it good luck, I suppose." He pointed at his empty cup. "As far as I'm concerned, my love of a decent rich roast coffee is to blame for my seeing the dangerous end of Fulton Hatfield's hunting rifle."

"Coffee?"

"Yep. If I hadn't accepted Shirley's offer of a second top off, I'd have been long gone before young Billy ever reached the truck stop." He shrugged and glanced up at the wall clock again. "I'd probably be rolling into Lucky Shores right about now. On such decisions whole lives can turn."

"Whoa, that's deep."

"Nope, it's the human condition."

Walker tried to conceal another deep yawn behind his hand, which Sheriff Hoover failed to mirror. She was clearly made of stronger stuff. Either that, or she hadn't been awake for nearly two days straight. Walker lowered his head and sucked in one more yawn. This one, he didn't bother trying to hide.

"So, you listened to Billy's garbled message and lit out to the Hatfield ranch. Then what happened exactly?"

For the second time that night, Walker went through the story, this time leaving nothing out. His memory, honed during his years in med school, stood up well to Sheriff Hoover's cross examination. He could remember each action and each spoken word close to verbatim.

"That's when you and your deputies turned up at the farm, and I have to say, a prettier sight than those red and blue flashing lights I haven't seen in a while. Not since … you know who."

Again, he pointed at the phone on the sheriff's desk. This time the Iron Lady's lips twitched and her smile actually seemed genuine. "Your partner in Lucky Shores?"

"S'right. My fiancée."

"You have anything more to add?"

"Only that when I took Hatfield's rifle and poked him in the head with it, I was in fear for my life, and in fear for the life of Mary Anne and her baby."

"Why did you think that?"

"From Mr. Hatfield's reaction to my presence in his house."

"In his daughter's bedroom, don't you mean?"

Walker clenched his jaw and leaned forward. He didn't like the slant of her question.

"What do you mean by that?"

"I'm covering what Fulton Hatfield's lawyer might bring up at his trial."

Walker forced his shoulders to relax and took a mouthful of the cooling coffee. "That's not going to be a problem, Sheriff."

"You sure?"

"Certain."

"Why?"

"Hatfield threatened me even though I announced myself as a doctor sent there by his son, Billy."

77

"So, you just up and launched yourself at a man brandishing a rifle. Sounds a little foolhardy to me."

"I didn't like the way things were going down. My presence in his house put Hatfield in an impossible position. No way was he going to let me walk out alive, not with what I'd discovered."

"That Billy Hatfield had gotten his half-sister pregnant?"

What was her problem? She either hadn't worked it out for herself, or wanted Walker to make the accusation independently. Again, he ground his teeth. So be it. Even though she may have been working some sort of legal ploy, Walker took the bait.

"Billy isn't the baby's father," Walker said, carefully studying the sheriff's reaction.

"He's not?"

"No. He most definitely isn't." Walker kept his voice flat. No need to show the emotion bubbling up inside.

"Well, who is, then?"

"Do you really need me to spell it out?"

Sheriff Hoover's unchanging expression told him she'd already worked out the answer for herself. Still, she refused to voice her suspicious.

"Yes, I do."

"Fulton Hatfield," Walker announced, still showing outward calm.

"Fulton Hatfield? You're serious?"

"As serious as an outbreak of Ebola. If you'd seen the way he looked at her and the way his hackles rose when he realized I'd worked out his dirty little secret, you'd have reacted the same way I did. Papa Hatfield raped his daughter and fathered her child. Do you need me to make it any clearer? The man is a pedophile who needs to be put away for a very long time."

The statement earned him the sort of reaction he expected. Gerrie's eyes closed and her jaw muscles bunched. The pen snapped under the force of her grip. Black ink bled onto her fingers.

"Darn it," she said, holding up her hand. She took a tissue from a box on her desk and tried to wipe the ink away.

Walker hadn't finished. "Sorry to say, I also suspect that Billy's developmental impairment is also the result of incest. If you interview the boy's mother carefully enough, she'll probably confirm it."

"Sorry, Doc, that won't be possible. Ellie May Hatfield died from complications suffered when delivering Mary Anne."

Walker nodded. It figured.

Post-partum fatality was a common complication of inbreeding. Walker had opened up a real cesspit, and Fulton Hatfield had crawled out from the ooze.

"Not a problem. I'll be able to prove my accusations with a paternity test."

"Are you absolutely certain of that?"

"As certain as I am of daylight replacing the darkness come tomorrow morning."

He'd never been more confident of a diagnosis in all his time as a fully-fledged medical practitioner. All two weeks of it.

"Okay. Anything more to add?"

"Only that it seems a shame to me that local child services didn't follow up on the writ Deputy McCloud told me he tried to serve a little while back. But I'm guessing the inquiry is going to look into the whole sorry affair."

"An inquiry?"

"The one you're going to set up when my accusations prove to be correct. Assuming I'm right about you, Sheriff Hoover, and you hate child abusers as much as I do."

"I do. Excellent. That's all I need for the moment."

Sheriff Hoover stopped the recording.

"Off the record, Doc, I promise you Fulton Hatfield's going down for incest, pedophilia, assault, kidnap, attempted murder, and anything else I can have thrown at him and help make stick."

Walker took a deep breath and let it out slowly. He didn't speak for a few moments.

"Sheriff Hoover, for a second back there, I was worried you were going to see things in a completely different way."

"Sorry 'bout that, Doc. I've had my suspicions regarding what's been going on at the Hatfield ranch for years, but never had enough probable cause to raise a warrant. My case wasn't helped by the farm straddling the state lines, neither."

Walker relaxed. He'd been right about the half-pint sheriff. She'd been waiting for him to make the formal accusations. As a stranger to Husqvarna County, he didn't have any historical axes to grind. He'd be classed as a totally independent witness.

"You can count on my support in any investigation you mount, Sheriff. I'll only be a few hours away. Josie and I'll be happy to visit and help you out all we can."

"Josie's your fiancée in Lucky Shores?"

"She certainly is."

"So, you're planning to settle in Colorado?"

Again, Walker nodded.

"I'll be taking over as head of the Lucky Shores Medical Center. They've had a highly paid replacement for the past four years and plan on buying my services for a knock down price."

"On account of you being newly qualified?"

"No. On account of me being happy to work for next to nothing in order to be with Josie. That and the fact I have other strings to my bow."

Six strings to be precise, and all attached to a guitar called Suzy.

Gerrie half-stood to lean across the desk and offer her hand.

"Well Dr. Walker—"

"If we've finished with police business for the time being, please call me Chet."

"Fair enough, Chet. And you'll call me, Gerrie. Okay?"

"Okay, Gerrie."

"On behalf of the citizens of Fort Wycombe, I'd like to thank you for all you've done here. If there's anything the town can do for you, just ask."

Walker winced. "Well, Gerrie. There is one thing."

"Name it."

"Would you point me in the direction of the nearest decent rooming house prepared to take in an exhausted medic in the middle of the night? A motel would do."

Gerrie rolled up the pieces of broken pen in a couple of tissues and dropped the bundle into a trash can at the foot of her desk. "You know what, Dr. Walker? I can just about manage to do that little ol' thing. You can be a guest of the county sheriff for the night. Can't promise you five-star accommodations, but the bedding's clean, the room's warm and dry, and we can even offer you a hot shower. How's that sound?"

"As long as there aren't any bars on the doors and windows, it sounds pretty close to perfect."

Gerrie flashed a genuine smile. "Follow me."

Chapter 9

The Happy Reunion

Walker gradually became aware of sunlight behind his closed lids and a growing level of background noise. He flipped over, turned his back to the window, and buried his head under the spare pillow, trying to drown out the noise or ignore it. Traffic rattled and rumbled past. In the street below, people greeted each other, welcoming in the new day with cheery enthusiasm. Dogs barked, babies wailed, children giggled and played, and Walker's calf ached.

He lay still, taking in the sounds and the smells of a strange room, a strange place, struggling to put the pieces together.

Where the heck was he?

Slowly, the fragments of memory pulled together and meshed into a semi-cohesive story. Upstairs in the sheriff's office, Fort … Wycombe.

Fort Wycombe, Wyoming.

He vaguely recalled climbing a dust-free staircase and following Sheriff Hoover, Gerrie, into a small apartment above the cells. She'd briefly shown him a bedroom and a bathroom, and bade him goodnight. He'd showered in minutes, dried off with a nice clean but scratchy towel, and flopped into a freshly made bed. He remembered nothing until being woken by the cacophony of life in a small town in the foothills of the Rocky Mountains.

His tongue, furry with sleep and foul-tasting from lack of toothpaste, stuck to the roof of his mouth. He peeled a gritty eye open and checked his watch. A little short of 7:15 a.m.

Damn it to hell.

So much for a sleep-in. Three hours' sleep and he was still exhausted?

Go figure.

"Must be getting old, Walker."

His sore eyes picked out a dark stain on the wall opposite the window, and his nose reacted to the odor of damp and mold wafting up from the floor.

"That's more than enough wallowing, Walker," he said to no one.

He threw back the covers and shivered as the cold, damp air hit his naked body. Where had he put his clothes? His eyes found the pile he'd thrown on a chair, but couldn't see his suitcase.

Hell on a budget.

He'd left it in the Ford. Last night's exhaustion had pushed thoughts of the morning from his head. As a result, he'd have to put on his filthy clothes or search for the Ford with nothing on but a towel wrapped around his waist. Not an option if the noise outside was any indication of the number of people whose paths he'd cross on the way—even if he did know where the deputy had parked his car.

What a mess. In his life, he'd spent enough time on the road to know how to prepare for waking in strange places, but all that had escaped him with the desperate need to sleep.

Walker ignored the undershirt and briefs, and made do with the bloodstained jeans. He tried not to smell the underarms or touch the blood as he worked to fasten the buttons of his plaid shirt, but his nose wrinkled when he lost the fight. He slipped on his boots, left the laces untied, and headed for the door to the top of the stairs.

The door opened inwards and he nearly tripped over a suitcase on the landing—his suitcase. At least someone had been awake last night. Gerrie, no doubt. He dragged the case inside, selected his attire for the day—all clean, all pressed by his mom, and all smelling as sweet and as fresh as a summer meadow.

After taking another steaming hot shower before dressing, he felt almost human again.

Before leaving the room, he tidied up, stuffed his dirty clothes into a black trash bag he'd found in the kitchenette, and headed downstairs, baggage in hand.

At 7:45 a.m. he was ready to start the day—or would be if he could find a place that served a half-decent coffee and a passable breakfast.

The sheriff's office hadn't changed much since he'd left it—not that he'd expected it to—but he had imagined it would be full of police officers already about their business. Still, after the night they'd had, a late start seemed appropriate and acceptable. With only four full-time officers, he doubted Fort Wycombe would run a twenty-four-hour police service.

The coffee machine on the hospitality table by the side of Nancy's desk stood cold and lifeless—a hideous sight for a recently woken man. A superficial search for coffee and a mug to put it in revealed nothing, and he wasn't about to rummage through the drawers and cupboards of a sheriff's office without the cop's express permission.

He stood scratching his head, wondering what to do next, when the front door opened and in marched the woman herself.

"Morning, Doc," she said, smiling as bright as a polished button.

"Sheriff." He dipped his head and pointed to his suitcase and the black bag sitting next to it on the floor in the middle of the room. "Do I have you to thank for my bag?"

She lifted her chin in a nod.

"Thought you'd appreciate a fresh set of clothes this morning. Didn't want you wandering around the place scaring the townsfolk with all that blood splattered over your clothes."

"I certainly do appreciate it. Thanks." Walker stretched out his first smile of the day—it almost hurt. "How long have you been awake?"

"Thirty-six hours, give or take. Didn't bother going to bed last night. So"—she rubbed her hands together—"can I interest you in a hearty breakfast?"

Walker straightened. Before his gritty eyes, the sheriff had turned from law officer into an angel of mercy.

"Gerrie, I thought you'd never ask. Please lead the way."

She stood aside and showed him out the door, locking the office behind her.

A watery sun cast pale shadows and Walker took his first daylight view of the Fort. A wide street flanked either side by two-story buildings with orange brick and stucco walls with flat roofs, mainly store fronts, but a few dwellings. To the south and west, steep wooded hills leaned over the town, cradling it in a protective embrace. To the north and east, the land sloped gently down to the flat plains already shimmering in an early morning heat haze.

Gerrie headed east along a concrete sidewalk and they ran a gauntlet of greetings and inquisitive stares from a street with an unexpectedly high population. Somehow, word must have gotten around about the strange doctor in town and the ruckus of the previous night. As he'd learned during his lamentably short time in Lucky Shores, small towns had comprehensive and intricate grapevines. Few secrets survived their operation.

One hundred yards along a paved sidewalk, Gerrie ducked down a narrow side street that led to a row of quaint arts and crafts shops and a large café that took up at least three buildings.

A sign on the plate glass window—painted in Old Wild West copper plate—screamed, *Beth's Eatery: The Best Darned Food in Wyoming*. Nothing if not a modest claim. They crossed the road and made straight for the glass door.

The fragrance of freshly ground coffee and newly baked bread—better than any perfume ever created—brought light to Walker's darkness and joy to his heart. His stomach growled in anticipation, and his mouth watered. Ivan Pavlov, the Russian dog torturer, would have been delighted.

Beth's Eatery was jammed with customers, mostly men, who sat with heads down, concentrating hard on their breakfast victuals. Even from outside the Eatery, Walker could hear cutlery scraping flatware and the low murmur of conversation.

Gerrie pushed open the door and silence fell in a wave from the front of the room to the back. Dozens of pairs of eyes took in Walker, all of them staring, all of them curious.

The sheriff made for the furthest corner and the only empty table in the place. Set for two, although large enough to seat six, a folded, hand-written card on the surface read, *RESERVED*.

"Morning folks," Gerrie said. "Can I help you with anything?"

A few of the men returned her greeting, but most simply lowered their heads and continued their task of stoking the furnaces in preparation for a hard day's graft.

By the time Walker and Gerrie took their seats, most of the crowd had settled down, but the group at the closest table kept side-eyeing him. Walker waited for Gerrie to explode until he recognized one of the men as Deputy Horace. The others at the table, three men and two women, wore the dun-colored uniforms of volunteer deputies. Walker didn't recognize any of their faces.

"Morning, Deputy," Walker said, dipping his head to the grizzled lawman.

Horace tipped his hat, but didn't relax the frown. "Hi, Doc. Sleep well?"

Walker scratched his chin's three-day stubble. "Never better, thanks."

"Should hope so, too."

Gerrie tapped the table with the flat of her hand. "Now, Horace. The Doc doesn't know about your alternative sleeping arrangements. It's not his fault you had to go home and suffer an earful of abuse from Martha for waking her up in the middle of the night. Poor woman."

Horace's breakfast partners chortled. The old man's scowl deepened, and he shot Walker a look of pure venom.

A middle-aged, middle-sized waitress with muddy blonde hair, dark at the roots, arrived carrying a notepad and the stub of a pencil. She ignored Gerrie and studied Walker with the intensity of a medical examiner sifting through the insides of a cadaver.

"The usual, Sheriff?" she asked, still looking at Walker.

"Yes please, Rhonda."

"And you, sir?"

The "sir" elicited another loud guffaw from Horace's table, but Rhonda silenced them with a sideways glare that could have stopped molten lava in its tracks. Even Horace looked away abashed.

Walker smiled pleasantly. "What's good here?"

"Honey, everything's good here. That sign on the window ain't bull jerky. You like bacon and eggs in the morning?"

"Yes please, and all the trimmings together with a bucket of your strongest coffee."

"Coming right up, sir."

Rhonda turned away, deliberately ignoring Horace's table. When she'd left, Gerrie turned her chair so she could take in both Walker and her deputies. "Horace, any news on Fulton Hatfield?"

The old lawman sniffed. "Busted nose, a couple black eyes, cut lip, and two broken teeth, but he'll live. When the Doc hits someone, they stay hit."

"Self-defense, Deputy," Walker said, adding a head tilt and a shrug.

"Weren't accusing you of nothing, Doctor Walker. Just offerin' an observation," the old man grumbled.

"Glad to hear it."

"Beats me how an unarmed medic on his own can overcome a backwoodsman with a rifle," the old lawman mumbled, half to himself.

"What are you suggesting, Horace?" Walker asked, his blood rising.

"Who's with him now?" Gerrie asked, interrupting a conversation that was only headed downhill, and rapidly.

Horace held Walker's eye for a beat before answering Gerrie's question. "They're keeping him in for observation. Worried about concussion. Like I said, this here medic packs one hell of a punch."

Before Walker could respond, Rhonda returned with a carafe of coffee and two large cups. She poured and left without saying a word, taking the carafe with her, much to Walker's disappointment.

"Who's watching him?" Gerrie repeated.

"Two of Laramie's finest law officers. Don't worry, Gerrie. I left him handcuffed to his hospital bed. That piece of bull excrement ain't going nowhere but lockup."

Walker must have looked confused, because Horace winked.

"Don't mind me, Doc," Horace said, "I'm just yankin' your chain. Far as I'm concerned, you went easy on that child molesting bag of sh—"

"Thanks, Horace," Gerrie said, holding up her hand. "And for the Doc's benefit, I spoke to the OB-GYN at Laramie Mercy about an hour ago. Mother and baby are both doing real well. Mary Anne's underfed, but they're working on that by giving her double portions of everything. They've also hooked her up to a drip for fluids and suchlike. Seems the poor child thinks she's in heaven."

"And Billy?" Walker asked.

"Awaiting a psych exam, but otherwise calm and eating his way through the hospital's food stores. You did a good thing yesterday, Doc. We all appreciate it."

"We surely do," Horace said.

He stood and actually smiled as he thrust a gnarled hand in Walker's direction. Walker suffered under a grip so strong, he worried for the safety of his fingers. The others took their lead from the veteran and left to go about their off duty business.

Rhonda brought their food, topped off their cups, and they tucked in. Gerrie's portion size matched Walker's, and he wondered how she was going to pack it inside so small a frame. She managed well enough and cleaned her plate first.

The food was good, almost as good as the breakfast Josie served him the morning after he pulled her father from the car wreck three years earlier. The company didn't quite match up, and neither did the fresh-baked bread rolls, but everything else hit pretty close to the mark.

Gerrie pushed her empty plate away, only just beating him to finish the supersized portion, and leaned back in her seat, coffee cup cradled in both hands.

"What next?" he asked, cleaning the yolk from his plate with the last piece of roll. He popped it into his mouth as she answered.

"After Nancy's typed up your statement and you've signed it, you'll be free to go."

He swallowed the bread. "Really?"

"Yes, and why not? I know who you are and where you're headed. There's no reason to hold you any longer than absolutely necessary."

"Again, really?"

"Why do you find that so hard to believe?"

"My experience of law enforcement leads me to expect things to work a lot slower. How come you're so happy for me to be on my way?"

She drained her cup, raised it to signal for a refill, and waited for Rhonda to top off both their drinks once again and head off before answering. "It may surprise you to learn that while you were sleeping the sleep of the just and the righteous, this local sheriff was hard at work. We have these wonderful pieces of modern police technology called telephones. We also have a couple desktop computers and a fax machine."

"I'm relieved to hear it."

"You should be. Last night, I faxed a copy of your passport photo to a sheriff friend of mine. A man named Caspar Boyd."

Walker allowed his eyebrows to shoot towards his hairline. "You called the Ghost of Lucky Shores in the middle of the night and he answered?"

Gerrie put down her cup and crossed her arms. They were so slim, he wondered how she would be able to hold the big handgun she carried in her holster, let alone fire it with any accuracy. The fact she wore it with the retaining strap buttoned down gave him peace. He hoped to never see her draw it in anger.

"The Ghost of Lucky Shores? On account of his given name?"

89

Walker's nod drew a warm smile from his host.

"Yeah, I like that. And it seems Sheriff Boyd likes you too. He told me I could trust you with my life. Caspar's normally a close-mouthed SOB. He's not the sort to sing people's praises without good cause."

"You know him?"

"By reputation, and we've met a couple times."

Walker relaxed his hard-working eyebrows. The first time he'd met Caspar Boyd, the veteran sheriff drew a gun on him and patted him down for weapons. The Ghost also interrogated him for five hours straight—and through the middle of the night.

Happy times.

Walker kept those particular details to himself and made do with a non-committal, "Sheriff Boyd is a good police officer and clearly a man with great intuition."

"He also confirmed you'd been offered the post of chief medical officer at the city's main health facility."

"That sounds really impressive until I tell you I'll be the *only* doctor in town and it's the town's only health facility."

Gerrie smiled again. When she wanted it to be, she had a nice smile. Warm and friendly. "Sheriff Boyd said that very thing, almost word for word. He also told me how you saved the life of that fiancée of yours, Joey Donoghue, and helped recover a whole bunch of stolen money. Despite your Brit accent, it seems like you're an all-American hero."

"Stop it, Gerrie. Gushing doesn't suit you, and you'll only make me blush. And most of that story is bull. I did very little."

"That's not what the papers and local news said at the time. I read up on you from the internet. Very impressive considering you arrived in Lucky Shores with nothing but a guitar on your back and a couple hundred dollars in your back pocket. And look at you now—three and some years later, a fully-fledged doctor soon to be in charge of your own hospital."

Walker shrugged. He didn't have a better response. He finished his coffee and set the cup on top of his dirty plate. The world always seemed a much better place after a good breakfast.

He wiped his mouth with a paper napkin, crushed it into a ball, and dropped it alongside the cup. "You said something about Nancy and my statement. Since you're letting me go, I'd like to head out and check on my patients. After that, I'll make tracks for my new home."

Gerrie checked her watch, as did Walker. 9:16 a.m.

"She should have started the transcription by now. Won't take her long. She's quick and accurate. We should have you on your way well before noon. Fancy taking a little stroll around the Fort while we wait?"

"You can spare the time to play tour guide?"

"Nothing else to do until I have your statement signed and the doctor gives me the all-clear to interview Fulton Hatfield. I have my radio handy if anyone needs me."

She stood and headed for the till. Walker reached for his wallet and she waved him away.

"Your money's no good here, Doc. Breakfast is on the Fort Wycombe PD. We owe you that much."

One of the patrons called out, "Hear, hear, Gerrie. You done good, Doc."

The rest of the crowd broke into a spontaneous round of applause. Blood rose to warm Walker's face. He raised a hand in acknowledgement and hurried through the door. The temperature had climbed a little since they'd entered the café, and the warm air did little to dry the sweat clinging to his face. He took a breath and held it until the sheriff exited the café.

"How come everyone knows?"

"Small town, Doc. Little else to do here but gossip."

"Yes, but … we only finished our interview a few hours ago."

"Like I said …."

"Yeah, yeah. I get it. Small town. Lucky Shores has the same magical bush telegraph." He undid the top three buttons on his shirt and pumped the air. It only helped a little. "Where we headed?"

Gerrie's eyes sparkled in the sunlight. He hadn't noticed how blue they were the previous night. Hadn't noticed the humor

91

behind them either, but then again, neither of them had seen much cause for humor at the Hatfield ranch.

"Back to my office to collect the wagon. Thought you might like a chauffeured tour. Umiak Falls are beautiful this time of the morning. And, since you're in a hurry, we can check on Nancy's progress before we go."

"A car ride suits me. I've done more than my share of walking over the years. Can't remember the last time it turned up my nose at the offer of a lift."

They took a different route to the sheriff's office, strolling in amiable silence, Walker relieved not to feel as though he were the object of suspicion. The sun on his back warmed and relaxed his shoulders and all felt right with his world. With fewer people around to impede their progress, they made the turn onto High Street and started the climb.

"Are you limping?" Gerrie asked. "Need to slow down?"

Walker's immediate reaction was to make light of his injury with one of his well-tried jokes. In the past, he'd used everything from falling off his skateboard in El Paso, to wiping out in a tube in Maui. This time, he felt comfortable enough to go with the truth.

"It's an old calf injury from when I was a paramedic. Doesn't worry me too much if I have time to warm up properly, but last night's little escapade likely ruptured a few thousand muscle fibers. I'll mend soon enough, though."

"Want me to take you to the clinic? Old Bones will be up by now."

"Old Bones?"

"The town's medic, Dr. Leonard Goodbody. Dear Old Bones has been practicing in Fort Wycombe for more than fifty years. Way past retirement age, but the town still can't do without him."

"Thanks for the offer, but all I need is rest. I'll pop a couple of ibuprofen if the ache gets any worse."

"Not far now," she said, pointing to the Fort Wycombe PD building. "We can slow it down if you want."

"This pace is fine."

Gerrie opened the door and Walker followed her into the dark of the office.

In the admin corner, Nancy—a sixty-something, gray-haired, and well-rounded matron—looked up from her keyboard and smiled a greeting. "Morning, Gerrie. I've made a good start on transcribing the interview. Shouldn't take too much longer."

Gerrie said something in response, but Walker wasn't listening. His mind had stopped working and no sound made it past the pounding in his ears. Another person in the room, who'd jumped to her feet as they entered, took the whole of his attention.

Walker's heart pounded, his stomach lurched, trying to twist itself into a reef knot. His mouth dried as she stood before him, all sixty-three-and-a-half, beautifully packaged inches of her.

She looked up at him through those huge, liquid brown eyes, and again his heart turned somersaults.

"Morning, Dr. Walker," she said, her face expressionless, but her eyes alive and shining.

He swallowed hard.

"Morning, Josie Donoghue."

Chapter 10

Hugs and Long-Delayed Kisses

The world stood still and disappeared into the background.

Josie. My Josie. How?

Walker's beautiful, feisty, wonderful fiancée stood in front of him, taking all the air from the room and leaving him lightheaded. How should he react? He wanted to whoop and holler, scoop her up into his arms, hold her tight, smother her with kisses. But in a sheriff's office? How would that go down? Would Gerrie class is a "lewd and lascivious" behavior?

He pushed away from the door and took a hesitant step closer. Josie did the same. What followed was a sort of slow motion, faltering dance.

"How you doing?" he asked, aiming for nonchalance, but hitting nervous schoolkid. He kept his hands in his pockets and made fists to stop them from reaching out and pulling her into a hug.

"Okay. You?" The merest uplift at the corners of her mouth betrayed the tiniest hint of a smile.

"Been worse. Nice day."

She looked past him, tilting her face toward the brightness of the morning. "Yep. Not bad."

Two more steps each and they stood inches apart. She had to crane her neck to maintain eye contact. The orange flecks in her brown eyes caught the sun's light and sparkled. They hadn't changed, nor had the effect they had on his heart rate, or his mind.

So damned gorgeous.

"What are you doing here?" He tried to make it sound casual, but it spurted out like an accusation.

Josie wrinkled her nose. "Just passing through."

"You promised not to drive through the night."

She made a great show of reading the time off her watch. "Ninety seconds."

"Sorry?"

"We're together ninety seconds and you're already picking a fight?"

He smiled. Couldn't help himself. His parents included, she was the only person alive who could make him feel like a geeky little kid.

"Sorry. Worried about you driving the mountains at night, is all."

"Now you're questioning my driving skills?"

"Stop it, you."

"Okay." Again the smile, this time wider, warmed his heart.

In the three months since she'd last visited him in Baltimore, Josie had let her hair grow out a little. Its soft waves now reached her shoulders and silver clips held it back from her face. The new look suited her, and she'd put on a couple of pounds in weight, still slim, but now extra curvy. Less elfin, more womanly. That suited her, too.

Hug her, Walker. Kiss her, damn it.

Something held him back. Held them apart.

Walker became aware of a heavy weight in the room. Other eyes stared. Other ears listened. Walker cleared his throat and made a half-turn. "Josie Donoghue, meet Sheriff Geraldine Hoover, and I guess this is Nancy?"

Gerrie nodded. "Morning Ms. Donoghue, my friends call me Gerrie. Very pleased to meet you."

They moved further into the room and the door shut softly behind them on an automatic closer. Gerrie and Josie shook hands.

"And yes," Gerrie continued, turning to Walker, "this is Nancy Greenwich, the real driving force of the Fort Wycombe PD. The place would fall apart without her."

Nancy tittered and played with the gold cross dangling from a chain around her neck. "Aw Sheriff, now you know that's absolutely correct."

Gerrie dipped her head towards the computer. Nancy took the hint and settled the ear buds back in place. She smiled at Walker and Josie, hit play on the recorder, and resumed her typing. Her long-nailed fingers flew over the computer keyboard.

"Shouldn't be too long now, Doc," Gerrie said. "I'm guessing you guys would like some alone time while you wait?"

"I was right before. You *do* double up as Fort Wycombe's chief of detectives."

"Way you two are looking at each other it doesn't take much to make the deduction, Doc." Gerrie turned and ushered both him and Josie back out the door. "The town park's just around the corner." She pointed towards the rising sun. "It's got bench seating and a killer view of the river and the mountains. C'mon, I'll show you. It'll be quiet this time of the morning, too. Why don't you two go sit and take a load off. When Nancy's done, I'll come fetch you."

"Thanks, Sheriff," Josie said. "It was a pleasure meeting you."

Walker reached out his hand and Josie took it, squeezed tight, and held on. Touching her sent electric tingles up his arm. God, he'd missed her so much.

They headed out, three abreast, and Walker couldn't drag his eyes from Josie. They'd taken no more than a few steps before Josie stopped and held him back. "You're limping again. What happened?"

"Nothing," he said. "Touch of cramp. Altitude always has that effect on me. You know that."

He looked over her at Gerrie, frowned, and shook his head. The sheriff gave him an almost imperceptible nod.

"Sheriff Hoover," Josie said, still looking at Walker, "how do you deal with witnesses who lie to your face?"

Gerrie grinned knowingly.

96

"Hell, honey, I either beat the truth out of 'em with a nightstick or lock 'em up and mislay the keys for a couple days until they see the error of their ways. Works like a charm."

"You have any space in your cells?"

"Plenty. Want me to throw him in jail right now?" Gerrie's grin widened into a full blown smile, and she carried on walking uphill, heading toward the sound of water crashing over rocks. "Doc Walker, I really like this one. She's a keeper."

Walker scrunched up his face and massaged his neck with his free hand, the one not clamped to Josie's and not letting go.

"Not quite so sure about that, Gerrie. If I caught something so small on my fishing line, I'd be inclined to throw it back in the water."

Josie punched his arm with so much force, he almost felt it land. Lord, but it was good to have her back in his life. He'd never let her go again. Not ever. He kissed the back of her hand and whispered. "Love you, Josie Donoghue."

Again, her eyes sparkled.

"Love you too, Chester Atlee Walker."

Gerrie stopped and indicated a sign attached to the side of a grain and hardware store that read: *Fort Wycombe City Park*.

"That there's the scenic route, much shorter than driving. Follow the path a couple hundred yards and you'll find one of the prettiest beauty spots in the whole of Wyoming. Not that you'll be interested in the view, I guess."

The glint in Gerrie's eyes and the mirth in her words showed what a difference daylight could make.

"If I'm busy, I'll send one of my deputies to fetch you when Nancy's done."

"Thanks, Gerrie," Walker and Josie said in unison.

They watched the sheriff retrace her steps before following the sign, which pointed them down a narrow alley lined with evergreen shrubs. Purple, white, and orange flowers dotted the verges, their perfume wafting on the wind, blowing into their faces.

"She seems nice," Josie said.

"Yep, effective, too. Professional. Things could have deteriorated badly last night if she'd lost her cool."

"Nice looking, too. If a little on the mature side for you."

"Is she?" He raised both shoulders in a deep shrug. "Hadn't noticed. The good looking part, I mean. No idea about her age, mind you."

"Liar."

He squeezed her hand. "It's true. It was dark last night and I had ... other things on my mind."

Like defending myself against an attack, and protecting a daughter from her child-molesting father.

"And this morning I was blinded by the light of your beauty."

"Cut the crap, Walker," she said. "You're not writing one of your tacky song lyrics now."

"Tacky? Really? That's so hurtful."

"There's no room for more than one liar in this relationship."

"Agreed."

The minute they reached the alley and were out of sight between two rows of bushes, Walker scooped her into his arms. She squealed and pretended to fight him off before throwing her arms around his neck.

"Chester Walker, put me down this minute."

"Really?" He held her away and gave her his patented hurt puppy-dog look.

"No. Kiss me, you fool."

"If you insist."

"I insist."

Walker planted the kiss he'd been promising himself since leaving Syracuse. She responded warmly and hugged him close and tight. They embraced and, for some strange reason, the world continued spinning.

He came up for air and she nuzzled his neck. "Hmm, that was just what—"

"Don't say it," he butted in.

"Say what?"

"Don't say that was 'just what the doctor ordered.'"

"You think you know me so well. What I was going to say before you interrupted me so rudely was, 'That was just what I've been looking forward to.' Now, put me down you big muscle-bound lug. I can walk on my own."

"I know you can, but I'm happy like this until my arms get tired."

He carried on walking, Josie feather-light in his arms.

"Fine. Anyway I promised not to drive here this morning, and I didn't."

As she spoke, her warm breath tickled his neck. It felt wonderful.

"How'd you get here then? Teleportation?"

She nibbled his earlobe.

"Stop that. I might drop you."

She nipped his neck instead and he loved it. If he knew Fort Wycombe any better he might have lost all self-control and carried her to the nearest hotel room. He stopped for a moment and breathed in her aura. She sighed.

"This is lovely."

"Yes, it is," he said, "but answer my question. How'd you get here if you didn't drive?"

She pulled away a little and fixed him with her most serious expression.

"One of CC's regular delivery routes takes him to Cheyenne. The moment you hung up the phone last night, I called him. He was happy to make a little detour and drop me off in this one-horse town."

Curtis Carling, locally known as CC, owned the biggest haulage firm in Lucky Shores. Walker and CC had met under trying circumstances on Walker's first day in town. They'd been fast friends ever since. The trucker had even made it to Baltimore during Walker's second year and they'd painted the town if not exactly red, they'd at least made it blush.

"CC always did think he owed me a favor after nearly running me off the road. Where is he?"

"Most of the way to Cheyenne by now, I'd imagine. Said to tell you 'Hi' and the drinks are on him the next time you play the saloon."

Walker shook his head. "That's not going to happen. Imagine the scandal. I mean, what would the dignified members of the Chamber of Commerce and the Hospital Board think of their highly paid and well-respected doctor twanging a guitar at the local saloon? I'd never hear the end of it."

"Given that my aunt chairs both organizations and owns the saloon, I doubt any of them would mind at all. In fact, most of them are members of the Chet Walker fan club."

"I have a fan club?"

She nodded. "Facebook and Twitter pages and everything. Some of the fans are crazy about you."

"And you?"

"Me? Nah, not so much. You're not a bad singer, but give me Justin Bieb—"

Walker silenced her with another long, slow kiss. It wasn't a hardship.

"Want to get down?" he asked, with their lips still touching.

"You saying I'm too heavy for you?" Her eyes shone.

"I'm not as young as I once was, and my leg. You know." He pretended to wince.

She ran her fingers through his hair. "A few more gray hairs since we first met and a couple more wrinkles, old man, but you'll do well enough. Okay, let me down."

He lowered her and they hugged. The top of her head reached his upper chest. Josie was small, but perfectly formed in every conceivable way. "God, I've missed you, Josie Donoghue."

"I know. You've already said that."

She took his hand once more and started marching, uphill, toward the sound of rushing water.

"So," she said, "tell me what really happened last night. I know you, Chet Walker. Ten minutes in a new town and you're already hip deep in danger and doing your best to save the world."

"I told you what happened on the phone last night. Nothing exciting. Nothing dangerous."

She looked up, patient sufferance etched on her beautiful face. She'd never let it drop, and he knew it. Walker tried to form his thoughts into some semblance of order, but having Josie close again was messing with all sorts of things—and not just his head.

"Before you and the cute-but-professional sheriff returned from your quiet breakfast, I spent some quality time with Nancy Greenwich. Honestly, Chet, the woman's such a gossip. Loves to hear herself talk. I couldn't shut the woman up. Not that I tried much."

She cut in front of Walker and put her hand to his chest to stop him dead.

"You faced down an armed lunatic pointing a rifle at you and chose not to tell me about it. Are we going to start our new life together with secrets?"

"Josie, Josie, Josie. What am I going to do with you?"

Walker cupped her face in his hands and leaned in for another kiss, but she pulled away.

"Stop that, Walker. We're going to have this out right now. The canoodling can wait for later."

"Canoodling? Have you been reading cowboy romances in my absence?"

"Stop sidestepping the issue."

Her hurt frown cut him in half and he relented.

"Okay. Here's how it goes down. First off, I'm not even in town when it started. I'm in a truck stop diner, faced with a distressed kid who's covered in blood and rambling about his dead sister. The ambulance is the best part of an hour away and I'm a recently qualified doctor—"

"By the way, congratulations, Chet," she said, the smile returning in all its heartwarming, jaw-dropping glory. "I'm so proud of you."

"Thanks. You want me to continue, or what?"

"Yes. Keep going."

He draped an arm across her shoulders, she hooked a thumb into one of his belt loops, and they continued walking toward the muffled roar of the waterfall. He cut his paces shorter and she lengthened hers until they matched. Walker told her everything.

"When I saw that poor little girl and her baby in all that squalor, and then that animal threatened us all … something flipped in my head. I didn't think, just reacted. Given the circumstances, if it happened again, I'd probably do the exact same thing."

"I could have lost you, Chet." Tears welled.

"Yes, well, you didn't. So let's just enjoy the view and the company and … wow. Will you look at that?"

The path opened into a wide park, with blue-green grass, cut short and well-tended, a play area, swings, and climbing frames for the youngsters, and a bike and skateboard track for the older kids. On their left, rock-strewn hills dotted with Douglas fir, spruce, and ponderosa pine rose in rippled, undulating beauty and grew into mountains that kissed the deep blue sky.

Not bad. Not bad at all.

Ahead, the grass ended in white-painted railings and sloped away to the southeast. A white water river boiled and tumbled down a rocky crag into the valley below. Mist-formed rainbows shimmered in the sunlight and took the words clean out of Walker's mouth.

With a gentle breeze in their faces and a stunning vision ahead, they found a bench and sat in silence, luxuriating in the stillness. Josie tucked herself under Walker's arm, and he hugged tight, keeping her warm, safe. He never wanted the moment to end. Close on four years largely spend without her. Four years of loneliness. Four years of study and stress melted away as though they had never been apart. Josie in his arms was the way life should be, and he never wanted it to end.

"Those red and yellow flowers growing in the borders, what are they called again?" he asked, although he knew full well.

"Blanket flowers. They grow wild all over this part of the country. Beautiful aren't they?"

102

"Not a patch on you."

"Pack it in, Chet Walker. You won't make me cry."

"I love you, Josie Donoghue."

She leaned back and looked up. "I know."

"That all you have to say?"

Her smile and the light shining in her eye said more than words could cover. "What do you want to do now?"

"What I *want* is to take you someplace quiet and secluded with a nice big bed and … well you can fill in the blanks."

"Sounds lovely, lead the way. Hotel, motel, back of your car. After all the time apart and everything we've been through, I reckon I can handle anything you have in mind."

She offered her lips, and he pecked them.

"But," he said, breaking off, "I promised to look in on Billy and the girls, so our private reunion"—he doubled hitched his eyebrows—"is going to have to wait until after our trip to Laramie. Do you mind?"

"I've waited two months and twenty-seven days since our last visit. Guess I can hold off a couple more hours. If I have to." She gave him a slow burn look and rested a hand on his thigh.

"Josephine Donoghue, you are wonderful."

"I know."

"Sorry, but it shouldn't take long. You're coming with me, right?"

"Chet, I spent the night bouncing around in the cab of CC's truck just to be with you. I'm not letting you out of my sight for a second."

He covered her hand with his and squeezed gently. "By the way, how is good ol' CC? Run down any more innocent hitchhikers recently?"

"Like I said, he's fine and sends his regards. He's expanded his haulage company since we recovered most of the city's money. Bought himself two new eighteen-wheelers and finally retired old Rayleigh. In fact, the whole town's thriving. For some reason, the townsfolk think you're some sort of a hero. They can't wait to see you again."

He shook his head at the nonsense and focused on her eyes. "Can I just sit here and look at you for a while?"

"As long as I can do the same."

An age later, a car horn interrupted their reminiscing and announced the arrival of Gerrie's deputy, Cooper. He waved at Walker, but stayed in his seat.

Walker kissed the top of Josie's head. "No rest for this busy country doctor. Let's get this over with. Coming?"

"Just try stopping me."

"That'll never happen."

"You said it."

"Are you ever going to let me have the last word in a conversation?"

"Never."

Good.

Chapter 11

The Hatfield Children

Laramie Mercy Hospital—an enormous complex that included a four-story psychiatric wing of yellow brick and white stucco—occupied a three-acre plot to the south of the town. Walker knew the size of the plot because a billboard at the entrance boasted that the site would soon house a new development. It would double the size of the hospital and include a fully equipped rehabilitation center for military vets.

Walker parked the Ford in the employees' assigned lot. He made sure any patrolling security guards would see the blue "Doctor on Call" card he placed on his dashboard—the one he'd brought with him from Johns Hopkins. They wouldn't mind, especially since they didn't know.

"Sure you want to come in with me? Psychiatric hospitals aren't exactly the nicest places to visit. Look"—he pointed over to their right—"there's a visitor's garden over there, or you could try that diner across the street. No idea what the food's like though."

"No way, Dr. Walker. You don't get rid of me that easily. I'm staying with you the whole time. There's no telling how long you'll be, and I'm not kicking up my heels alone in a strange town while you swan around in a top-dollar medical facility."

"I'm going to be in and out in a flash. They're not my patients, and I'm just honoring a promise."

"Doesn't matter, Chet. I'm sticking with you."

"Okay, but don't say I didn't warn you." Walker sighed. He'd never been able to change her mind once she'd come to a decision.

They hurried up the path to the main entrance. Automatic doors slid apart and allowed immediate access. Modern and clean, the lobby inspired confidence. The smell of polish and hospital disinfectant reminded him of Johns Hopkins and made him feel right at home. Josie stood close, but they didn't hold hands. Walker tried to maintain as professional a demeanor as possible despite how much he wanted to hold her tight and bury his nose in her hair.

Control yourself, Walker. Plenty of time for "canoodling" later.

The receptionist recognized his name and greeted him with open enthusiasm.

"Dr. Lannister—she's our head of psychiatric medicine— asked me to send you straight in the minute you arrived. The emergency psych ward is on this floor. Head through the double doors and carry right on to the end of the corridor. I'll phone ahead and make sure she's waiting for you."

As promised, Dr. Lannister greeted them at the second barrier to entry, a locked antechamber. It was guarded by a big man wearing the uniform of a private security company—gray, starched, and with military sharp creases. Instead of a holster, the guard's leather utility belt held a pouch for pepper spray and a loop for a cop's nightstick.

Who the hell are they holding in here?

Worry must have shown on his face because Dr. Lannister—a middle-aged woman with a trim figure and gray hair cut severely short—stepped around the counter and extended her hand.

"Hey there, you must be Dr. Walker. Please don't worry about Marvin"—she indicated the guard—"his presence is mandated by our insurance provider. You see, as well as treating the county's general psychiatric population, this facility is licensed to evaluate remand prisoners. Sometimes we also have overspill from the local penitentiary during the appeals process, or for parole hearings. But have no fear, Billy Hatfield is not in our secure wing. Oh no, Billy's a darling. Calm and well behaved. We've not had a single moment's problem with him. Dr. Walker, please call me Evelyn. Howdy do."

Evelyn pumped his hand with the enthusiasm of a thirsty man drawing water from a well. Walker introduced Josie and the psychiatrist's smile grew wider. "Well now, so pleased to meet you, Ms. Donoghue. Deputy McCloud told me all about what went down at the farm last night. You have yourself a fine man here."

"I know." She hugged Walker's arm and gazed up at him through falsely adoring eyes. "He's my absolute hero."

"Quit that, Josie," he whispered. "Sarcasm doesn't become you."

Josie winked and the sycophant dissolved away.

Evelyn cleared her throat. "Let's go to my office. It's private and we can have a quiet chat."

Josie glanced at Marvin and the locked and barred door he guarded. "Should I stay here? Are there any confidentiality issues?"

Evelyn put her hand to her chest.

"Oh now, bless your heart. Aren't you the sweet one? There's a family waiting room you can stay in while Dr. Walker and I have our consultation. Don't worry, dear. I won't keep him long. I know from past experience that not everybody can be comfortable in a psychiatric facility. Please, do follow me."

The overly effusive doctor punched four numbers into a keypad on the wall behind Marvin and pushed through the steel security door—she didn't bother to hide the code. It led to a reception area large enough to house a desk, a chair, and a filing cabinet. It also had room to allow a full turning circle for a hospital bed. Two more security doors, one to the right of the desk, the other to the left, completed the layout.

A sign above the right-hand door read: *Secure Wing - No Entry to Unauthorized Personnel*. The other door remained blank.

The lack of a view to the outside gave the space the feel of an enclosed white box. Despite the brightness and the large, landscape posters hanging on the walls, there wasn't enough money in the US health system to make Walker work in so confined a place. He barely managed to suppress a shiver.

107

Josie took his hand and squeezed. She knew how he felt about enclosed spaces. For that reason, she hadn't argued when he'd laid out his plans to drive rather than hop a flight to Pitkin County Airport, Aspen, the nearest commercial airport to Lucky Shores. For Walker, a two- or three-day drive across America held far more appeal than a five-hour flight in a steel and aluminum tube, even if it did mean delaying his reunion with the love of his life.

Evelyn punched the same pattern of numbers she'd used outside into the keypad adjacent to the left-hand door. It opened onto a long corridor. This one had windows all along the south-facing wall. Real windows with clear glass which allowed bright yellow sunlight to flood in and warm the hallway. Walker forced his shoulders to relax.

They left Josie in a nearby waiting room, flicking through the pages of a celeb gossip magazine, and decamped to Evelyn's spacious office next door.

"Before we talk about Billy, you should know that his father, Fulton Hatfield, is currently occupying a single room in our high security wing."

"He is? I thought he was being monitored for concussion."

Evelyn nodded. "He was until"—she consulted her notes— "6:32 this morning, at which time he suffered what can only be described as a psychotic break. He began ranting about how the Devil himself had sprung forth from the pits of hell and was walking this land of plenty. The poor man tried to gnaw his thumb off in order to slip out of the handcuffs."

Walker sighed. "I think Mr. Hatfield considers me the Devil. Hence the reference to 'walking.'"

"Could be. Could well be," she said, nodding sagely. "Anyhow, the on-call doctor sedated him and ordered a psych evaluation, but we can't do that until he's calmed down and we're able to lower the dosage of his medication."

When she paused to read her notes, Walker jumped in. "You want my advice? Treat everything Hatfield says and does with suspicion. He's facing serious charges. Very serious charges, all of which carry heavy sentences. I wouldn't put it past him to

108

angle for a diminished responsibility plea. He's gotten away with some pretty hideous crimes over at least two decades, and you don't do that unless you're extremely cunning. Add desperation and rage to the mix, and you have a highly dangerous combination."

He expected the same indignant reaction he'd received whenever he'd voiced an opinion to a more senior colleague at Johns Hopkins.

"Thank you, Dr. Walker. I do hear what you're saying, especially since you've experienced Mr. Hatfield's actions first hand," she said with very little hint of condescension. "We'll be monitoring his condition closely to conform to the full judicial process. Before long, this clinic will need to present a report to the proper authorities. I'll handle the case personally and will elicit a second opinion if there is any doubt as to my diagnostic conclusions. But rest assured, Dr. Walker"—she pointed at the paperwork on her desk—"I have a great deal of experience in the area of legal competency. Mr. Hatfield won't be able to pull the wool over my eyes. No, sir."

All Walker could think to say was, "Good," but for some reason, her relaxed complacency instilled precious little confidence. Big Marvin's presence should have been a comfort, but how valuable would a rent-a-cop prove if Hatfield kicked off? He'd make Gerrie aware of the situation. From what he'd learned about the Fort Wycombe sheriff, she'd have more of a clue than most, and she might be able to bring pressure to bear on the authorities in Laramie.

Evelyn closed one file and opened another. "Now, let me see. Billy Hatfield." Her lips moved as she read from the first page, using an index finger to keep her place. "Yes. A much more definitive diagnosis. Of course, he's completely exhausted after what happened last night, and he is suffering from chronic malnutrition, but that's easy to treat. I've prescribed extra rations and he's eating everything we put in front of him, poor boy, but he will recover. Physically, he's strong and resilient, and that's likely down to his being a farmer."

109

She paused for breath and Walker filled the silence. "He's wiry but strong. Have you had a chance to assess his developmental status?"

Evelyn wagged her head as if weighing the answer. "We had a short session this morning which was exploratory and very gentle. I didn't want to overburden him after what he's suffered in life. I've made a tentative and preliminary diagnosis based on our very short conversation and Billy's physical characteristics. No doubt you've noticed his facial features?"

Walker sighed. "Elongated head, prominent jaw and forehead."

"Couple that with the intellectual deficiency and your diagnosis is?"

"Fragile X syndrome?"

Evelyn nodded slowly, her lips thin. "My thoughts exactly. I've sent a blood sample to the hospital lab for confirmation. The syndrome is quite rare, but I haven't seen a more severe case. Billy might have other underlying conditions, but the blood work will tell us more."

"Are you aware of his family situation?"

"With his father? Yes, I am, and I think close familial association is an obvious causal factor."

Inbreeding. A turd by any other name would smell as rank.

"What can you do for him?"

Evelyn screwed up her face.

"I've tasked one of my staff to run some developmental tests to quantify Billy's impairment, but we'll let him settle in for a couple of days first. My sense is he'll score between fifty and sixty on a standard IQ test, but ..." she trailed off when Walker started shaking his head.

"Won't put money on it, but I think you'll find it's a little better than that. He'll be in the seventy to eighty range, I'd say. He's higher functioning than you'd expect."

"Really?"

"Despite his physiological challenges, Billy was able to drive a vehicle down a steep and dangerous track at speed and in near dark conditions."

Evelyn's eyes widened. "Really? That is interesting. Nobody told me that. Drove a car you say? Interesting. In that case, I might be able to sponsor him into one of our vocational outreach programs." She put an index finger to her lips, made a note in the margin of Billy's file, and nodded. "Yes … yes, if things pan out, I really think that'll work nicely. You see, our Social Services Department runs a city farm that doubles as a dude ranch. Billy might be able to cope. That's marvelous. I think there might be a positive outcome here after all. But it's early days. Leave it with me, Dr. Walker. Yes, leave it with me."

She jumped to her feet with the speed and agility Walker didn't expect from a woman of her age. "Would you like me to take you to him? He's in the day room. Follow me, please."

Walker held up five fingers to Josie as they passed the waiting room. Josie waved him along and flipped another page in her magazine.

Evelyn stopped at the fifth door along the corridor and showed him into a room filled with natural light and smelling of fresh cut flowers. An air-conditioning unit hummed in the background, but the gentle sound barely made it over Billy's contented giggling. He and four other patients sat with eyes glued to a large TV screen.

"I'll leave you to get reacquainted," Evelyn said. "When you've finished, press the red button and Nurse Chambers will let you out. We keep the doors in this unit locked at all times, of course."

"Of course. Thanks for everything, Dr. Lannister."

She waved away his words. "It's my job. I'll be in my office when you want me."

Walker studied Billy for a while before making his approach. He couldn't believe the change in the young man's appearance since his dramatic arrival at the roadside diner. He'd showered, shaved, and combed his hair, and someone had given him a set of clean clothes—white T-shirt, faded blue jeans, and hospital crocs.

No doubt about it, Billy would never play the lead role in a Hollywood romance, but he scrubbed up well enough and watched cartoons on the big screen with wide-eyed enrapture.

"Hi, Billy. How are you this morning?"

Billy tore his eyes from the TV. "Hey, th-there …"

"Dr. Walker. Remember me from last night?"

Recognition spread slowly across his freshly scrubbed face. "Y-Yeah, I remember. Look"—he waved at the screen, as excited as a kid in a toy store at Christmas—"they got color TV here. L-Looks like real life! And I-I had raspberry Jell-O after dinner. I like raspberry Jell-O. N-Never had none afore."

"That's great, Billy. I'm glad. Have you seen Mary Anne and the baby?"

Billy's gap-toothed grin spread even wider.

"Y-Yeah, I seen 'em. The baby's only a little bitty thing, and she pooped her diaper. Smelled something awful. Worse than the pigsty at home." He held his nose for a second before lowering his head. "Guess I shouldn't say nothing 'bout it since she's a baby, and she can't help herself none, huh?"

"That's okay, Billy. Sometimes babies have accidents."

Billy nodded a couple of times and then scrunched up his face. A hand crept up to twist a lock of his hair.

"Something wrong, Billy?"

"Mary Anne said I-I was to tell you somethin' if you was to come back like you promised you would, but can't remember. I-I's sorry." Tears filled his pale eyes. He sniffled. "C-Can't remember none, but it were i-important."

"It's okay, Billy. I'm going to see her next. She can tell me herself."

"No!" Billy said, voice rising in agitation. "I gots to remember for myself. It's important, else she wouldn't'a told me." He tugged harder at the clump of hair. "Papa always said I weren't no good for nothin'."

112

Walker took hold of Billy's hand and lowered it to the side. "Billy, that's not true. You saved Mary Anne's life yesterday. Saved the baby, too. You are a good brother. A brave brother."

"I-I is?"

"You are. Everyone in Fort Wycombe is going to think you're a hero for what you did."

He blinked and tears fell. "I drove the car on the road. I's bad. Sheriff Hoover's gonna … gonna send me to jail."

"No, Billy. That's not going to happen. Sheriff Hoover will probably say thank you for doing such a good thing for Mary Anne and the baby. Everything's going to work out fine."

Billy slapped his forehead with the heel of his hand. "I-I remember, I remember! Mary Anne said I was to stand up"—he stood and stuffed the hem of his T-shirt into his jeans—"and I was to say"—he squeezed his eyes tight shut—"'Thank you … Dr. Walker. We all … 'preciate what you done for us.' There, there I-I remembered, didn't I?" He beamed with pride and relief.

"You did well, Billy. Very well indeed, and I'll tell Mary Anne you remembered it word for word."

"You will?" He puffed out his narrow chest and the beam widened.

"I will, Billy. You take care now. Mary Anne and the baby will need their big brother to look after them."

"Yeah. I-I know, and I-I can do that. Who's that?"

He pointed at the door. Josie stood on the other side of the glass, her hand raised in a greeting.

"That's Josie. She's my fiancée."

"Fi-ancée?"

"It means Josie and I are going to get married."

"Married? You and her's gonna have babies?" he asked, flushing bright red.

Walker grinned. "Hope so, Billy. Lots and lots of them. One day."

"I knows what that means, Dr. W-Walker."

"You do?"

Perhaps the lad wasn't as naïve as he looked.

113

"Means you's gonna have lots of stinky diapers to change, huh?"

"I expect so, Billy. Want to meet her?"

Billy shook his bowed head. "Uh-uh, no. S-She's too p-pretty, and N-Nurse C-Chambers w-won't like it." A shadow clouded his eyes and his toothy smile faltered.

"Nurse Chambers?"

Billy's chin trembled and he lowered his head.

"Is there anything you want to tell me, Billy?"

A head shake, but no words.

"Billy?"

"A-Ain't nothing, Dr. W-Walker. I's trying my best, but sometimes I-I gets confused. S-Sometimes, I-I makes mistakes."

He looked up. Frightened eyes stared up through bushy dark eyebrows.

"You know you can tell me anything, and I won't be angry, right?"

"I-I knows, Dr. W-Walker. But it all g-good, honest it is."

"Okay, pal. You sure you don't want to meet my Josie?"

The kid flushed bright red, shook his head again, his other worries apparently forgotten.

"Not to worry Billy. Some other time?"

"Yeah. S-Some other t-time."

"I'm going to see Mary Anne and the baby now. Listen to what Dr. Lannister has to say. She's good people."

"I-I will. Thanks for what you d-done for us, Dr. W-Walker." Billy raised his head, forehead wrinkled. "Wh-Where's P-Papa?"

"Don't worry about your father. He can't hurt you or Mary Anne anymore."

"Ya promise?"

"Yes, I promise, Billy. You'll be okay. So will Mary Anne and the little one. See you soon."

Walker clapped the boy on his skinny upper arm and turned. By the time he reached the door, Billy had retaken his seat in front of the TV and resumed his happy giggling. The cartoons' immediate and total joy clearly overcame the nebulous fear of his father's potential reappearance, and perhaps that was a good thing.

Rather than hitting the red button and disturbing Nurse Chambers, a person he'd yet to meet, Walker tried repeating the number pattern he'd seen Dr. Lannister use on the keypad, 7-9-8-2. Worryingly, the electronic lock disengaged at his first attempt. He pushed through the door and almost bumped into a large male nurse. Dark hair, deeply tanned, six foot three, at least 225 pounds—most of it pure beefcake—the man stood with feet shoulder-width apart and folded massive arms across a chest the size and shape of a thirty-gallon beer barrel. His acne-dotted face gave Walker a cause for concern.

"Would you be Nurse Chambers, by any chance?"

He looked behind the big man, but Josie was no longer in the corridor. She'd probably returned to the waiting room. Her absence gave Walker slightly more room to maneuver.

"That's right," Chambers answered, his voice incongruously higher-pitched than expected from a man of such bulk. "And you must be Dr. Walker. Am I right? Lannie, sorry, Dr. Lannister said you were here. How'd you get out of my day room?"

Walker told him.

Chambers sneered. He leaned forward and pungent body odor wafted across the narrow space between them. "Well now, ain't you the enterprising meddler?"

Walker held his position. "Didn't take much enterprise. I understood this to be a secure facility. Someone with half a brain could get out of here."

Chambers' sneer changed into a scowl. "People with half a brain's all we got around here, Doc. Ain't never had a breakout before, so I suggest you just mosey yourself along 'fore I get angry."

Walker stared hard at the irate man, but didn't budge. In Chambers' one aggressive response, the reason for Billy's discomfort became clear. Walker hated bullies with a passion and had difficulty keeping his temper in check.

115

"Yes," Walker said, smiling without mirth, "and I imagine you're someone who's rather easy to upset."

The big nurse deepened his chest. His biceps bunched.

"What exactly do you mean by that?"

If Walker ever allowed himself to be frightened, this might be one of those times, but he didn't and it wasn't. His growing anger wouldn't allow intimidation to take hold. Instead, he maintained his smile and spoke slowly and quietly.

"As a nurse, you should know that, apart from stimulating muscle growth, one of the side-effects of AAS abuse—that's *anabolic-androgenic steroids* for those of us in the medical profession—is anger control issues. Facial acne is one sign. Another is reduction in testicular size and function. Furthermore, steroids are listed under the Controlled Substances Act, which makes possession and use of such substances without a prescription a federal crime punishable by up to one year in prison for the first offense."

As Walker spoke, Chambers' arms dropped to his sides, his tan faded, and his blink rate increased. His fingers flexed and straightened. Walker eased his right foot back a fraction, turning his body sideways to the big nurse, in preparation to defend against any aggressive action.

"Now, Nurse Chambers, before I say anything else, I'm going to ask you two questions. Ready?"

Chambers tucked in his chin in much the same way Billy had done earlier. His hands formed fists, and his arm muscles tensed, but they stayed down at his sides. Walker raised his hand a little, readying himself for the man's lunge.

"First question. If I got my very close friend, Sheriff Gerrie Hoover, to ask her colleague, the Laramie Chief of Police, to search your hospital locker, or your home for that matter, would they find any anabolic steroids? Second question, if those police officers did find any such 'medication,' could you provide them with a legitimate prescription?"

Chambers shook his head. His shoulders slumped and his fists unclenched. The immediate danger had passed, but Walker remained on guard.

"Fair enough. Here's what you and I are going to do. Listening?"

Silence.

"Nurse Chambers," Walker said, a little louder, but still not shouting, "I asked whether you were listening."

"I'm listening," Chambers mumbled after a momentary hesitation.

"Come with me and I might just be able to save your career."

Walker turned and, after a quick glance in the waiting room to confirm Josie's presence, marched straight into Evelyn's office without knocking. Nurse Chambers followed close behind, meek as a five-day-old kitten.

Walker let the heavily-muscled nurse pass and shut the office door behind them.

Chapter 12

Babies and Hoovers

The elevator doors slid shut, bouncing as they met in the middle. Walker pressed the button for the fourth floor. Ordinarily, he'd have used the stairs, but he'd had a tiring couple of days, and his calf still ached like someone had forgotten to loosen a tourniquet. Even the irrepressible Josie had started to flag after her through-the-night journey.

As the elevator started its ascent, she leaned against him for support as much as for a cuddle.

"What was that all about?" she asked, looking up, fatigue clouding her eyes.

"Huh?"

"Your second meeting with Dr. Lannister. That big guy who followed you into her office looked really miserable. Close to tears."

"Nurse Chambers you mean?" Walker made a serious face. "Yes, a sad case indeed."

"How so?"

"Poor chap broke down and told me he was addicted to steroids. Kept feeling angry, flying into rages. He was concerned about how it would affect his day-to-day patient care. I suggested he should come clean to the hospital board and enter a rehab program. He agreed instantly."

Josie shot a look that told him she didn't believe a word of it. "A complete stranger walks up to you and confesses to a felony offense?"

Walker shrugged and opened his hands. "What can I say? Must have one of those faces people feel comfortable talking to. Johns Hopkins runs excellent training modules on how to develop a first-class bedside manner." He finished with his version of an innocent grin.

She sighed. "You were in her office quite a long time. Did I hear raised voices at one stage?"

"Oh that." Walker scratched his stubble. He hadn't made time to shave that morning. Maybe he'd grow another beard, but not without asking his partner first. Wouldn't want to upset her.

Hen-pecked? Yes, sir.

"After dealing with Nurse Chambers' little … condition, Evelyn and I had what the politicians call 'a free and frank exchange of views' when I recommended she overhaul her unit's security protocols."

Josie pulled away. "When you did what? Chet, you can't simply walk into someone's domain and start laying down the law after being there fifteen minutes."

"That's pretty much what Evelyn said. Only she used a little more volume." He stretched out another grin, this time rueful.

The elevator dinged and the doors retracted. Walker stood aside and allowed Josie to exit first. They entered another bright corridor, this one empty.

"I'll explain later it all later," he said. "First, let's see how the little ones are doing, eh? Oh, before I forget, remind me to call Gerrie. I need to talk to her about those same security matters."

"Chet Walker, you are impossible."

"Probably," he agreed, "but I have the best of intentions."

They found the maternity ward, full to bursting with new moms and newer babies. Twenty beds, twenty cots, and a sun-filled room full of hope, joy, exhaustion, and diapers. The smell of freshly bathed newborns filled him with pleasure and, judging by Josie's gleeful reaction, she felt the same way.

During his time as a paramedic in Syracuse, Walker had delivered five babies. He used the fact to avoid a rotation on the maternity ward in Baltimore, but the magical act of childbirth—in the medical jargon, parturition—still had the power to blow his two-week-old professional mind.

In the far corner beside a sunlit window, Mary Anne sat in a padded chair, nursing. Hair washed and brushed back from her face, she smiled down at her baby, a picture of maternal contentment. She looked up as they approached and re-adjusted her loose-fitting top. When recognition hit, a broad grin lit her impossibly youthful face.

"Dr. Walker! You came."

"Hi there, Mary Anne. How are you, and how's the little one?"

"She's a hungry one. Don't hardly give me a moment's peace," she answered, looking at Josie.

Walker made the introductions.

"Hey there, Ms. Josie. Wanna hold her?"

"No, no, that's okay. She looks so content."

Josie tried to appear cool, but couldn't hide her delight when the baby disengaged from the nipple and gurgled contentedly. Josie took the empty chair next to Mary Anne and accepted the offered bundle of new humanity. Eyes alive with excitement, she held the little one up to her shoulder and gently rubbed her back.

They chatted pleasantly for half an hour until a heavy-lidded Mary Anne yawned. "Sorry, Dr. Walker. This little girl kept me up most of the night."

"Not a problem," Walker said. "We need to be heading for home, anyway."

Fear showed on the innocent face. "You ain't stayin' in Laramie?"

"Mary Anne," he said, settling on his haunches in front of her, "we're headed for Colorado, a little place called Lucky Shores. It's where we live."

At least it will be, if we ever manage to get there.

"What's me and the baby gonna do after you're gone?" Her eyes grew wide and her lower lip trembled.

Walker took time to explain how she and the baby would be made joint wards of the state and assigned a guardian. He spoke gently, but Mary Anne didn't seem to understand.

"They gonna take away my baby?" She wailed and snatched the infant from Josie. The baby grumbled at being shaken.

Walker placed a hand on Mary Anne's shoulder. He couldn't answer what he didn't know. The terror on the new mother's face upset him as much as it clearly hurt Josie, who leaned across and hugged mother and baby.

Hell, that didn't go so well.

"Mary Anne, listen to me, please." The girl looked up, blinking tears from her cornflower blue eyes. "Whatever happens, whatever anyone says, call me and I'll do all I can to help. Understand?"

She nodded, holding the baby tight to her chest, lower lip curled out.

He handed her one of his recently printed cards. "This has my clinic number in Lucky Shores. My personal cellphone number's on the back. Keep it safe."

Mary Anne stuffed the card into a pocket in her smock. "Thank you, Dr. Walker. 'Preciate it a whole lot. You're being so kind to me. Ain't never had that before. 'Cept for Billy. He's always been a good brother, even when Papa ..." She sniffed and the tears fell.

Josie handed her a box of tissues she found on the bedside table, and Mary Anne blew her nose.

"Ms. Josie, can I ask you somethin'?"

Josie nodded, unwilling or unable to speak.

"Can I call my baby after you? Josie's a lovely name and you're so pretty."

"'Course you can, honey. 'Course you can," Josie said, turning her face toward Walker, as tearful as the new mother.

"Not Barbie, then?" Walker asked, forcing the question past the huge lump in his throat.

Mary Anne shook her head. "In the daylight, baby don't look like no Barbie, but she do look like a Josie. Lovely name for her, don't you think?"

"Sounds good to me," Walker said.

He gave Mary Ann and Josie time to put Little Josie in her clear plastic crib before tapping his watch at adult Josie—he'd never be able to think of his darling girl as Big Josie.

"Sorry, but if we want to be home today, we really must get a hustle on."

#

Walker fired up the Explorer and rolled out of the hospital parking lot. They hadn't spoken since leaving the maternity ward. All the way through the hospital, Josie had been content to hug his arm and rest her head against his shoulder, silent after the extended and highly emotional goodbye.

He turned right at the exit and soon picked up the WY-230, heading south, toward Colorado and home.

Josie curled into a ball, feet tucked under her firm little butt. Eyes closed, content smile, she looked wonderful. He struggled to get used to the fact that, after all this time, they were finally back together.

For the first time in ages, a new tune bubbled up from the recesses of his tired mind. A ballad, slow and strong. No lyrics yet, but they'd come. Working on the old songwriter's code, "if you find an easy rhyme, use it," the song would probably include the lines, "She came to me in Laramie. All the while she made me smile."

Got to work on that, buddy.

He hit the power button on the GPS. While waiting for it to lock onto the satellites, he cut a swift look at Josie.

"You were great with the baby," he whispered in case she'd fallen asleep. "A natural."

"Faking it, Chet. Don't go getting any ideas."

"Me? Not a chance. I've never had an idea in my life."

She stretched out a hand and rested it on his knee.

The GPS bleeped its readiness. Walker hit the preset destination, "Home," and waited for the map to form and the numbers to arrive.

"By the way," he said as she turned to face him. "Have I ever told you how much I love you?"

"Yep, but it'll never get old."

"So, two hundred ninety-eight miles to go, and the GPS gives an ETA of six hours."

"Sounds about right."

"We won't get in until well after dark. Want to push on through, or find somewhere for the night and make a fresh start in the morning?"

"That's up to you, Doc. I'm done making decisions for the day. All tapped out. Whatever you say, I'll need a pit stop for food and a freshen up. I'm pretty bushed after travelling through the whole of last night."

Damn, what a fool. He hadn't even stopped to consider food.

"How long since you've eaten?"

"Been a while. I packed breakfast before we left Lucky Shores. CC and I ate on the move. He didn't want me to miss you and we drove straight through."

"Hell, girl. You must be starved. Why didn't you say?"

"Didn't want to interrupt a doctor at his work. Made me proud just to be in your presence."

"Stop that, you."

"Stop what?"

"Sarcasm doesn't work when it comes out of such a gorgeous mouth. Listen, why don't we stop at Shirley's place? She does a decent coffee and her food's almost as good as yours."

"Glad you said 'almost.' Who's Shirley, and how far away's her diner?"

"She runs the place I stopped at when I more-or-less crashed into Billy Hatfield. Thirty miles away, give or take. Can you wait half an hour for your grub? The alternative would be to turn around and search for someplace decent in Laramie."

She took in a deep breath and arched her back. "I can wait. You look tired. Are you okay to drive?"

"I'll be good for thirty miles or so. Shirley might know a place we can rest up for the night. How does a motel or guest house sound?"

"Lovely, although I'd be happy on the back seat if you're with me."

123

"Josie Donoghue, you say the nicest things."

"I know. Get used to it."

"Never."

Walker waited, but she didn't respond, just closed her eyes. *Finally had the last word.*

A full minute later, she said, "You will."

Walker grinned and left well enough alone.

#

Josie pushed away her empty plate. Walker always wondered how she managed to pack such huge portions into so small a frame and still weigh no more than a six day old kitten left out in a thunderstorm.

"Looks like that filled a hole," he said, after swallowing a bite of homemade pepperoni pizza.

"It did, and you were right," she said, dabbing her lips with a napkin. "Shirley knows how to grill a steak and rustle up some fries, and that pepper and mushroom sauce was a triumph. You know what?"

"What?"

"I'm going to ask her for the recipe."

He watched her sidestep between the empty tables on her way to the serving counter. Knowing he was looking and not minding, she sashayed a little, exaggerating the effect. She'd definitely filled out some. Gone was the elfin twenty-two-year-old girl he met on his first day in Lucky Shores. She'd become more rounded, more womanly. Her curves, firm in the tight jeans and cotton shirt, were perfect. If he had to wait much longer to be alone with her, he might just explode.

Josie and Shirley, heads together, chatted away like longtime friends. From time to time they threw a glance in his direction, smiling and laughing. Apart from being a similar age, they must have had other things in common besides working in a diner. They clearly got along well.

124

By the time Walker finished his apple pie and cream—a rare indulgence—and drained his coffee, Josie was on her way back, a big wide grin plastered on her beautiful face.

"You look happy."

"We're in luck. There's a cottage out back for rent and it's empty." She jangled a set of keys between finger and thumb. "What are you waiting for?"

Walker leaned back. "The bill."

"Shirley said we can settle up in the morning after breakfast. Come on. Apparently, there's a TV and a games room."

"We're not going to need either of those time wasters," he said, but still he didn't move.

"Well?" she asked, a frown started to form. "What's wrong?"

"Nothing. Just savoring the moment. I've never seen anything more beautiful than you, and I don't ever want to forget the way you look right now."

"Aw, you say the sweetest things, but get off your ass and follow me. I have an ache only one specific doctor can cure."

He jumped to his feet. The chair legs scraped on the tile floor.

"Doctors aren't supposed to fraternize with their patients, but in this case, I'm going to make an exception."

"Too dang right you are."

She took hold of his hand and pulled him toward the door.

"Goodnight, Doc," Shirley called. "Don't do anything I wouldn't do."

Walker didn't have the time or the inclination to respond.

#

Walker woke to the sound of Josie singing in the shower. He smiled in recognition of the song he'd written for her. Their song. Unrecorded and sung only to each other. She had a nice voice, high and clear. Not powerful, but always in tune and a good foil to his grumbling baritone. Despite his coaxing, she'd always refused to duet with him during his winter-long residency in the

125

Lucky Shores Saloon. Although she claimed stage fright, he knew it was more down to her not wanting to steal his limelight.

Back then, she thought he still had his eye on the big brass ring. She thought he hankered after a record deal with a big recording company, but she'd been wrong. That winter, he sang for his supper and for the excuse to stay close to the woman he wanted to spend the rest of his life with. So, he accepted the weekly gig at the saloon for the money and her company, and all the time he laid his plans.

Last night, when they lay spent and naked, he kissed the jagged scar he'd hacked into her stomach. The operation that saved her life also changed his. It reminded him of who he really was. All his life, he'd only ever wanted to be a doctor, but nearing the end of his medical training, he'd lost his way. He'd dropped out.

Burn-out had been a terrible thing.

The operation on Josie, carried out in the harshest of conditions—a mine halfway up a mountain in the middle of nowhere—gave him back his girl and gave him back his life's mission. In exchange, Josie had lost a kidney and gained an ugly-assed scar. Not a fair exchange, but she didn't seem to mind. In the long term, she'd also gained a newly qualified doctor who would love her forever. No doubt about it.

Walker stretched out in the comfortable bed and listened to his future wife singing. He reached for the velvet-lined box with the diamond ring and placed it on her pillow before padding toward the bathroom. Time to see whether they made shower cubicles in Wyoming large enough and strong enough for two.

Chapter 13

Homeward Bound

One hour into their trip home, with Josie fiddling with her engagement ring and holding it up to the sunlight the whole time, they passed a hitchhiker. A young man with shaggy blond hair and a guitar strapped to his backpack, he carried a placard with *Aspen* written in red ink. Walker eased his foot off the gas and cut a glance at Josie.

"What do you reckon? Stop?"

She shook her head. "Aspen's way out of our route and I don't like the look of him. I mean, a guitar and all that hair? Worrisome."

Walker laughed. "You're the boss."

He added some pressure to his right foot and they sped past. The hitchhiker threw them the finger. Remembering a similar event the last time he hitchhiked along a road in the area, Walker dropped his smile and concentrated on his driving for the following few miles.

Later, with one hundred mountainous miles still to go, he pulled into a dusty, two-pump gas station and turned to face Josie. He reached for her hands and held tight.

"What's wrong?"

He stared into her eyes for a full minute without speaking.

"Chet, you're worrying me."

Sighing, he kissed the back of each hand. "You know how precious you are to me, right?"

She nodded, still frowning. "But?"

"No buts, that's it. I love you and always will." He kissed her hands again. "Well, maybe there is a 'but.'"

"Which is?"

"We're going to have to stop all this."

"Stop all what?"

"I'm getting too old for all this excitement. Can we settle down and live a boring, quiet life, please? Maybe grow old together and raise a passel of rug rats?"

"You think living with me in Lucky Shores will be boring?"

It was his turn to frown. "Stop that, girl. We'll have plenty of excitement, but let's make it the normal kind. No more guns. No more rushing off in search of clues or bad guys. Just normal, honest to goodness, small town living. Okay? We got a deal?"

She grinned. "I'm fine with that, Chet Walker. Let's go home."

"Only ..."

"Only what?"

"Only we need some gas or we'll be stranded in the mountains overnight. Whereas I'm okay snuggling together for warmth, I'd much rather be snuggling together in a nice comfy bed. Assuming your Aunt Jean will still let us share a room before we're married."

Josie laughed. "She's my aunt, Chet. She's not a nun."

"There's one more thing."

"More? Heck, Chet, you have a shopping list?"

"Is the Old Logging Road up to Lucky Shores still open? It's heading toward the end of the summer, but I'd like to visit where I met your dad. Mark the place, you know? Make a proper farewell. I never really had the chance last time I was here."

"Chet, that's a lovely thought." Sadness crossed her face at the memory, but something else too, something Walker couldn't interpret. Pride? Joy? "I forgot to tell you. Since construction started, they patched up the old road. These days, we use it year-round."

"Excellent. Let's do that, then. Shouldn't add too much time to our trip, even though I'll be taking it steady."

They gassed up, restocked with bottles of water and snack bars, and hit the road again. Two hours later, they reached the turn Walker had taken a little under four years earlier, only that time, he was hiking with a backpack, Suzy, and a near-empty wallet.

Not everything had changed. His wallet hadn't gotten much heavier. It still felt lighter than it deserved to be.

He stopped the Ford at the turn off. "Where's the billboard?"

The sign advertising *Open Mic Sessions at the Lucky Shores Saloon* had gone. In its place stood a simple green road sign announcing, *Lucky Shores – 18 miles*. A smaller sign below read, *Danger – Road Liable to Flood in Winter*.

Josie sighed. "We took it down. Since our first and last resident singer left to become a doctor, the saloon stopped the open mic sessions and started booking real professional acts. Good ones, too."

Walker put his hand to his chest and feigned disappointment. "You mean I wasn't a real professional act?"

"It's not that at all. You were just irreplaceable."

He dropped his hand. "Good answer, Ms. Donoghue. Remind me to sing you something I've been working on during this trip."

"You've started writing again?"

Once again, excitement shone in her eyes. No doubt about it, Josie had made it to the top of Walker's fan club, and he loved it that way.

"Not taking it seriously, but Suzy's been calling to me since I qualified, and I've been neglecting her far too long."

"You've been neglecting me, too." She gave him a little girl pout that looked out of place on her normally self-confident face, but still made him sit up and take notice.

"Not any more. I promise."

"And I'm going to hold you to that, *mister*."

"Hey, that's *doctor* to you, missy."

"Keep saying that to me, and we'll have a falling out."

"I'll never say it again. Shall we go?"

Before she could reply, he selected drive and stomped on the gas pedal.

Even driving well below the limit and taking extreme care on the switchback curves, the drive to the place where Josie's father

129

crashed his car took less than forty minutes. The same uphill journey had taken Walker nearly five hours to hike back in the bad old days before he'd seen Lucky Shores. Before he'd met Josie. Before she'd helped turn his life around.

The asphalt surface, patched and looking a million times better than when he'd hiked it, wound up into the foothills. The pines, dark green in the low evening sunshine, spread out on either side of the road, interspersed with stands of trembling golden aspen. As the gradient increased and the twists and turns tightened, Walker started to wonder whether he'd be able to pick out the accident site. After all, it had been dark that afternoon and a thunderstorm had raged. Driving rain had plastered his long hair into his eyes and lightning flashed its blinding fury. And he'd had to scramble into a crushed, cramped car. Although it all seemed such a long time ago, the horror of crawling into the confined space of the Dodge's crushed driver's compartment still had the power to make him shudder.

As it turned out, he needn't have worried about missing the spot.

"Wow," he said, pulling to a halt halfway along the only straight stretch for miles and miles. "Didn't expect that."

Josie showed him a sad but proud smile. "The city council built this picnic area as a memorial to Daddy. After the court case, the whole town felt guilty for accusing him of something he didn't do. This was their way to apologize. Too little and eight years too late, if you ask me."

A small stone cairn marked the place where Mickey's ancient Dodge had blown a tire and left the road. In deference to the man's atheism, it wasn't topped with a cross, but a carving of a bug-eyed rattlesnake—Mickey's artistic logo. Behind a glass panel, recessed deep into the stonework to protect it from the bleaching effect of the sun, rested a photo of his final unfinished painting, his reworking of Da Vinci's *The Last Supper*. The painting had contained a clue that led to Walker and Josie finding most of the town's stolen money, nearly twenty-five million dollars of it.

Set back from the cairn, in the middle of a graveled flat area, three rustic tables hewn from weather-silvered oak with attached benches allowed wayfarers to stop and take in the astounding views. Mountains fringed with trees and top-dusted with snow, snarled at the sky. Thanks to Josie as his guide, Walker could name at least three of the obvious peaks, the most conspicuous being the molar-shaped Tooth Mountain.

Walker shut off the engine. The exhaust crackled and popped as the metal cooled in the thin air.

"Are we going to get out and chill?" he asked, pushing open his door.

"You go on, I'll phone Aunt Jean and tell her where we are."

"There's a stable phone signal up here now?"

She tapped the screen on her cell phone and nodded. "It still drops out during winter storms, but we should be good right about now. You go commune with nature, I'll be with you in a minute."

Walker left her to it and squatted in front of the little monument to a reluctant accountant, a great painter, and a brave, brave man. He'd have loved the chance to get to know Josie's father, but the tragic accident and the town's murderous doctor had conspired to rob Walker of that undoubted pleasure. He blinked away blurriness to his vision and stared at the inscription etched into a small brass plate below the painting.

Why must I always draw snake eyes?

Walker smiled at the line from one of his songs. No passing stranger, no one outside of Lucky Shores, would have understood the reference. After eight years spent in the wilderness—literally—Mickey had not only identified the real thief, but had found a way to send a message even from the grave.

A brilliant, brave man.

Yes, Walker would have liked the man who'd given him the world, given him Josie. He stood and ran his eyes over the side of the road, but all signs of the actual crash had been removed, either by the weather or during the landscaping. Perhaps that was for the best. Scorched earth, scraped asphalt, and dried blood wouldn't have lent much to the peace and tranquility of such a stunning view.

Josie joined him at the shrine. She leaned against him, resting her head on his arm, and they stood in silence until the sun boiled the mountains and the shadows lengthened to darken the memorial.

"Stunning," Walker said, his voice an awed whisper.

She looked up at him through glistening eyes. "Yes, it is."

"I wasn't only talking about the view."

"Stop that, you'll make me cry."

His vision blurred. "What is it with you women? Cry-babies, the lot of you. Real men don't cry."

"Oh no?" She reached up and wiped a tear from the corner of his eye. "What's this then?"

"Dusty here. All this wind." He sniffed and blinked again.

"Yeah, right."

Walker swallowed hard. "Did you get through to Jean?"

"Yes. She's expecting us at the house within the half hour. Wouldn't surprise me if she'd baked a cake."

"The mayor of Lucky Shores baking a cake?" He grimaced. Josie certainly hadn't inherited her baking gene from her aunt. "Can't wait. Shall we go?"

Josie smacked his arm. "What's that sneer for? Aunt Jean's a great cook."

"I grant you, she can open a can of beans and stick some steaks on a grill, but she's no Josephine Donoghue."

"Aw, you're so sweet."

He grinned. "I know. C'mon girl, let's get home."

Walker held the door open for her. For once, she said nothing about being able to manage her own door-opening, but simply slid into the passenger seat and said, "Thank you."

Ordinarily, such meek compliance from his sparky little darling would have sounded the warning bells and he'd have asked why, but they'd already endured a long day and he let it go.

132

During their brief stay at the *Michael Donoghue Memorial Picnic Area*, more than a dozen vehicles had rolled past, far more than had used the road the first time Walker traveled it. A sign of the change in prosperity and popularity of the area.

He kept the Ford in low gear all the way to the summit, and again as they dipped down on the other side. Bright daylight still reigned on the western side of the mountain pass, the sunset delayed an hour by the topography. Two miles later, and five hundred feet lower, they negotiated a hard right turn, slowed to a crawl, and once again, Walker stared out in awe over the horseshoe-shaped valley.

With its steep granite mountains, wooded slopes, wide alluvial plain, and stepped terraces—both manmade and gouged out by retreating glaciers—he'd never seen a more beautiful spot.

And there, slap bang in the middle of the valley, dominating the view, spread the huge, elongated circle of Big Lake, the largest body of freshwater in Sequestra County, and one of the largest in the state. Clinging to its southern shore, lay the twinkling, sunlit roofs of his new home, Lucky Shores.

On the valley floor, the small city itself clung to the lake's southern shoreline, dazzling in its beauty.

"What a view," he whispered. "Takes the breath away."

"Always does."

Buildings sprouted on the terraces beneath them. On the topmost, the sheriff's office crouched low and squat, in command of all it surveyed. On the terrace directly below it stood the *Lucky Shores Medical Center*. A converted girl's school, with a wrap-around parking lot and helipad, it comprised two ten-bed wards, four private rooms, one fully equipped operating room, and an outpatients clinic—Walker's new place of work. His new domain.

With white walls, a single story, and a flat roof, the place had a quietly imposing atmosphere; a competence. The first time he'd seen it, a dog-tired Walker hadn't been impressed with its cracked windows or its tired and dirty walls. Right now, as Walker carefully steered the Ford around the dangerous curves in the road, the newly qualified doctor in him saw the place in a totally new light. Knowing he'd be in charge in a few days, it both impressed and scared the hell out of him.

His heart rate leaped and his stomach churned as fear and excitement battled for supremacy. Was he really capable of running a hospital, however small, so soon after qualification? True, he'd have the help of the hospital board, but so much responsibility, so much pressure. He'd either sink or swim, and it wouldn't take long to find out which.

On the other hand, Walker was a fast learner—he could tread water well enough and didn't fancy drowning.

"Bet you can't wait to get started," Josie said.

Walker eased his foot off the accelerator and slowed the Ford to a crawl once more. "Mind if we drop in to say hello?"

She screwed up her face. "Can't it wait? I'm hungry, exhausted, and need a long soak in a hot bath. Besides, Consuela won't be happy to have you mess with her schedule."

"Dear old Consuela still runs the place with an iron fist inside a razor wire glove, huh? How's she doing?"

"Full of beans and beside herself now she knows you're coming back. She hated the first three replacement doctors the HMO provided. The latest one's the worst so far. A foreigner. Doesn't fit in here. Barely speaks the language."

"Where's he from, India? Pakistan?"

She showed him an impish smile. "Nebraska."

Walker laughed. "A Cornhusker? Does he have all his inoculations?"

"He'd be okay but no one can understand a word he says. Pity the town can't afford a translator."

"You're terrible. If you guys can't understand a Nebraskan, how am I going to fit in?"

"You'll do okay, Doc. The locals will go easy on you or they'll have me to deal with."

"My little protector." He blew her a kiss and fed a little more gas into the engine. The Ford increased speed, but not by much. "Let's go home."

The serpentine road clung to the northern side of the valley, wound past the turning to the new road that eventually hooked up with I-70, and leveled off at the valley floor.

Walker kept his eyes on the road and concentrated on the driving. The rusted iron guard rail on the outside of the road had been replaced by a reinforced concrete wall, very strong, very safe. At least they'd repaired the damaged surface where Doc Matthews had plummeted over the edge in his desperate bid to escape capture. Walker wasted no tears for his predecessor. After all, the sociopath had been prepared to kill Josie on the operating table, the same way he'd ended Mickey's fight for survival.

Somewhere between the summit of Tabletop Mountain and the outskirts of town, the Old Logging Road became Main Street. Nobody seemed to know where exactly, it just did. Vertical cliffs on the right and sloping precipices falling away on the left flattened out into the wide valley floor. More and more buildings sprouted as the gradient eased.

Although the overall scene hadn't changed much from his first visit, it was easy to see the subtle differences. Where before they stood empty, most of the buildings on the outskirts of town—both business and residential—were now occupied. Most sported a fresh coat of paint. Broken windows had been replaced, guttering re-hung, roofs fixed, and front yards tended. The shops that had been closed during his residence, now showed signs of life. The neon sign above the four-pump gas station glowed bright in the encroaching dusk. Shiny vehicles sporting *For Sale* signs filled the front lot and showed an optimistic face to the world. Far more optimistic than it had during his previous visit.

Main Street ended in a T-junction when it reached the shoreline, right onto East Lane and left onto West Boulevard.

Big Lake welcomed him with a sparkling smile as sunlight danced on its rippling surface. The promenade on the far side of the road, dotted with wooden benches and streetlamps, still offered an unobstructed view of the water and a stunning outlook beyond. Half a mile or so to the east, the steel and concrete jetty seemed to hover over the water. Boats bobbed at anchor, small trawlers, leisure craft, rowboats, similar to before, but greater in number and more brightly painted. The whole lakeside and valley seemed happy and thriving. Even the fire station had received a lick of fresh paint. Bright red woodwork and the windows' white glazing bars gleamed in the sunshine.

He made a left onto West Boulevard and crawled past the diner where he'd first seen Josie, and she'd saved his life by giving him the best darned breakfast he'd ever tasted. Not to mention filling his coffee cup with pure nectar. Two women he didn't recognize stood in the doorway waving and shouting their names.

"Who are they?"

"My staff. The tall blonde on the right is Peg, and Allie's the brunette."

"They look excited to see us."

"Excited to see you, Chet."

"Even though we've never met?"

"I've told them all about you. Everything."

"Oh dear. They're both tall and the blonde one's curvaceous, but they're not my type. Not my type at all."

"And who exactly is your type?"

He winked. "I'm looking at her."

She grinned and shook her head. "Just as well, Doc. Man-eaters, the pair of them. I've banned them from attending any of your clinics unless they're at death's door, and even then you'll need Consuela Cortez as chaperone."

"As I said, you are my little protector, and you know what?"

"What?"

"I love it."

"Good."

Walker grinned—he still couldn't have the last word.

He parked on the Boulevard outside Jean Hallibone's guest house—their temporary home. Like the other houses on the street, the three-story Colonial had benefitted from a recent paintjob and new guttering. As always, the garden was neat and well-tended, the flower borders burst with vivid color, and the wrap-around

136

porch still housed a swing. Millie, their shaggy dog, barked in a frenzy at their approach, straining at the leash tied to a fencepost.

"Be quiet you daffy pooch," Walker said as he slipped the dog's leash off the post and fended off its slathering tongue-lashing. He kneeled and ruffled the fur behind her ears. The dog keened with delight.

Until that precise moment, Walker had no idea how much he'd missed the silly hound.

"What nasty person tied you up, eh girl? Was it evil Aunt Jean, eh? Was it, girl?"

Millie jumped up and Walker caught her, but held her lapping tongue away from his mouth. There were limits to his love for the animal—for any animal.

Josie laughed. "Told you she'd remember you. Typical. You've been away four years. I've only been away a couple days and you're already her favorite. Crying shame. A girl can get jealous, you know."

"Wait until nighttime. Only one of you is getting into bed with me, and it isn't going to be this scrappy little mutt."

He set Millie down and headed for the steps up to the front door, but Josie blocked the way.

"Where do you think you're going?"

"I thought Jean baked a cake? Better get it over with, I suppose."

"Yeah, but she's in the saloon. She can't afford not to open on a Friday night. And I don't know about you, but after the past couple of days, a drink would go down like a treat right now. What do you say?"

"I dare say I could force down a cold one, if my life depended on it."

Her smile eclipsed the setting sun. "Let's go."

Josie took his hand and they wandered toward the saloon, Millie tugging at her lead the whole way. To their right, Big Lake lapped the shoreline, driven by the gentlest of fall breezes. The air, with its pine-clean tang and its freshwater chill, brought with it the promise of peace and tranquility. In the age since he'd last

137

tasted that same air, he'd never forgotten the sense of wellbeing it brought him, although much of the peacefulness came from the woman resting on his arm.

Oh, how he'd missed Josephine Donoghue and the place she called home. The place he'd make their home together. He just needed to get his feet under the table, set up his practice, win the trust of his patients, not screw up his doctoring …. The list grew as he contemplated the immediate future. The pitfalls lay everywhere.

Baby steps, Walker. Baby steps.

With Josie at his side, his pocket-sized bodyguard, there wasn't a thing they couldn't do together.

The two-hundred-yard quiet saunter ended far too quickly, and they ducked left into the saloon's parking lot. It stood largely empty, just half a dozen SUV and pickups—essential vehicles for life in the high mountains—filled the spaces nearest the entrance. Curtains covered the windows and the lights were off, but the red neon sign announcing the place as, *Lucky Shores Saloon*, was complete. The last time he'd seen it, the sign was missing its "*c*". It being whole showed off the city's financial recovery as much as anything he'd seen up to that point. A sign of wealth. Progress indeed.

"Looks pretty quiet," he said.

"It's early, Chet. Aunt Jean doesn't usually open 'til six o'clock these days. Not unless there's a special event. Weddings, funerals, and such."

Walker checked his watch. 5:53 p.m.

He cast his eyes to the sky. Another half hour until sunset. In the mountains, the working day pretty much started and ended with the sunrise and sunset, that much he'd learned during his short stay. Logic dictated that the saloon would synchronize its opening times to the working day.

He pulled open the door, stood aside to let Josie in first. When he followed her inside, the whole room erupted into pandemonium.

Chapter 14

Welcome Home, Doc

The house lights flashed on, a couple of hundred people roared "Surprise!" and raucous applause rattled around the room.

A flustered Walker leaned close to Josie and shouted over the noise. "A surprise party? Just you wait. You're going to suffer for this."

Josie shrugged. "Man up, Doc. Act happy."

She didn't even have the good grace to appear embarrassed.

A huge banner stretching across the bar read:

Welcome home, Doc Walker.

Happy, smiling faces, most remembered, a few not. Names attached themselves to some of the people as they continued the applause. CC and his family smiled, whooped, and jostled. Ellie May Harrison, Josie's high school friend, volunteer fire-fighter, and wanton man eater, leaned against the bar, giving him the slowest of slow burn looks. It hadn't worked on him before and it never would. Maybe she'd grow tired of it someday. Abel Dunleavy and Pete, two of the Three Stooges sat on either side of Dunleavy's petite wife, Izzy. The third member, George, was absent.

Others hugged the background, people he didn't expect to see at a party thrown in his honor.

Pride of place, and leading the welcoming howls, the Lucky Shores dignitaries took center stage. Jean Hallibone, mayor, owner of the saloon, and guest house proprietor, held a

139

microphone to her lips, but waited for the initial roar to die down before speaking. To her left stood Sheriff Caspar Boyd, The Ghost of Lucky Shores, and a few others he couldn't name. All wore goofy smiles and applauded loud enough to hurt his ears.

A far cry from the welcome he received the first time, but Walker could handle it. Probably.

Jean started talking, but couldn't make herself heard over the noise until she flipped the switch on the microphone.

"This thing working now?" she said, quieting the crowd with a raised hand. "Keep the noise down, darn it. The poor man probably can't hear himself think."

She stepped forward, separating herself from the rest.

"I'm going to keep this short—"

At least twenty of her audience cheered. They'd clearly heard her campaign speeches.

"Yes, okay. Point taken. Just wanted to welcome home the new head of the Lucky Shores Medical Center, Dr. Chet Walker!"

#

The celebration extended into the evening in a blur of welcoming, hair tousling, back-slapping, and flowing booze.

By the time the noise settled to a gentle roar, Walker's cheeks ached from all the hours of unaccustomed smiling. Around midnight, he and Josie made their excuses and hurried home to a bedroom decked with cut flowers and another *Welcome Home* banner.

Walker pulled Josie close and kissed the top of her head. Despite the long hours in the car and the extended session in the saloon, she still smelled fresh and clean and ... edible.

"Wow," he said, "that was intense."

Josie looked up through half-closed, tired eyes. "But you handled it so well, my big bwave soldier."

She stretched up and offered her lips. They kissed, and she gave a little moan. He picked her up, carried her to the bed, and laid her gently on the folded-down sheets.

"The food, the free booze, the floor show ... when did you arrange it all?"

She smiled and stretched out, indulging in the soft sheets and the firm mattress for a moment before slowly undressing. "Aunt Jean and I have been planning this for months. All I had to do was tell her when we left Fort Wycombe this afternoon. She had everyone in town prepped and ready to go. You nearly messed things up when you demanded we stop off at Daddy's mem—"

"That's why you were on the phone?"

"Sure was. I had to get the timing right."

"And you had your spies out, marking our arrival?"

"Surely did. Now stop talking and kiss me."

A few minutes later, he leaned back, eyes roaming her naked, perfect body. The scar on her belly had faded to a silver "S," but still stood out against her lightly tanned skin. Somehow, she was more stunning than she'd appeared the time he'd seen her half-naked in that same room. He'd burst in on her unexpectedly, mistaking her bedroom for the bathroom. Serendipity, a happy accident. Impossible as it seemed then—he'd known her less than a day—he was already certain she was the only woman for him.

Walker smiled at the memory of her sitting in front of her mirror, in her black underwear, staring back at him, unfazed, unabashed. Self-contained.

"What are you smiling at, Walker?"

"Remembering the first time you let me into this room."

"When you broke in here and grabbed a sneak peek at the goods, you mean?"

"You didn't lock your door. How was I to know?"

She didn't say anything for a while, but lay still and allowed his eyes to feast.

"Well?" she asked.

"Well what?"

"Are you coming to bed, or not?"

"Okay. Shuffle across then. Give me some room."

She did.

#

Walker woke to paradise. Or at least, Colorado's version of it. Bright yellow bars of light framed the windows and he noted details in the room. The edge of the mirror, the pale brown of the dressing table, the lavender colored bedding. A long shaft cut a vertical slice through the room and picked out the highlights in Josie's hair.

He lay on his back and, naked and still asleep, Josie cuddled close, arm draped across his chest, leg interlocked with his. Her breath tickled his chest hairs. He ran a fingertip over her exposed shoulder, raising goosebumps. She whimpered in her sleep.

His wristwatch read 8:53 a.m. He hadn't slept so late in years, but on the first Saturday morning of his new life, he'd take a pass on an early reveille.

The house stood quiet. He imagined that downstairs, breakfast for the guests—assuming there were any—would be tapering off. His stomach grumbled at the thought of bacon and eggs, but he could wait. Waking Josie after their journey and the missed sleep would be a criminal act—possibly a felony, definitely a misdemeanor—and he wouldn't want to incur the wrath of his mighty Josie. The pocket dynamo. His future wife.

He lay still for another thirty minutes until the bathroom called and he could wait no longer.

Showered but without a shave, he pulled on a T-shirt and jeans and padded downstairs. He returned to their room with a tray of coffee and a long-stemmed rose, taken—with Jean's permission—from the border running around the front yard.

Josie sat up, disappointingly wearing one of his polo shirts, and greeted him with a smiling yawn.

"Coffee in bed? I could grow accustomed to this kind of service."

"Make the most of it, girl. I've been reading up on country practice. Doctors in the Boonies get called out at all hours of the day and night."

"But you don't take over from Dr. Cornhusker until Monday."

He balanced the tray on the dressing table, used it to slide across some of Josie's magic girlie potions, and sat on the bed.

"Don't you believe it. Peg, your blonde short-order cook, just tried to book a physical. Something about inner thigh strain."

Josie jerked straight up in bed. "And you said?"

"What could I say? I told her to contact Marcy and arrange an appointment. You needn't worry, though. I only have eyes for you."

She relaxed back and took a sip of coffee. "Hmm, not bad. You have the job."

"Every morning for the rest of our lives?"

"Walker, you are such a romantic."

"Aren't I though. Shall we have a little more light on the proceedings?"

He drew back the curtains and was knocked back by the view framed in the window. Unlike his old room at the front of the house, which showed the whole of Big Lake and the promenade, the view from Josie's room took in the western shore of the lake. The panorama included a major portion of the western mountain range and was dominated by the spectacular Tooth Mountain.

"Wow, will you look at that? I wondered why you chose this room and not one at the front."

"You know me, Chet. I'm a mountain girl. That's the only view for me."

He scrunched up beside her on the bed and they sat, staring through the wide window, delighting in the changing colors and atmosphere as clouds passed in front of the sun and dappled light rippled over the mountain slopes. Could life get any better?

Josie pulled him down and nibbled his neck.

"Hey, stop that, girl. How professional would it look for the town's new doctor to wander the streets brandishing a high school hickey?"

"Just making my mark."

"You've already branded my heart, my darling girl," he said, wincing at the sickly words.

"Oh Lord, that's awful. Wouldn't have passed as the lyrics of one of your love songs."

"Sorry. Out of practice. To be honest, I haven't finished a new song or played Suzy in public since leaving this place."

"Is that why you refused to take the stage last night despite all the calls for a set?"

"Yep, but this place does something to me. Already, I feel the creative juices flowing."

"I know."

She let out a throaty giggle that Walker couldn't ignore no matter how hard he tried.

#

"Do we have any plans for the day?" he asked after they'd finished their drinks and indulged in a more intimate and pleasurable activity—twice.

"Unlike you, Dr. Walker, I have work to do. The diner needs restocking, and I need to set the menu for next week. I can't trust Peg or Allie with anything more intellectually demanding than the coffee machine."

"Really? I thought we'd use the down time to take a trek up to Little Lake and see about organizing the cabin reconstruction."

"Lovely thought, Chet, but that'll have to wait until spring. Can't start building this late in the year, and you'll have your work cut out at the medical center."

"Will I?"

"Of course. With three different doctors in four years, you'll need to put your stamp on things. The place will need a total reorganization."

"You think?"

"Of course. You need to set proper clinic times, outpatients appointments, and such. And you'll need to liaise with the chief of medicine at the Douglas Ferry Hospital. After all, you won't be doing anything other than minor surgical procedures. Serious operations will have to be transported to—"

Walker stopped her with a kiss.

"What was that for? Not that I'm complaining."

He smiled. "Ms. Donoghue, you might be surprised to learn I've been working on a business plan for the medical center since I started back at Johns Hopkins. Everything's in hand. I've even arranged to spend the second half of next week in Douglas Ferry with our old friend Gerard Andrews. You know, the surgeon who saved your life on the operating table after my butchery?"

He traced the line of her scar with the tip of his index finger. Her little rounded belly rippled under his touch. He leaned down to kiss it.

"No, don't remember a thing about it. I was out cold, remember? And stop playing with that ugly-assed scar, you butcher."

"I did my best, honey. To think I nearly killed you."

"You know I'm kidding. I'd have died up on the mountain without your magic hands. What's a little scar against that? You don't really think it's ugly, do you?"

"Of course not, it's just when I think how close I was to losing you ... I ... Damn it, girl, this is supposed to be a happy day. Right?"

"It is, and I've never been happier than I am right now."

"Oh, now who's being a big old softie?"

"You said it, honey." She pecked his cheek, rolled off the bed, and grabbed his robe. At least five sizes too big, its hem dragged on the floor when she draped it over her shoulders. "Don't know about you, but I could eat a side of beef.

"And I could manage the other side."

"How about I have a quick shower, and then I cook us some brunch before we go our separate ways for the day?"

"Sounds like a plan. After brunch, I really should show my face at the clinic. During last night's meet and greet, I told Dr. McCrery I'd check in this afternoon."

"So that trip to Little Lake was a whole load of baloney?"

"Not so much. I'd have cancelled the Cornhusker if you'd said yes. He has another month on his contract here. There's plenty of time for a proper handover period. And by the way, I could understand every word he said last night, despite the background noise in the saloon and the amount of booze he was sucking down."

"Yes, he does like his alcohol, but it never seems to affect his work, and I was only kidding about his accent. Nebraskans are almost like cousins. Give me a few minutes and we'll go downstairs together. I'd love to show you off."

"A woman in a shower for a *few* minutes? I'll believe that when I see it. Want me to come in and scrub your back?"

"Do that and we'll be having lunch, not brunch."

"Hmmm. Sounds good to me." He scratched his chin. "I'll need a shave."

"Really? I love that five o'clock shadow thing. Reminds me of the first time we met. And you'll be growing your hair back again, right?"

"If you insist."

"I do."

"Only if you quit being so bossy."

He threw a t-shirt at her. She dodged and scooted out the door laughing. It was so good to be back, Walker couldn't stop smiling. Everything from here on in would be steady, workmanlike, and normal. Or as normal as it could be in a new town, with a new career, and a woman with a gentle secret, who for some reason didn't want to share with him.

Give her time, Walker.

He took a deep breath, stared at the stunning scene beyond the window, and listened to Josie singing happily in the shower. Whatever her reason, Walker would give her time. She deserved all the time in the world after waiting so long for him to qualify, and he would do nothing to make her uncomfortable.

Walker reminded himself that Josie's world had changed beyond recognition, too. She, a wealthy and self-made woman, was taking on a relative stranger with nothing to his name but a six-string guitar and a doctor's shingle.

Yep, he'd give her all the space she needed to come to terms with the changes in their lives. Nonetheless, he did finagle his way into scrubbing her back, and she didn't complain at all.

As it turned out, Lucky Shores shower units were plenty roomy enough for a big guy and his petite fiancée.

Chapter 15

Settling in for the Long Haul

To avoid the inevitable inquisitive nature of any tardy guests, Walker, Josie, and Jean ate in the privacy of the kitchen. Brunch stretched from ten thirty through to midday. Plates piled high with the savory works, led to pancakes and maple syrup, and left him pleasantly full if not downright bloated.

"That was wonderful. Thanks, darling," he said, pushing the cleaned plate away and wiping his mouth with the napkin.

He stood and started bussing the table, but Jean held up her hand. "Leave that, Chet. I'll clear it later. No doubt you have better things to be doing on your first day in town."

She held his gaze for a beat longer than necessary and left him in no doubt as to what the mayor of Lucky Shores expected of the city's new medical practitioner.

"I have indeed, Mayor Hallibone," he answered, forcing a serious expression onto a face that wanted to do nothing but grin like a loon.

He owed her a great deal, not least for looking after Josie since she'd become a virtual orphan after her mother's death from cancer and her father's disappearance when the *Savings & Loan* was robbed some twelve years earlier. The fact that Jean had ensured Walker's appointment as the town's chief medical officer after an interview consisting of nothing more than a video call with the rest of the city's medical board, only added to his obligation.

He'd repay the debt with interest, and he'd start right away.

"Thought I'd pay a visit to the medical center while Josie works her magic in the diner."

Jean nodded and topped off their coffees for a second time.

148

"Aunt Jean, don't go forcing Chet to work all hours to prove himself." Josie shot a glance at Walker who shook his head, but she refused to heed his unspoken warning. "He's a damned fine doctor and the town's lucky to have him."

Jean frowned and pursed her lips.

"You know that, and I know that, but the rest of the townsfolk are taking his skills on faith. At least to begin with. Chet will have to prove himself to the community the same way any other newcomer does. Isn't that right, Chet?"

"It certainly is, Mayor Hallibone," Walker answered, still straight-faced.

Jean lowered her cup to the table and jabbed an index finger at him. "Keep on calling me Mayor in this house and you and me are gonna have a falling out, Doc."

Josie tapped the table, mirroring Jean's finger-pointing antics. "Chet finished second out of over two hundred in his class, and I've seen the evidence of his work first hand." She let a hand rest on the area of her stomach which held the scar. "As I said, the town's lucky to have a doctor of his skills at such a cut price. After what happened in Fort Wycombe, I wouldn't be surprised to find headhunters from all the big hospitals in America banging on our doors."

"What was that?" Jean's head snapped around and her eyes drilled into Walker's. "Have you been getting into trouble again?"

"Nothing like that, Jean. Josie's just being overprotective again."

"What exactly happened at Fort Wycombe? Caspar Boyd told me their sheriff got in touch asking about you."

Walker broke the eye contact and once again frowned at Josie. "Nothing much. I ... Sheriff Hoover just wanted proof of my good character."

Jean's doubtful expression showed him what she thought of his explanation.

"Won't take but a minute to call Caspar and get the skinny."

Josie leaned forward, hands formed into fists, excitement and pride clear in her every movement. "Chet helped deliver a baby and save the mother from her pedophile father. He took a rifle from the man and was responsible for him being arrested. And after that, in the hospital, the way he was with his patients was wonderful."

"He did what?" Jean jumped to her feet and rounded on Walker. "Have you gone out of your tiny—"

Walker rose with her.

"It's not as wild as Josie makes it sound. I didn't actually deliver the baby. The mother managed that feat all by herself, pretty much. I simply cut the cord and persuaded the father to hand himself over to the local police, in the shape of one, Sheriff Hoover. Nothing more exciting than what happens in the Boston ER every weekend. In any event, I'm not allowed to say anything about it, Jean. It being *sub judice* and all that. The sheriff told me not to talk about it. Right, Josie?" He frowned again for emphasis.

"Yeah, whatever. Chet broke the Hatfield case because he's a damned fine doctor, Aunt Jean. There are no two ways about it. Lucky Shores is finally living up to its name."

Walker formed a simultaneous grimace and smile. He wasn't used to having someone fight in his corner and still drop him deep in the smelly stuff.

Jean didn't share his mirth. "If you don't tell me what happened right now, I'm calling Caspar and *he'll* tell me." She turned side-on to Josie and gave Walker her full attention. "You wrestled with a man pointing a rifle at you?"

Walker raised his hands in surrender. "Listen. I'll let Josie explain exactly what happened while I go check in with the medical center, okay? I'm needed there, and Josie clearly likes the retelling part."

Jean sighed. "Yes, she does."

Walker turned to Josie, wincing. "If you look after Millie today, I'll take her tomorrow. Okay?"

"Sure. She's good with me in the diner. Used to it. Go play with your new friends, but play nice, and don't get mud on your jeans." She winked.

He sighed. "I'll see you guys later."

150

Despite Jean's presence, Walker kissed Josie full on the lips, nodded goodbye to the town's mayor, and hurried from the room as fast as his legs would carry him. So much for his tranquil new life. He'd broach the thorny issue of finding a place of their own with Josie as soon as things calmed down. Which would probably be sometime in the middle of next summer.

With the cell phone pressed against his ear, he hurried to the front door and grabbed his heavy coat from the rack in the hall along the way. From his earlier stay in town, he knew better than to stray outside in the high mountains without the correct clothing, no matter how benign the weather appeared.

As expected, the Ford was exactly where he left it, out front, and pointing the wrong way. After spending the best part of four days driving from Syracuse, the last thing he needed was to slide behind the wheel. Lucky Shores Medical Centre was only a five-minute drive. How long would it take to walk? He ran the math in his head and ended up with forty-five minutes.

Doable, but bit of a challenge.

He stood on the porch waiting for his call to connect, trying to make up his mind. Walk or drive.

"Lucky Shores Medical Center, how can I help you, Dr. Walker?"

Walker smiled. He'd recognize Marcy Greenbaum's scratchy but eager voice anywhere. As well as being the medical center's main daytime receptionist and backup administrator, she acted as the roots of the town's news grapevine. Best of pals with Polly Dukakis, owner of LSLR, *Lucky Shores Local Radio*, nothing much reached broadcast quality without Marcy having a say in it first. Marcy also happened to be a staunch friend of Nurse Consuela Cortez, the Medical Centre's chief nursing officer.

"You have my number on the call log already?"

"No need, Dr. Walker," she said, smugness smoothing her words, "I have an excellent memory for phone numbers. I suppose you'd like to arrange a meeting with Dr. McCrery?"

"Yes, please."

"Sorry, Dr. Walker. He hasn't arrived yet, but he's due to take a mother and baby clinic in an hour and sometimes … occasionally arrives early to set up. Want me to call him at home?"

"No need to bother him, Marcy. I'll come by to say hello and help out if he needs it. I'll use it as part of the handover process. What's he like to work with?"

"Not my place to say, Dr. Walker," Marcy answered, snappily.

Her reluctance to gossip over the phone was entirely out of character and spiked Walker's interest. What was going on there?

"Would he accept an offer of help?"

"Oh yes. He'll definitely accept help. There's no need to worry yourself on that score."

"Right, I need to stretch my legs. I'll be there in about half an hour, okay?"

"Excellent. I'll tell Consuela. She's looking forward to working with you again after all these years. We all are."

Marcy mumbled the last three words.

"Thanks, Marcy."

With the phone still pressed to his ear, Walker strode down the path, turned right after opening the gate, and headed toward Main Street. Gulls screamed and argued overhead. A light wind drove pine-scented air into his nose and rippled the surface of Big Lake.

Marcy coughed. "Wait, you said 'stretch your legs,' Dr. Walker? You don't plan to hike all the way up the hill, do you? It's such a long way from the mayor's guest house."

"Only a couple of miles. I'll be there in plenty of time."

"Please forgive me, Dr. Walker, but … you being new in town and all, you know about the passing places on the Old Trucking Road, don't you?"

The feel of pavement under his walking boots brought back the old days. Tough old days, but they'd brought him to Lucky Shores and to Josie, which made them good old days.

"Thanks Marcy, but I do know to keep tight to the cliff face and stay well clear of the open side."

He knew that now, but hadn't known it during his first day in town. Walker still hadn't forgiven Caspar Boyd for not issuing the warning when he'd left the LSPD offices that first morning. On the other hand, he'd made the acquaintance of CC, who nearly killed him on that same road. Happy days.

"See you in a few, Marcy."

He ended the call and increased his pace. The breeze had stiffened in the two minutes since he'd left the guest house, and clouds had bubbled up from the south. A car passed, heading in his direction. It slowed to match his pace. The driver, a bearded man in his sixties wearing a fur-lined coat, lowered his window. Walker recognized him from the surprise party, but couldn't recall his name. Walker returned the man's beaming smile, which revealed a perfect set of pearly white dentures.

"Afternoon, Doc. How you doing?"

"Fine thanks. It's a wonderful morning."

"Surely is but it's going to rain 'fore dark. Where you headed?"

Walker's kneejerk reaction was to ask what business that was to a relative stranger, but small town Americans worked by different rules. The concept of privacy didn't seem to hold the same sway as in the cities. He bit back his immediate response, said, "Medical center," and managed a cheery grin while pointing up the hill.

"Your shiny new Ford out of gas or something?"

Not only did this stranger know his name and business, but he also knew Walker's ride.

"Nope. Just fancied a walk."

The stranger's mouth dropped open.

"Really? What you wanna go and do that for? I can give you a lift, if you like. It's a heck of a long way. Uphill, too."

"But downhill all the way back."

The man, still keeping pace with Walker, pondered the concept for a moment before nodding. "That it is, Dr. Walker. You're a deep one. Very deep. If you're going to walk up that far

153

remember to keep in tight to the rocks. Wouldn't want to lose our new doctor before he even gets the chance to settle in."

"Thanks for the warning. I'll make sure to duck into the passing places the moment I hear a vehicle coming."

Walker decided that playing so nice could get very old very quickly, but he held off sighing.

"You do that, Doc. Can't never be too careful."

"Have you been talking to CC recently?"

"Sure have. He was in the saloon last night. Why?"

"It's nothing. CC was the one who pointed out the passing places when he gave me a lift my first ever day in town."

"He did, huh?"

Walker nodded.

"Well," the man said, "if you're sure you don't want a lift, I'll be on my way. Have a nice day, now."

"You, too Mr. …"

"Riley Hickman. Retired weatherman, but I like to keep my eye in. I have an appointment to see you Tuesday."

"Really?"

"Yes, sir. I'll need a repeat prescription for my pain meds. Sciatica's kicked in early this year. Always does when the air pressure plummets. Going to be a long, cold winter. Be seein' you, Doc."

Riley gunned his engine, and Walker waved him off. He considered the value of having a sign made to tell people he knew what side of the old road to walk on, but decided that would make him look churlish. The locals were only being friendly, trying to help.

Walker passed the diner and waved to Peg and Allie, but hurried along when it looked as though they were about to rush to the door and buttonhole him.

After the fire station, with its bright new paintwork, he turned right at the only set of traffic lights in town and headed up the hill. Unlike the smog of Baltimore, the air tasted clean, fresh, and invigorating.

154

The chorus from Haircut 100's *Fantastic Day* ran through his head, but he couldn't recall the lyrics to any of the verses. Could barely recall the main melody, either. During his medical training, he'd relegated music to the back burner of his life.

Behind him, a car horn blared and rubber squealed on asphalt. He spun around. A dark blue Toyota Tacoma—shiny and chromed, tinted windows all around—stopped hard, its nose dipping and its rear wheels skittering in the dust. The front doors flew open. Two huge men jumped out and stood watching him from behind matching sunglasses.

Oh hell. Not again.

Although he'd only met them a couple times, Walker would have recognize William "Hooch" Geddes and his cousin, Angus "Bull" Argyle, anywhere.

The first time they'd come face to face, in the medical center, they'd set out to beat him to a pulp. However, through luck and their bad judgment, Walker had gotten the better of them that time, but that was then, and over his years in med school, he'd become soft—or at least, softer.

Could he outrun them? He tensed his calf, pain free for the moment, but it wouldn't hold together for an extended sprint.

He tried to swallow, but a dry mouth wouldn't allow it. Walker could take a beating—he'd done so plenty of times in his life—but he couldn't afford to damage his hands. They had doctoring to do.

Could he talk his way out of whatever they had in store for him? He'd tried that with these two the first time, and a fat lot of good it had done.

Walker searched his surroundings for help, but Main Street stood empty. His mouth dried further, his heart rate climbed, and his breathing rate increased. The adrenal glands pumped adrenaline through his system. Preparing him for action.

Fight or flight?

Flight was out of the question. Only fight remained.

Walker took half a step back, drew close to the stone wall guarding the side of the fire station. It would protect his back.

155

Assuming a defensive stance, he raised his arms, but kept his hands open and loose. At the very least he'd get a few punches in. He'd target Hooch first. The leader. The faster one, and the better fighter. Bull, the larger man, but slower in thought and action, would have to wait.

Hooch Geddes pushed away from the car door and slammed it shut. He'd lost the paunch since Walker last saw him. Looked lean and fit. More powerful and dangerous than his beefier cousin.

The big man's mouth curled into a crooked smile. He'd had work done to straighten and clean his teeth. "Me an' Bull's been looking for you, Walker."

Hooch sauntered closer, his swaggering gait as noticeable as ever. Bull Argyle followed three paces behind, frowning.

Walker tensed, balled his hands into fists.

Chapter 16

Dr. Cornhusker and the Clinic

Hooch stopped a couple of paces away, out of range for a flying fist or a snap-kick. He stood square on, feet planted shoulder width apart, hands on hips. Bull stopped and mimicked his older cousin's stance. Only he didn't look as cool. Or as menacing. In different circumstances, Walker might have laughed in the face of the big dumb ox.

They both wore blue jeans, white shirts, and western-style suede leather jackets. Bull's coat even had tassels. Hooch wore a string tie. They looked like a pair of storefront cowboys. The only things missing were the hats. Although their Stetsons probably rested in special holders inside the Toyota's cab—along with their rifles.

Walker sighed. Funny how his mind worked. He was likely about to take a beating, but he took in the fashion details while his attackers waited to pounce.

Walker tensed again, ready to deflect the first punch.

Hooch's right hand twitched—the gold signet ring on the middle finger could do some serious damage as a knuckleduster—and reached up to remove his shades.

Here it comes. Get ready. Watch Bull.

The elder cousin threw him an apologetic smile.

"Guess me and Bull owes you a big goddamn apology, Dr. Walker."

Hooch passed the sunglasses to his left hand and stretched out his right, offering to shake.

"Sorry?"

"You heard me, sir. First time we met up in the hospital, me an' Bull was in the wrong. Way off beam. Shouldn't have attacked you the way we done. But we got what we deserved, I

157

guess. So, you gonna leave me hanging, or what?" He waggled his fingers. "Don't worry, Doc. This ain't no ruse. What you done for the town, putting it back on its feet, was good for us all. Me especially. We got our land back and our ownership of the gold mine. The Geddes family owes you and little Joey Donoghue. And we owes you big time. Put it there, Doc." He thrust his right hand further forward.

With some reluctance, Walker took Hooch's offering, expecting to have his fingers crushed, but the shake was good. Firm with rapid pumps, but no aggression.

Walker breathed a little easier, but still didn't drop his guard. Not completely.

Hooch turned to his cousin. "Well? Your turn."

Bull lowered his head, rounded his shoulders, and stuffed his hands into his jeans pockets.

"Yeah. I'm sorry too, Dr. Walker," he said, his mumbled words barely carrying on the stiff breeze, "but I ain't shaking your hand."

Walker couldn't blame the man. Their first meeting ended up with Bull suffering two broken wrists, shattered knuckles, and both hands in plaster casts for six weeks.

"That's okay, Bull. I understand. Apology received."

Olive branch offered and accepted, Walker finally eased the tension from his neck. He didn't close the gap between them, though.

"We were gonna come to your welcome home party last night, but Larry said it would pro'bly be best if we waited until today. He figured you'd be tired and maybe a little … defensive."

Nice one, Larry. The very best of the whole Geddes clan.

"How is he?"

Hooch nodded. "He's doin' real good. Looking after the ranch. Said he'd catch up to you later. Apparently, you still owe him a drink."

Walker would never be able to thank Larry Buchanan enough. Another of the Geddes clan, one he'd seriously misjudged, Larry

158

was one of the people instrumental in saving Josie's life back on Tooth Mountain.

"I certainly do. Has he fallen off the wagon?"

Larry's temper when drunk had dropped him in hot water in his past, but it hadn't stopped him becoming the second best mountain tracker in the county. Second only to his Josie.

Bull snickered, but shook his head.

"No," Hooch said, scowling sideways at Bull. "Larry's still teetotal, but enjoys a night in the saloon drinking his alcohol-free beers."

"And how's your mother?"

Hooch sighed heavily. "You ain't heard? No reason you should have, I guess. Poor Ma passed away. Couple years back. Heart attack."

"Sorry to hear that, Hooch. She was good people."

That wasn't exactly true—Ma Geddes ruled her clan with a harsh tongue and a rod of pig iron—but Walker didn't want to hamper the development of such a blossoming new friendship.

The three men stood in a triangle, the silence dragging. Walker still didn't want to turn his back on them, just in case. Bull kept silent. He did nothing more than stare at his boots and ease his weight from one foot to the other.

Two cars drove past, one heading uphill, the other down. Where had they been when Walker thought he needed help?

Hooch scratched his chin. "You headed to the hospital?"

"Sure am."

"Need a lift?" he asked quickly, squinting up the hill toward the mountains.

"Thanks, but no. I wanted to take a walk."

Bull snickered again.

Hooch smacked him on the shoulder. "Shut that, Bull. The Doc's got every right to take a walk if he wants to. Free country, ain't that so, Doc?"

"It is," Walker said, agreement being simpler than opening an in-depth political debate.

"Take care to—"

"Don't worry, I'll use the passing places if I need to."

"You do that. Well, me and Bull's likely to see you around, Doc."

"Reckon so."

"Thanks again for what you done for Lucky Shores."

The cousins turned and climbed back into the Toyota. Five seconds later, the pickup peeled away from the sidewalk, tires squealing. Hooch waved out the window and yelled, "Yee-haw!"

Walker watched them go, finally able to drop his guard completely. If Josie had told him during brunch that the head of the meanest clan in the county would apologize and offer the olive branch of friendship, he wouldn't have believed her. Things really were looking up.

He checked his watch—getting late for his meeting—and strode up Main Street. He kept tight to the cliff side of the road and listened out for roaring engines.

#

During his stroll, no vehicles hurtled down the hill threatening to drive him over the cliff, but an intermittent procession of slow-moving cars and SUVs passed him, headed uphill. Mostly driven by young women, he presumed they were booked into the mother and baby clinic. Most of the moms smiled at him as they drove past, but none stopped to issue the safety warning. Sticking close to the cliff wall showed them Walker knew his way up the side of a mountain.

He made it to the turn into the medical center with no more than a slightly aching calf, a stitch in his side, and raw lungs from sucking in cold air at high altitude. The parking lot was full of the same vehicles that had passed him earlier, station wagons and small SUVs—modern day chariots for existing soccer moms and soon-to-be soccer moms.

Walker paused outside the entrance until his breathing settled before waiting for the automatic doors to open and stepping into the foyer.

160

Before he'd made it into the reception area, Marcy stood and welcomed him as though he were a returning football hero.

"Dr. Walker. Come in. Come in. Glad you made it up that hill safely."

The beaming smile was the first he'd ever seen on her. He wasn't sure a grin suited her wizened features, but no doubt she'd settle back to dour normality before too many seconds had passed.

She clasped her hands close to her chest. "Just let me look at you."

Walker hesitated, wondering whether to give her a twirl, but decided it wouldn't do much to secure his gravitas or his position in the community.

"Good afternoon, Marcy. Great to see you again. How are things?"

And there it was, the worried frown returned. "Things will be so much better now that you're here, Dr. Walker. So much better."

Marcy's over-effusive greeting set off Walker's internal alarm. Something had happened. Something bad. He stared at the slightly built receptionist, but she refused to meet his eye.

"What's wrong, Marcy?"

She dipped her head.

"Not for me to say, Dr. Walker."

Interesting.

Marcy Greenbaum wasn't noted for her reluctance to spread news, however bad. His internal alarm changed from warning buzz to emergency shriek.

"Is Nurse Cortez on shift?"

"She'll be right here. Checking on Mrs. Schuster's bandages right now." She interlaced her fingers as though in prayer. "We are *so* happy to see you, Doctor."

"You already said that, Marcy."

"Yes, yes, and I meant it, too. Four years is far too long to be without a permanent doctor. And a good one," she said, sounding both apologetic and desperate.

161

Walker couldn't figure out what was going on, but premonition told him it didn't bode well.

"Are you going to tell me what's happened?"

Marcy returned to her seat, face serious, fingers now playing with the gold crucifix dangling from a thin chain around her wrinkled neck. "You know me, Dr. Walker. I'm not one to speak out of turn ..."

"No, Marcy. Of course not." Walker mentally crossed his fingers behind his back.

She leaned closer. "Let me just say *everyone* here is delighted you qualified and chose to set up your first practice in our beautiful city. And I mean *everyone*." She added a conspiratorial nod and would probably have tapped the side of her nose if her fingers weren't already occupied.

"Dr. Walker, Chet! Thank the Lord."

Walker turned toward the voice.

Consuela Cortez, head nurse and co-founder of the Lucky Shores chapter of the Chet Walker fan club, rumbled along the corridor, arms open, breathing hard, heels squeaking on the polished floor tiles. Her happy screech could have deafened a herd of bison at one hundred paces. She practically fell into him and wrapped him in a pillow-soft embrace. She smelled of donuts, hard candy, and coffee. No one could ever accuse Consuela Cortez of providing the best example of a healthy diet.

"Hi, Consuela," he managed to say, peeling himself out from under her powerful grip. "Great to see you."

"So sorry we couldn't make your party last night, Chet—Dr. Walker—but no one else would cover for ... Dr. McCrery."

The way her lips curled when she mentioned the temporary medic—as though she'd bitten into an apple and found half a maggot—told him a great deal. The light of revelation started to glow.

"Not to worry, Consuela. I thought you might be busy caring for your—our patients. Where *is* the good doctor?"

162

She lifted one of her eyebrows and her nostrils flared. She was clearly fighting the desire to sneer. "You and I need to have a chat about him. Will you follow me, please?"

Walker frowned. "Sounds ominous. Where are we headed?"

"The clinic. The mothers are getting restless. Follow me. Marcy, I'll be right back. Don't forget to mark Dr. Walker as being in attendance."

The revelatory glow flared and Walker knew this was not going to be a good day.

"But I'm not here officially. Not yet," he said, following her along the same corridor she'd arrived from.

Consuela looked up at him from her five-foot-six-inch height and almost-as-wide frame, smiling. "You're a fully qualified doctor in a small town medical center. Trust me, you're here officially."

"But I need to register with the state board and sign a truckload of insurance papers."

"Hell, this is Lucky Shores, Doc. Paperwork's already been done and part-registered. All you need do is put your John Hancock on a couple dozen forms and things will be hunky-dory. You, me, and Mayor Hallibone can finish up all the housekeeping Monday morning. Meanwhile, you're on the payroll. Thank the Good Lord A'mighty."

She made the sign of the cross and increased her pace so much, Walker had to lengthen his stride to keep up. Her breathing became ragged, but still she didn't slow.

They hurried past the place where he'd first danced with Hooch and Bull, and turned left at the end of the hall where a shorter corridor terminated in a pair of doors marked, *Group Therapy*.

Without breaking stride, Consuela burst through one door and held it open for him. They entered a room full of chattering women, most in different stages of pregnancy, some post-partum carrying squealing babies. Two of the moms were breastfeeding. Dr. McCrery was conspicuous by his absence.

163

All the women turned toward him. Silence fell and each one smiled.

"Ladies," Consuela announced in a voice loud enough to command attention, but quiet enough not to scare the newborns, "this is Dr. Walker. He'll be taking the clinic this afternoon."

Walker grabbed hold of Consuela's pudgy arm and pulled her to one side. "I'll be *what*?"

"Don't worry, Doc," she whispered. "This'll be a cakewalk compared to what you handled at Fort Wycombe. It's easy stuff. Checking developmental progress of the babies, vaccinations, blood tests, answering questions. The usual stuff. I have everyone's case files over on the desk, and I'll be here if you need me. Unless I'm called away."

"Where the hell's Dr. McCrery?"

"Who knows?" Consuela scrunched up her face keeping her voice low. "The old drunk left town this morning. Seems he didn't like the idea of playing second fiddle to the homecoming hero. Mind you, there ain't no one in this town who's going to miss him for a single second."

"You're kidding."

She shook her head and nodded toward the expectant patients.

"Over to you, Doctor. Your patients await."

Walker gulped, turned toward his audience, and dragged on his game face. "Who's first?"

Half a dozen hands shot into the air.

"Holy crap," he muttered. "What am I doing here?"

Consuela chortled. "Mrs. De Souter, you first."

An older, care-worn woman in what appeared to be her third trimester struggled to her feet. Walker took a breath and led his first official Lucky Shores patient toward the desk in the corner. He pulled the confidentiality screen into place and set to work.

Chapter 17

Josie Donoghue

Josie peered through the fogged window of the diner as she headed to the front door. The place was near empty. Four customers sat at separate tables eating late lunches.

She pushed open the diner door, entered, and moist heat leaped out to smother her in its comforting embrace. Before the door closed behind her, she tore off the light jacket, removed her wool hat, and headed toward the staff changing room.

Peg and Allie sighed in sympathetic harmony. Before Josie had time to take more than two steps, they rushed out from behind the counter and formed a reassuring barrier to her progress.

"So?" Peg asked in hushed tones, trying to make sure none of the customers could overhear.

"So what?" Josie answered, on the defensive.

The waitresses looked at each other as though to say, "This torture is too much to bear."

"So how'd it go?" Peg demanded, her voice hushed—at least using her version of hushed.

"How did what go?"

"The reunion, silly," Allie said, bunching a dishcloth in her reddened hands.

"Yes," Peg added, "the *reunion*. Was it all you expected it to be? Did he take you in his arms? Sweep you off your feet?"

Josie's scalp prickled in the warmth from the diner and under the heated stares of her concerned but overeager employees. But on this day of all days, she wouldn't let their well-meaning support ruin her good mood. She made a great play of checking the interest of the few remaining customers. Deciding that they were in too public a place, she beckoned her the girls to follow her behind the serving counter. She forced her lips into a brave smile and leaned closer to the women, who looked ready to burst into anticipated tears.

Josie grimaced while shaking her head and.

Peg's sympathetic smile deepened into a heartbroken frown. "Aw, Joey. He needs to know. It's only fair. He's a doctor now. He'll understand. He can take it."

Allie added to her friend's questioning. "When you left for Fort Wycombe, you told us you'd be back the next day, but you've been away nearly two. We were on tenterhooks. Weren't we, Peg?"

"Sure were. You know how much we care about you, Joey. We've been here all this time dying to know his reaction."

Josie pulled them further away from the customers' prying ears. Heads had started to cant and ears had started to twitch. Cutlery stopped scraping flatware.

"Peggy-May Ransom, lower your voice. I don't need the whole of Lucky Shores knowing my business."

Peg's shoulders sagged, as did Allie's.

"Didn't tell him, did you?"

Josie lowered her gaze to her feet. A few crumbs of bread dusted the floor area around the cutting board. She shook her head. Away less than three days and already the place had started to look like a canteen on Skid Row.

"No," she said, barely making it above a whisper.

Peg and Allie rushed forward to embrace her. Both had inches on her in height and pounds on her in weight, despite her recent changes.

"Oh, honey," Peg said, reaching out and pulling her even closer. "Why on earth not?"

"I couldn't," Josie said. "The … The timing wasn't right. And … well I-I …"

The two women—her long-time employees and close friends—only meant the best for her. Their expressions of sadness and empathy did something to Josie. Without warning, the emotions rose and threatened to overwhelm her. She swallowed past the tightening in her throat and reached into the pocket of her

166

too-tight jeans for a hankie. She dabbed her eyes. When was she going to be able to control her emotions? Everything was so overwhelming—Chet's return, his love, his bravery, the danger he'd faced and overcome. Everything.

She'd intended to tell him, of course she had, but the timing had never been right, what with the business with the Hatfields and the police involvement. How could she have added to his concerns? He had to be worried with his new job and his new life. How *could* she tell him?

Chet had already changed his life for her. He'd given up his music and returned to medicine. All for her. Oh, he told her he'd done it for himself, of course. He'd told her he knew he'd never make it as a singer, and that he'd only been running from the nightmares of his past, but Josie knew better. Chet Walker, the man with magic in his voice, had given up a promising career in music for her. And now, she was going to lay even more hardship on the shoulders of such a wonderful man. How could she?

She hated keeping secrets from him. Hated the way it made her feel. Hated the barrier it threw up between them. A few days, no more. She'd let him settle in a little first, then she'd lay the news onto him. He'd react well. He'd stay with her. Of course he would.

Wouldn't he?

Standing at the center of the little group hug, she soaked up Peg and Allie's goodwill, and it made her stronger.

They'd been amazing. The gabbiest women in town—Marcy Greenbaum excluded—yet they'd not only worked out her secret, but they'd kept it for over a month. It must have been pure torture for them, and Josie loved them all the more for it.

Josie worked herself free from the cuddle. She smoothed out the creases in her dark blue Lucky Shores Diner T-shirt with its tacky, Peg-and-Allie-created cursive legend, *The Best Little Place to Eat in the City*, above a jaw-droppingly beautiful picture of Big Lake.

She blew her nose. Time to knuckle down to business.

167

"Peg, get on with cleaning the grill. Allie, there are tables to bus and floors to clean. I'm going to start the inventory."

Peg reached out a hand, brushed a bang of Josie's hair out of her eyes, and tucked it behind her ear. "Sure thing, honey. We're on it. And we're both here for you if you need us. You know thar, right?"

Josie stuffed the hankie back in her pocket. "I know you are. Now, shall we get to work, ladies? I don't want to be here all afternoon. I have other things to do."

Her friends both cackled.

"Speaking of Chet," Allie said. "Where is he right now?"

"At the clinic, of course. Taking the chance to familiarize himself with his new practice."

"By talking to that no-good Cornhusker, McCrery?" Allie asked, a sneer wrinkling her full lips.

"Fat chance of that," Peg said. When she wagged her head, her dangling silver earrings danced.

Josie's ears pricked up. "What do you mean by that?"

"Goddamned lush. McCrery rented a house a little up the road from our house. I watched him pack his car first thing this morning and drive off. Wouldn't surprise me if he's half way to Nebraska by now."

"Darn it, Peg. Why didn't you tell me before?"

She shrugged. The earrings and her "girls" pressed against the cloth of her T-shirt. "I don't know. It might have been nothing, but the way he was looking around all secretive and furtive-like … Who knows. Maybe I'm wrong."

"You know what that means, don't ya?" Allie said, even more sympathy showing on her expressive face.

Josie nodded. "Yep. It means that Chet's going to be on call from day one." She tried to smile but couldn't make it work.

Peg draped a motherly arm around her shoulders. "Never mind, honey. You an' your hunky doctor will have plenty of time to get to know each other again … If'n you know what I mean." She double hitched her eyebrows.

Josie blushed and ducked away from Peg's heavy arm.

168

"Okay, you two. That's more than enough of your gossiping. Are we ever gonna get any work done today?"

A couple of hours later, Josie's cell phone vibrated, disturbing her in the middle of counting stock. Chet's caller ID flashed up on the screen.

About time.

She rushed to answer it with fumbling fingers.

"Hey there, honey," she said, turning her back to a grinning Peg and Allie. "You okay?"

"I'm fine, thanks. You?"

He sounded fraught, and the background noise of gabbling women and gurgling babies told a their tale.

"Not bad, thank you. What's up?"

"I've encountered a bit of a ... um ... challenge here."

She sighed and faced Peg and Allie again. They were all ears and eyes but for once, silent. "Don't tell me. Dr. McCrery's let you down and you've had to fill in for him at the Mom & Baby group?"

Chet whistled through his teeth. "Wow. Have you become a psychic since I've been gone?"

She laughed. "No. It's just—"

"I know. News travels fast in a small town. I'm go—"

"Good job you called ahead, I was worried for you. Aunt Jean said you left this morning without a heavy coat and you walked. Darn it, Chet, do you even have a flashlight?"

"No, but the sun's still up. And I did dress warmly. Took my quilted jacket," he said. "I know how cold it can get here overnight even in the early fall. I get it. I really do." He laughed. "In my defense, no one let on I'd have to run a darned maternity clinic on my first full day in town. I expected to be back home an hour ago. I've had a heck of a day but it's nearly over."

"What happened to McCrery?"

Walker told her. Allie and Peg shared a glance and nodded.

169

"Typical," Allie said, "wouldn't expect anything else from a doctor sent to us by that no-good, penny-pinching HMO. Every one they've sent has been useless. Either drunk, or lazy, or both."

Chet said something, but a double-wail in the background, stereophonic crying, drowned out his words.

"What was that, Chet? I couldn't hear you."

"Sorry. It's been mayhem here." He spoke up. "I'm just about done though. Only one more patient and her twins to see. Are you still at the diner?"

"Yes. I'll be here a little while. There's a couple more hours' worth of work to finish up."

"Great. I'll be through here soon. Missing you like crazy." The warmth in his voice melted her heart and all her concerns. She'd tell him soon. Really she would.

"Missing you, too," she whispered, trying to ignore the heat rising to her face.

Peg clearly noticed her reaction to Chet's words and put a hand to her chest and made a silent, "Aw." Allie gave up a dopey smile and fanned her face with her hand to dry a mock tear.

Josie scowled at them, but it didn't do any good.

"Let me know when you're done and I'll come collect you."

"Thanks, love. That'd be great. I'll call you as soon as I'm free, if that's okay."

"Okay, honey. I'll be waiting."

"Make sure there's a coffee on the go."

"Always."

He ended the call and Josie slid the cell phone into her back pocket, trying to avoid making eye contact with the two fools who rushed toward her, giggling and throwing another group hug.

"Oh stop it, will you? This is too much. Get on home while I finish off here."

"Are you sure, honey?" Peg asked through her giggling. "It's Allie's turn to swab the floors."

"Hey, no fair. I did it yesterday."

"Yes, but I've done it three times this week, and you know it always make my back ache."

"Darn it, me and Joey both know what makes your back ache. It's on account of having to hold up them huge boobs without any decent scaffolding, girlfriend."

"You're just jealous, honey. My 'girls' are self-supporting. Always have been."

The comment generated another huge cackle from both girls, but Josie refused to respond to the low tone of the conversation.

"That's okay, ladies. I've been away most of the week and have to wait for Chet's call anyway. I don't mind cleaning up if you open up tomorrow morning. I'll be needing a sleep-in." She avoided adding a double eyebrow hitch.

Darn it. She was getting to be as bad as Peg and Allie. Hardly the best way to keep the staff in check.

The two giggle-heads rushed to the cloakroom to fetch their coats, and Peg started singing, "Her boyfriend's back. Her boyfriend's back! Gonna hit the sack, now her boyfriend's back!"

Allie joined in with a reasonably passable harmony as they hurried toward the exit, repeating the chorus over and over. Josie grabbed a dishcloth from the counter and snapped it at Peg's butt, deliberately aiming short.

"Any more of that and I'll be looking to make some staffing changes around here."

Peg interrupted her song long enough to say, "Bye Joey, have a nice evening with your *man*."

At the word "man" she mock-swooned, Hollywood style, and the two idiots rushed through the door. Still giggling, they crossed the street and fell straight into Allie's car. Josie returned their excited waves and broke out a great big smile. Chet was back and life was good. Now all she had to do was choose the right time to lay her secret on him—the only slight blip on the horizon.

Chapter 18

Baby Spit and a Summons

Walker finished washing the baby spit—a viscous and particularly rancid form of yellow vomit—from the sleeve of his shirt with a surgical wipe and collapsed into the chair, as exhausted as he'd been in months. Tension and stress could lead to nervous collapse, and he wasn't far off.

Suck it up, Walker.

In his time, he'd faced down gunmen, snipers, and lunatic medics armed with scalpels, what was so scary about a few moms and their babies?

"Thanks for the help, Consuela," he said, avoiding any trace of sarcasm.

She chuckled.

"As we expected, you're a natural. Sure enough, they all loved you. Wouldn't surprise me to find the place even more packed next week once the young moms all start singing your praises."

"Full? We've just seen fifteen moms-to-be plus babies and you're telling me this wasn't a full clinic?"

"Sure thing. Most of the pregnant women in town avoided Dr. McCrery unless there was an emergency or they needed a new prescription. You could say his bedside manner left a lot to be desired."

"You mean he used to—?"

"No, no. Nothing like that. Nothing nasty. No unnecessary disrobing or manipulation. It's just that he didn't seem to care about his patients none. That, and the fact his breath stank of booze when he ran out of the peppermint mouth spray."

Walker cast his eyes around the clinic. Light, airy, recently decorated, the place was comfortable, but not entirely suitable for private consultations.

"Exactly how many pregnant women are there on the list at the moment?"

"Eighty-seven."

"What?" Walker ran the math in a second. "For crying out loud. That's twice the average for the whole state."

Consuela chortled so much her chubby shoulders bounced up and down and her hair danced.

"Well now, Doc. Seems like you've been doing your homework. And you're dead right. Since the regeneration of the town, our demographics have changed beyond recognition. We now have a younger population, with a higher proportion of women still in their reproductive years. That, coupled with the increase in jobs and the recovery in income, it stands to reason the birth rate's going to pick up some. Nights can get pretty cold hereabouts."

Her smile dropped for a moment, and she continued.

"On a serious note, we've been advertising for a full-time midwife for almost two years now but, so far, there's been no takers. The city's not quite recovered enough to pay for highly qualified and experienced people, you know. We're waiting for the resort's completion and the influx of all the holidaymakers. The city council predicts an even bigger boom when that happens."

Walker rubbed the tightness from his neck and shoulders. "Seems like you and I have our work cut out if we're going to build this medical facility into a place that Lucky Shores can be proud of."

Her smile returned and stayed strong. "Looks that way, doesn't it?"

"So. Last night with that welcoming party, you were all playing me?"

Consuela leaned back in her chair and threw a hand up to her bosom. "Why Dr. Walker, whatever do you mean?"

173

"Nobody told me anything bad about Dr. McCrery. No one suggested he'd likely run off and I'd have to step in without warning."

"Oh, come now, Doc. None of us knew the old soak would up sticks and leave us high and dry. And besides that, Mayor Hallibone told us all to keep it to ourselves. She didn't want you upset on your first day back."

"And Josie, was she in on it, too?"

"Heck no. Joey's never been sick a day in her life … apart from that time she got shot and you had to operate and … well you know all about what happened." The hand released her chest and wafted the air between them. "Well, we'll let that matter drop. No point recalling all that nastiness. What I meant to say was how Joey never met Timothy McCrery in a professional setting. Only time they came into contact was when she was serving him lunch in the diner or whiskey in the saloon."

"Why did the hospital board keep him on so long? If he was that bad, you should have gotten rid of him."

"We thought about it, but didn't have grounds. Mostly, the old lush kept his drinking private and turned up to work just the right side of sobriety. Truth is he was the best of a bad crop of doctors the HMO sent us. The first two were positively dangerous. Neither could read English. Prescriptions were more random than the state lottery. Lucky Shores is hardly a major draw for quality medical staff. Nor is it a center for medical excellence. Stuck out here in the wilds, there aren't many top-flight medics queuing up to work here. Yourself excluded, of course." Her eyes twinkled and she added a wink.

"Of course. So," he said, sighing, "I guess I'm on permanent call-out twenty-four-seven?"

Consuela nodded. "Pretty much. At least until the city starts collecting enough taxes to pay for more staff. We need a junior doctor to work under you and at least two more full-time nurses. We've been operating too long on a skeleton staff and well-meaning volunteers."

174

Walker puffed out his cheeks. He'd been board certified for less than three weeks, and in that time had run a grand total of one maternity clinic. Already, he'd been promoted up the ranks from junior doctor to senior consultant, and it could only happen in a place like Lucky Shores. Not for the first time, Walker wondered what he'd let himself in for. Could he handle the pressure?

Only time's going to tell.

Before he had the chance to ask Consuela another question, the phone on the desk rang. Walker checked the caller ID before lifting the handset.

"Hi Marcy, what's up?"

"I have Sheriff Boyd on the line, are you free to take his call?"

Now what?

"Of course. Put him on."

The phone line clicked once. "Chet, that you?"

Walker recognized the gravel-voiced lawman right off. He sounded less laid-back than usual. The worry wagon returned at full tilt.

"Yes Sheriff, it's me. What can I do for you?"

"Hold on a moment, Chet. Marcy, the phone line didn't click," Caspar growled and waited for Marcy to disconnect and quit her eavesdropping before speaking again. "Damn woman, one day I'm gonna charge her for snooping on official police business."

Walker smiled and winked at Consuela, who could hear the sheriff from way over on her side of the desk.

"One second, Sheriff." He hit the mute button and nodded to his favorite nurse. "Thanks Consuela. Can you organize a meeting of the full hospital board at the earliest opportunity? Next week if possible. I need to present my business plan."

She stood and headed for the exit. "Marcy's already on it, Doc."

"Thanks, and maybe we should call a meeting for all the hospital staff plus as many volunteers as can attend. I'd like to introduce myself and get to know all the staff."

"She's on that, too. We thought Monday morning at shift handover's best. Nine o'clock in the a.m. suit you?"

175

Clearly, Marcy wasn't just a listening post.

"Sounds good to me. Thanks for everything. I'll have my cell phone on and fully charged if you need me before then. Do I need to see anyone before I go?"

"Uh-uh. There aren't any in-patients at the moment, and we keep Sundays clear whenever possible. Treat emergencies only." She waddled out the door, waving goodbye.

Walker released the mute. "Sorry, Sheriff. It's kind of busy here."

"I guessed it might be," Caspar said, with a voice deep enough to shatter granite.

"You heard about Dr. McCrery leaving town?"

"Yep. Marcy just told me. Never did take to the quack. Too keen on the rye, if you see what I mean."

"Is there something you needed, Caspar? I'm pretty keen to head for home now that the maternity clinic's over."

"No, nothing special. Didn't mean to worry you none. Just thought you might like to pop into my office and shoot the breeze. Since you're in the area, an' all."

Walker snorted. "How come you knew where I was? No, no, don't tell me. A small town holds few secrets."

Caspar delivered his version of a laugh—a cross between a hacking cough and a buzz saw chewing into an oak log. "Something like that, Doc. One of my deputies saw you hiking up the hill and ducking into the med center. I called Marcy and she gave me the skinny."

"*One* of your deputies?" Walker asked, unable to keep the surprise from his voice. "You have more than Lionel these days?"

"Sure do, Doc. A thriving town needs a strong police department."

"So, you've been hiring new staff?"

"Yep. Come up and meet the team. You okay to walk, or should I send Lionel to fetch you in a prowl car?"

"No, I'm good to walk. I've seen him drive."

The buzz saw sliced another plank from the log. "Don't be like that, Doc. Since you've been gone, the city's sent Lionel on a whole heap of specialized training courses. High speed and defensive driving, sharpshooting, something fancy called 'cognitive interview techniques.' These days, I actually use him as my chief of detectives. The boy's turned into a damned fine police officer."

"Under your expert tutelage, no doubt."

"You said it, Doc."

After a final pass, the log was stripped and dressed, and the lumber stacked for delivery to the drying kiln. After that, it would head to the builder's yard.

"I'll be there inside ten minutes, Caspar. Put the coffee on. First though, I'll need to let Josie know where I'm headed."

"Fair enough. Tell her I'll drop you back in town. Wouldn't want her to fret none. It wouldn't be telling tales out of school to let you know how much she's been pining for you these past four years."

Me too, Caspar. Me too.

Caspar ended the call without saying goodbye, as was his way.

Walker dropped the handset into its cradle, grabbed his coat, and strolled from the room. On his way past Marcy at the reception desk, he waved his cell phone at her.

"You know how to get hold of me. I'll keep this thing charged and powered up from now on. See you Monday morning, if not before."

He didn't stop to chat, or to answer any of her inevitable questions.

Chapter 19

The Ghost's Lair Revisited

Once through the medical center's main doors, Walker marched to the end of the drive and paused to dial Josie. While he waited, he took in one of the most beautiful landscapes the Colorado Rockies had to offer. He'd never tire of the scenery in this part of America. The greatest country on earth.

"Hey there, handsome," Josie answered before he had the chance to speak, "you ready for the pickup?"

"Sorry, honey," he said, trying not to sound too tired or breathless. "Just received a call from Caspar. He asked me to pay him a short visit while I'm next door."

"You're not exactly next door. You're a hundred feet below him."

"Okay, okay. No need to be so pedantic. Is this what I've got to look forward to for the next fifty years?"

"Only if you want to."

"I do."

"Correct answer," she said, a smile lifting her voice. "What does he want to talk to you about?"

"No idea. Just a chat. I guess he's keen to show off his new team. You didn't tell me the LSPD is now more than a two-man operation. Turns out, The Ghost has staff."

"No, I didn't. We had so little time together when I visited, I didn't want to waste a moment on idle gossip."

"Fair enough. Your flying visits were short, but precious and wonderfully sweet." He paused, but when she didn't respond, he carried on. "This shouldn't take too long. No need to wait at the diner, Caspar said he'd run me back into town."

"It's ok, I'll be here a little while longer. I'll keep the coffee warm for Caspar. You take care, Chet Walker. I'm already missing you again."

Walker responded in kind and they chit-chatted the whole time he trudged up the hill, neither wanting to be the first to hang up. He felt like a teenager gabbling to his first serious crush.

The blustering wind in his face, an aching leg, and the steep incline all combined to hamper his progress. Another right turn off the Old Logging Road—or was it still Main Street—found him at the turning to the final terrace before the mountain rose sheer to the sky. A fifty-yard track led to the *Lucky Shores Sheriff's Office*.

At first glance of the outside, the place hadn't changed at all. The windows didn't even sport a new coat of paint.

A single-story, stone building with a flat roof, it was clear someone had converted the family residence into a precinct house by attaching iron bars to the large front windows and the half-glazed door. Before loaning it to the town during its eight-year long financial hiatus, the place had been Caspar Boyd's private home and, according to Josie, the old lawman still lived the widower life in two rear rooms.

Walker climbed the stone steps up to the wide veranda. Without knocking, he opened the door and strode right in. After all, he did have an official invite.

The noise struck him first, and then the number of people. Five of them, all in the smart, blue-grey Lucky Shores PD uniforms. Walker took a moment to recover. The last time he'd been in the office, the town could only boast two full-time officers, the sheriff and his deputy, Lionel Doge. They also had a part-time emergency backup officer, Deputy Maxine Burroughs. At the time, the town was so poor, Sheriff Boyd worked on deputy's wages and mostly lived off his pension from twenty-five years at the Denver PD—the last ten as chief of detectives.

No one ever told Walker how much the twenty-year-old Lionel Doge earned as a deputy, or how the town could afford to pay him anything at all. Walker once suggested they'd plugged into some sort of state-funded youth opportunity scheme. When no one had said anything to contradict his joke, he thought he might have hit on the truth.

A quick scan of the bustling room showed how much the town's restored fortunes had benefitted its police department.

Six desks, two more than Walker remembered, and three of them occupied, showed the detritus of heavy use—PC monitors, paper files, pens, dirty coffee cups, photos in frames, trash cans full to overflowing. The ancient CB radio setup in the far corner had morphed into a modern-looking telecommunications center with a flashy unit covered in switches and dials, none of which Walker understood.

The addition of IT infrastructure was particularly impressive, and Walker suspected it to be the result of Lionel's influence rather than Caspar's.

To one side, Uncle Albert, the giant, antique, pot-bellied stove, stood dormant, awaiting the full onset of fall when he would work non-stop through the winter and into late spring. The old standby would throw out a wave of superheated air so scorched you could use the room to grow tomatoes, or sweat the truth out of close-mouthed witnesses and reluctant suspects.

Caspar and Lionel stood in front of an expensive-looking coffee machine, heads together, talking quietly with their backs to Walker.

He pushed through the batwing doors set into the wooden banister that formed a waiting area and stepped into the office. The noise died as the first three pairs of eyes turned on him, and then Caspar and Lionel turned, too. Walker stopped, hand holding one of the swing doors open, and batted back the waves of inquisitive scrutiny.

Caspar spoke first, a grim smile cracking his face.

"Everyone listen up for a minute. This here's Dr. Chester 'Chet' Walker. You can introduce yourselves later. Treat this man with all the respect he deserves. Y'all hearing me?"

The three deputies, each even younger and fresher-faced than Lionel, mumbled, "Yes, Sheriff," but continued to stare.

"Unless he breaks the law," Lionel added, a wide grin forming on his still-youthful face. "In which case, you can treat him the same way as any other citizen of the city." He laughed and rushed across the room to shake Walker's hand and grip his forearm at the same time. "Welcome back, Chet ... I mean, Doctor Walker. Congratulations on the medical degree, by the way. Sorry I couldn't make your surprise bash last night, but I was on duty. I heard it went well, though. Place was jumping, yeah?"

The young deputies resumed their duties. Two tapped at keyboards, the other continued her phone call.

Caspar made slightly slower progress than Lionel, but didn't seem any less pleased to see Walker.

"Good to see you again, Doc," Caspar said, gripping Walker's hand as though he meant to crush it into pulp.

"Go easy there, Sheriff Boyd. I need these fingers for my work."

"Sorry, son. Guess you've gone all soft from living back east."

Caspar let go and Walker flexed his fingers, trying to restore some of the circulation. "I was too busy studying and working to spend time in the gym, Sheriff. Man, you're looking old."

The senior sniffed. "That's on account of me being in charge of this here kindergarten. Makes me feel like some kind of Methuselah."

"Yep, and you look it, too."

Caspar stepped closer. Walker tensed, expecting a dig in the ribs, but the old lawman pulled him into a man-hug that yanked him off his feet and caused a yelp of surprise. He doubted the grizzled sheriff could remember the last time he'd hugged another guy. Then, as if he'd come to his senses, Caspar slapped Walker hard enough on the back to force the air from his lungs. When the sheriff finally let go, Walker collapsed onto wobbly legs.

The three of them stood for a moment, locked in a mutual appraisal.

Both Caspar and Lionel had aged since Walker first met them. Caspar stooped a little more, but remained lean, and still looked as though he could crush rocks with his bare hands and fell trees with a scowl. Lionel had matured from teenage boy, to a powerfully built twenty something man who filled out his deputy's uniform and wore it with pride and confidence. Sergeant stripes on his epaulettes showed the benefit of Caspar's guidance.

"This place has changed," Walker said, pointing at the electronics. "New radio. Computers on every desk. You've dragged this place into the third millennium."

Caspar snorted. "You can blame that on Sergeant Doge, here. Kept pestering the mayor to invest in all these shiny new doohickies. More trouble than they're worth, you ask me."

Lionel leaned closer to Walker and lowered his voice. "Don't let his words fool you, Chet. The sheriff's all over the internet like a co-ed in an IT lab. Keeps abreast of all the latest in police software, too. I even caught him on the video phone to Interpol last month when one of the construction workers over at Middle Lake turned out to be on the European terrorist watch list."

Walker, partially recovered from the affectionate mauling, gawped at the sheriff. "Really, Caspar? I have to say, I am impressed. Do you use more than two fingers when you batter at the keyboard?"

Walker wondered whether Caspar's part-missing pinky finger affected his typing speed, but thought better of asking. After a rough start to their relationship, Walker counted Caspar as one of his closest friends. He was also a darned good sheriff and had earned Walker's respect as a consummate professional.

"So, Sheriff, you invited me here. How can I help? Any of your team need a physical? One of your prisoners require patching up after 'accidentally' walking into the pointy end of a nightstick?"

Caspar's shoulders straightened. "Very funny. You still into coffee, or have you really gone all East Coast on me and taken to drinking *frappe-mocha with spices and sprinkles* or whatever? Or, God forbid, you haven't started on tea, have you?"

Walker grinned at the sinewy lawman. "Coffee's plenty good enough for me. I noticed your fancy new machine over there. Is it any good?"

182

"Help yourself, and you can top mine off while you're at it. Mine's the big white cup marked 'The Boss.' Take them through to my inner office, and I'll be with you after I've finished the weekly debrief."

Walker ran the gauntlet of side-cast eyes and made it to the coffee machine. He filled two cups—both black, no sugar—and studied the young troops in action.

The female, Deputy Elle McFerrin according to the badge on her shirt and her desk, ended her phone call and smiled at him. A shy smile on a plain, round face that reddened under his steady gaze.

Stop it, Walker. Leave the kids alone.

Caspar stood at the head teacher's desk as though lecturing at a community college. "… and we need to add the new development at the far end of Chinook Rise to our nightly patrol. The developer complained about kids trashing his equipment. I'll do the drive-by tonight, but Mac"—he nodded to Elle McFerrin—"make sure you add it to the schedule. Just a quick ride-by people. No need to go overboard. I never knew a building site that wasn't a magnet for inquisitive kids. Lionel, arrange a daytime site visit to check their security. No rush. Next week's soon enough."

Lionel nodded and made a note on his—shock and horror—computer tablet. "We need to do something about the access road to Middle Lake, too. Construction traffic's tearing up the surface. If we let it get out of hand, it'll end up as bad as the Old Lumber Road used to be back in the day. We'll need to consider issuing the developers with a couple of code violations."

Caspar nodded. "Good idea. Who's our go-to guy for drafting legal paperwork?" He rubbed his hands together and five pairs of eyes, including Walker's, focused on the well-fed kid sitting adjacent to Mac. His named badge read Deputy Martin Jordan.

"That'll be you, Air," Mac said, her voice deeper than Walker expected.

Deputy "Air" Jordan moved the piece of candy he'd been crunching to the side of his mouth before responding. "Sure thing,

Sheriff. Thirty-day warning be enough, d'you think? Or will they need longer?"

Caspar deferred to Lionel with a nod.

"Thirty days ought to do it. We need that road up to standard before the winter snows or we'll be pulling bodies out of car wrecks all the way through 'til spring."

Air nodded with the enthusiasm of someone who actually enjoyed legal paperwork. "I'll get on it first thing Monday morning. Be ready and signed by Tuesday afternoon. Judge Driscoll won't want to be bothered before then."

Caspar and Lionel both nodded.

"Why not?" Walker asked, unable to rein in his curiosity.

Deputy Air swiveled his chair to face Walker. "Sorry?"

"Why won't the judge want to be disturbed before Tuesday?"

The chubby deputy pumped out a grin. "That's on account of Judge Driscoll being guest of honor at the Rotary Club's annual awards shindig this weekend. Everyone in town knows Amos Driscoll can't hold his drink. It won't be worth trying to talk to him before he sobers up."

"I see. Thanks."

"Lionel, you can take over here," Caspar said, holding out his hand to Walker for his drink. "Give out next week's assignments and make sure everyone's day reports are on my desk before you sign out. Right now though, I need some caffeine. With me, Doc."

He pointed to the door in the back wall marked "Office," and led a circuitous route between the desks. No doubt about it, the room was overcrowded. It smelled of laundry detergent, deodorant, and coffee, but mostly of people. Walker shuddered at the lack of space and batted down the sinewy tendrils of claustrophobia. He hadn't had a panic attack since the afternoon he spent treating Josie in Pastor Caring's goldmine and hoped he'd actually beaten the disorder.

Fat chance.

At least the lights glowed bright and the setting sun still shone through the barred windows. He swallowed and took a deep breath.

Walker negotiated the narrow walkways, concentrating on not spilling his drink, but still managed to brush a bunch of files from off one desk.

"Damn it."

He stooped to pick up the mess and returned the pile to the surface. A young family stared back at him from the silver-framed photo next to the PC monitor—a blond man, a dark-haired woman, and two pre-school kids, one of each. The smiling woman wore the uniform of a LSPD Deputy, and Walker recognized her as Maxine Burrows. When he'd last lived in Lucky Shores, Maxine had been the town's part-time deputy. An honest, friendly woman, he enjoyed her company on the few occasions they'd met out of uniform.

Caspar pushed through the door to his inner sanctum and held it open. Walker was transported back almost four years to his first night in town. Not his happiest memory, but his life had turned around since then.

Apart from the huge flat-screen computer monitor dominating Caspar's desk—an anachronism in such a traditionally furnished space that didn't even contain a TV—the room hadn't changed since his first visit. The posters behind the sheriff's desk still featured pictures of Woody Guthrie and other folk-singing greats. The same heavily laden bookshelves clung to the walls, and the furniture still smelled of wax polish, old leather, and smoke from the log fire. The kitchenette still stretched out along the back wall beneath a landscape window with a panoramic view of the western mountain range and a glowering sky. As always, the room reminded Walker of his grandfather's lakeside study in Syracuse, only this one was bigger and more lived in.

The stone fireplace held the makings of a fire, screwed up paper, kindling, and small logs, but remained unlit. To his left, two wingback leather chairs and a couch hunkered around a wood coffee table. Caspar's "comfy corner."

185

The Ghost dropped into one of the wingbacks. "Take a load off, Chet."

Walker didn't need a second invite. He'd half-expected the old man to take up his official interview position and force him to sit across the desk in one of two uncomfortable hard-backed chairs. He'd done it before, but it seemed that times had changed.

Caspar must have picked up on the sideways glance at the offensive seats and grunted. "Still haven't forgiven me for rousting you that first time, huh?"

"You ever sat in one of those damn torture chairs, Caspar?"

He laughed. This one sounded less buzz saw, more orbital sander, and the smile softened his heavily tanned and craggy face. "Only once. They're to stop visitors staying too long in my private quarters. I rarely invite people to sit here." He rubbed a hand over the soft leather of his wingback and stared at his steaming coffee.

"You saying I should feel honored?"

Caspar shrugged and tilted his head to the side. "If you like."

"You never did say why you gave me such a hard time that night."

"Didn't I?" He sighed and refused to meet Walker's gaze.

"No, Caspar. You didn't."

The lawman took a breath and looked up. "Look at it from my point of view. The same day the town's most hated man returns, you arrive with him. What was I supposed to do?"

"You didn't really think I had anything to do with the robbery? I'd have been seventeen years old at the time it went down."

"No, but ..."

"You used me to flush out the real thief, and you risked Josie's life doing it."

"Yeah, I know, I know. Made a big mistake, and I've felt guilty about it ever since. Joey's forgiven me, have you?"

"I'm here, aren't I?"

"So you are."

Walker paused long enough to make the point before breaking a slightly awkward silence.

"I can think of a way you can make it up to me," he said.

"Name it."

Walker leaned across to look through the gap between the sheriff's desk and his chair where the 1962 Braun Music-O-Gram stood in all its valve-boosted, pre-digital-age, stereophonic glory. "Play your original version of Woody's *This Land is Your Land* when Josie and I get married."

Caspar looked up and took no time making his decision. "On one condition."

"What's that?"

"I play it in here just for the two of you. Don't want that platter or the stereogram to leave this room. They're too valuable and I ain't takin' the risk."

"Sheriff Boyd, you have a deal."

"We good now?"

"We're good."

It didn't take much. Walker had forgiven the old sheriff the moment he helped carry the comatose Josie from the gold mine and into the rescue helicopter.

Walker stretched out his aching legs and squirmed deeper into the leather chair. He took a healthy gulp of what turned out to be a below average brew. The coffee machine may have looked impressive, but its product didn't match the promise. He leaned forward and placed the cup on a coaster sitting on the coffee table. To mask his rejection of the drink, he tilted his head toward the outer office. "Crowded out there."

"No kidding. The city's population has more than tripled in the past four years. A combination of old-timers returning and new-bloods arriving due to the construction. Lucky Shores had a new lease on life, and we needed a bigger police department."

"So I see." Walker stared at the coffee, but no matter how thirsty he got, nothing would make him drink the stuff. He could wait for his return home. "They say a sign of age is when cops start looking like school kids. I must be getting old. Although you were the one who mentioned a kindergarten."

Caspar took another sip, grimaced, and licked the taste from his lips. "Paid a Goddamned fortune for a top-of-the-range, all-bells-and-whistles machine, and the dang thing churns out coffee that could pass for river mud." He put aside his cup. "You're right though, the newbies are young. Keen, but inexperienced. Trouble is my budget doesn't stretch to poaching qualified officers from bigger towns. Lucky Shores doesn't exactly pull in the cream of the crime-fighting crop. At least, not yet." He looked through the window at the setting sun and shook his head slowly. "You should have seen the sorry bunch I had to screen with the town council the last time we did some recruiting. Washed-up drunks, college kids, and trigger-happy wannabes. I really hate the idea of going through the process again."

"You hiring?"

"Yep." Caspar nodded. "We're looking to fill three new vacancies."

Walker thought about that for a second. "I counted six desks out there. Does Lucky Shores really need a ten-person PD?"

"Ten?"

"Yes. Six desks out there, yours in here, and the three new deputies. That makes ten. Unless you need me to check the math with a calculator." He smiled.

"I didn't miss your sass Doc, but we're only going to have nine, for now."

"That means someone's leaving?"

"You always were sharp as one of your scalpels. I didn't miss that, either."

"So, Maxine's the only one missing tonight. Is she the one going?"

Caspar nodded. "'Fraid so."

"She hasn't cleared her desk yet, so where is she?"

"It's her turn for the outer patrol this afternoon. Won't be back in the office until morning. She'll be sorry she missed you. I reckon she wants to apologize for missing your clinic this afternoon."

"Why?"

"She's expecting again. Six months gone and getting bigger by the day." His smile was tinged with sadness.

"If I don't see her first, congratulate her for me, will you?"

Boyd's thin lips compressed. "Commiserate, more like. Her husband passed away a couple months back."

The news hit Walker like a sock to the jaw.

"Russel's dead? God, that's terrible. What happened?"

"Construction accident up at the resort. He left her pretty well covered financially with life insurance, but she's going to have to give up work to look after the kids when the new baby arrives. She loves her job. Good at it, too."

"That's a crying shame. I met Russell a couple of times. Nice guy. Friendly."

Caspar nodded again. "Yep. Russ was a good man and a fine husband."

Walker let the information sink in until he felt the need to break the silence before it became morose. "Where the hell you going to put them? The new deputies, I mean. Planning a hot-desk arrangement. A night shift maybe?"

"Nope. I finally managed to convince the city's appropriations committee to reopen the old PD building. It's the two-story brownstone the far side of the diner. They've put money aside to refurbish it starting in the spring."

"That's good news. I bet you're looking forward to getting your home back."

Caspar stared at the coffee cup and nodded. "Sure am."

"You'll be closer to the diner, too. You'll be able to get a decent fix of caffeine."

When Caspar didn't respond, Walker studied the old man more closely. Drooping eyelids suggested fatigue, but at five thirty in the afternoon?

"You okay, Sheriff?"

Caspar rubbed his eyes with the heels of his callused hands. "Tired is all. Not getting much sleep these days."

"Worried about something? Worry's a regular cause of insomnia."

189

Caspar filled his lungs, which, despite the man's age, sounded clear and showed the benefit of being a life-long non-smoker.

"Worry?' he asked, nodding. "The sheriff of a bustling town's always got something to worry about, but there's nothing you need to concern yourself with."

"You sure? Want me to book you in for a medical next week? I'll be running a special discount for senior citizens."

"Don't sass me, boy. I could still whoop your ass."

Walker took in the sheriff's lean frame, his steel cable forearms, and made the assessment. Caspar was old but tough. The scars above his left eye told of battles won and lost, but the glint in his eye showed a quiet confidence with no hint of bravado. Walker, younger, taller, and fifty pounds heavier, could probably have taken him in a fair fight during his days as a travelling man, but he'd spent four years treating patients in hospital wards and had grown soft. Nope, a fight between them right then would be too close to call.

In any event, who was to say Caspar Boyd would fight fair? And the firearm in his holster would tilt the balance in the lawman's favor. Walker sniffed at his ridiculous musings. He really liked the old man and would never deliberately pick a fight with anyone.

Walker raised his hands in surrender. "Yep, you probably could at that, Sheriff."

"You'd like to find out though, wouldn't you? I saw you taking my measure."

"Not guilty," Walker lied, adding an innocent, wide-eyed smirk.

Caspar slapped his hands to his knees and used them to lever himself upright. His joints crackled in complaint and he grunted. He pointed to the window. "Getting dark. Cold, too, most likely. You'd better let me drive you downhill."

Walker stood with about the same amount of effort. The outcome of their would-be battle stood even more in the balance.

"You sure? Wouldn't want to put you to any trouble. I could easily call Josie and ask her to collect me. To be honest, if I'd known Dr. McCrery was going to do a runner—"

"Do a what?"

"Sorry, British slang. If I'd known McCrery was going to hightail it out of town, I'd have taken my Ford this morning."

"You spent too long in London."

"Won't argue with you on that one. Cold, damp, and expensive, but the people were nice enough. Some of them, at least."

"C'mon then. You can join me on my patrol. Every now and again I like to show the townsfolk how their tax dollars are being spent, and I'll drop you off at the mayor's place when we're done unless the diner's still open."

"Thanks, Caspar. I always wanted to ride shotgun in a cop car. Can I play with the flashing lights and the sirens?"

"Hell, boy. How old are you?"

Caspar clapped Walker on the shoulder and practically pushed him through the door.

Chapter 20

On Patrol with the Ghost

Walker stepped onto the porch and coughed as the cold mountain air scorched his lungs. It never ceased to amaze him how fast the temperature could plummet after sundown at this altitude. He turned up the collar of his quilted jacket and settled his wide-brimmed hat more firmly on his head.

"Where is everyone?" he asked Caspar, indicating the empty outer office they'd just passed through.

"They've all gone home. We don't run a night shift."

"They don't say goodbye? Not even Lionel?"

Caspar snorted. "It's one of my cardinal rules. If I'm in my office, no one disturbs me unless it's an emergency. Have to have some privacy in my own home."

Walker shivered as another knife of frigid air sliced through his clothing. He rubbed his hands together. "Jeez, Caspar, hit the locks, will you? I'm freezing."

"Soft lowlander. You'll toughen up soon enough. Or buy some decent winter clothing. In you go."

He pressed the button on his key fob and the flashers on his truck—a brand new Chevy Tahoe 4WD with the full "special service" add-ons—blinked twice. Walker skipped down the steps, dove into the front passenger seat, and yanked on the door. It closed with a satisfyingly expensive rubberized clump. The cab still had the showroom squeak and smell only a new car could manage.

It felt good to be in the front seat of a police vehicle once again. During his time on the road, he'd been locked in the back more often than he cared to remember.

Caspar locked the front doors to his office and took his time to reach the car. His eyes took in the mountains and the sweep of the valley, and he smiled in obvious appreciation. Walker had to agree. With the sun hitting the peaks and washing the valley in its amber glow, few landscapes could match it for raw beauty and grandeur. No matter how often he saw a Lucky Shores sunset, Walker doubted its magnificence would fade. Clearly the sheriff felt the same way.

"God, I love this place," Caspar said as he buckled his seatbelt, a sad sigh adding a punctuation mark.

"Sounds like you're fixing to leave."

"Nope, but we've all got to go sometime, Doc."

"Is there something you're not telling me, Caspar? Are you really okay?"

The old sheriff turned his head to look at Walker, a strange expression darkening his face. "I'm fine. Tired is all. Looking forward to having my home back and maybe handing in my badge."

"Retirement? You? Hell, Caspar, I thought they'd bury you in that uniform." He smiled to lift the mood, but Caspar Boyd didn't reciprocate.

"Feeling my age, son. Coming up on my sixty-ninth birthday. Getting too damn old to do all this baby-sitting. I wasn't joking 'bout running a damned playschool. And I'm getting too damn old to be traipsing around the mountains chasing perps who should know better than to drive drunk or hunt out of season. Mine's a young man's game."

He sighed and stared off into the distance. Walker kept quiet, giving his friend time. He'd never heard Caspar so introspective. It was almost worrying.

"Lionel's a good right-hand man," Caspar continued, "and if he was ten years older, I'd encourage him to run for office, but ... Hell, Chet, listen to this tired old fool." He snicked Walker's knee with the back of his hand. "Let's go check out the town. Buckle up. I don't want to run the risk of injuring the city's new doctor in an accident. City Council would be a mite upset, and a certain diner owner would rip me a new one."

Caspar pressed the big red ignition button. The Chevy roared and then settled into a smooth-running growl. Walker barely felt the vibration.

The sheriff drove to the end of the drive and stopped at the junction with the Old Lumber Road. He pointed to the right, uphill. "Ordinarily I'd take a run up top and take a tour of some of the smaller towns along the upper ridge, but time's a-wasting, and I can set one of the deputies to do that tomorrow."

Walker scanned the mountain ridge, searching for signs of human habitation—lights for example. He found none. "I've never been to any of the outlying towns and villages. Guess I ought to show my face when I get settled in."

"At the last city council meeting, Mayor Hallibone said how the old Dr. Matthews used to run regular outreach clinics. She was hoping you'd reinstate them, but I doubt you'll have the time given what's going on over at Middle Lake."

"Something I need to know about?"

Caspar indicated left and nudged the SUV onto the resurfaced road, heading downhill.

"Nothing too serious," he answered after making the turn and checking the rearview, "but the city's tripled in size with the construction workers, and we've had a series of accidents recently. Apart from the three fatalities—including Maxine's husband—most of them were minor. You know, cuts, falls, broken bones, and suchlike. A few were ... what do you medics call them? Life-altering injuries?"

Walker nodded. "Usually means amputations and non-recoverable brain damage. Are you saying the construction companies are cutting corners?"

Caspar shifted into low gear to negotiate a hairpin curve and left it engaged, not taking his eyes from the road. "Not so much. But after the last incident where a crane collapsed, killing one man and injuring five others, Mayor Hallibone insisted the Consortium build a helipad to link the resort with the Douglas

Ferry rescue center." He cut a glance at Walker. "They kicked up a fuss and claimed financial hardship caused by the delay, but the mayor threatened them with an injunction and they folded."

"Good old Jean. Won't back down from a fight."

Walker grinned.

"Didn't win her any friends though. The Consortium's threatening to put up a candidate to stand against her in the next election."

"You're kidding, right? No one's going to waste money backing an opponent to Jean Hallibone. During the bad times, she practically kept the city going single-handed. Lucky Shores would have gone bankrupt without her."

Caspar negotiated the final sharp bend and cut a right turn into a side street Walker hadn't been down before. The road sign called it Steiniger's Crescent.

"People have short memories, and most of the newcomers don't care 'bout what happened in the past. Besides, the Consortium's the county's biggest employer and money talks loud."

"You don't think much of your fellow citizens, do you."

Boyd sniffed and flicked the headlights to high beam. "Seen it all before, Chet. Politics is bad business."

Caspar continued to the end of the residential road, played his searchlight on the three houses at the terminus, and made the tight turn where the road ended at the edge of the forest.

"This whole street's been bought by the Consortium and is earmarked for their executives for when the ski resort opens next fall. Some of the city's residents have been priced out of the neighborhood. Been a little friction brewing, especially by the environmental lobby. When the big construction firms move in, there's always someone or something as suffers."

"I thought the major changes were restricted to Middle Lake?"

Caspar nodded and rolled the SUV forward, still playing the spotlight on the houses.

195

"Most of them are," he answered, "but there's always going to be change and some people don't like it. Didn't Josie tell you any of this?"

"Hell, Caspar. Apart from video calls and emails, we've only seen each other three times a year for the past four years. We were hardly going to spend the time gossiping about Lucky Shores, now, were we?"

Walker studied the old man's reaction. Did he actually blush? No. Not possible. Must have had something to do with the color of the setting sun.

Caspar maneuvered his truck around a dark Nissan SUV parked half-on, half-off the sidewalk. A large oval badge adorned the driver's door. White background, green letters and logo—a stylized mountain with a ski lift stitched to the outside of one slope. It looked about as attractive as a zit on the nose of a supermodel. The italicized letters read, MLDC, the ubiquitous Middle Lake Development Consortium. He'd seen the logos all around town, on vehicles, billboards, and in commercial windows.

"Hell! Not again." Caspar stamped on the brake and the SUV shuddered to a stop ten yards beyond the Nissan.

"Stay in the car, Doc."

Caspar unfastened his seatbelt and jumped out the door.

"What's wrong?"

"Broken window. Stay here!"

"The hell I will."

Heart beating fast, Walker opened his door and slid out into the chill night. Damn it, why didn't he learn to dress for the mountains?

Caspar unclipped his Maglite and played the beam over the house. Sure enough, one of the downstairs windows of the nearest building—a log-built, two-story, Mountain Rustic cut into the side of the hill—had a brick-sized hole in the bottom quadrant. Glass shards sprinkled over the gravel path picked up Boyd's flashlight beam and sparkled like jeweled ice.

Caspar drew in a deep breath.

196

"This is Sheriff Boyd," he thundered, in a voice so authoritative it prickled the hairs on the back of Walker's neck, "better show yourselves if you know what's good for you."

He waited, torchlight quartering the front of the house and picking up nothing. With his free hand, Boyd signaled for Walker to step behind him. Walker obeyed. The tension of watching a real lawman at work beat anything he'd seen on TV and in the movies. How did cops do this sort of thing for a living without collapsing in a puddle of fear?

Staring down the barrel of Fulton Hatfield's hunting rifle had been different. Then, he had Mary Anne and the baby, Little Josie, to consider. Now, he had time to reflect on being in the potential firing line. If Walker hadn't minded showing Caspar his fear, he'd have dodged behind the SUV.

Boyd held the Maglite out to the side, well away from his body. Any shots fired at the light from the Mountain Rustic would miss them by a comfortable inch or two.

No problem.

Walker's whole body tingled with tension.

"Don't make me come in there searching. I'm hungry, and when I'm hungry, I lose all my sense of humor."

An angry cursing sounded over the top of the pine needles rustling in the treetops and reached them from around the back of the house.

"Hold you're damned water, Sheriff. It's me, Abe. Pete's here, too. Keep that pistol in your holster. We're coming out front. Okay?"

Caspar's shoulders relaxed, and his right hand released the handle of his holstered automatic. Walker hadn't even noticed it had come to rest there.

"Okay, Abe. Come on out. You too, Pete. But do it slow."

Two shame-faced wayfarers appeared at the side of the house. The first, Abel Dunleavy—six foot two, mid-forties with a bushy white beard and long hair—had increased in girth since Walker last saw him. The other, Pete, half Dunleavy's height and a quarter his bulk, had a huge overbite, a receding hairline, and an

197

ill-conceived chin. Walker never had learned Pete's surname. They were two thirds of Lucky Shores' version of the Three Stooges. George, the final part of the triple act, wasn't with them.

Caspar lifted the beam. The two men squinted and raised hands to shield their eyes.

"Stay where you are and show me your hands. Make sure they're empty. You hear?"

Dunleavy straightened. "Aw hell, Sheriff. You know us. Why you going Robocop all of a sudden?"

"Hands," Caspar repeated, his voice near a growl.

Dunleavy and Pete did as instructed and revealed four gloved paws. All empty.

"Okay boys, lower your arms and tell me what in the hell you're doing here."

Dunleavy, still shielding his eyes from the glare, shook his head. "You know right well what we're doing here. I'm going to reach into my jacket pocket and show you my security identification one more time. I'm getting awful tired of this, Sheriff Boyd."

"Yeah, me too," Pete agreed, his high-pitched voice matching his slight stature.

"Explain yourselves one more time," Caspar said, closing the gap between them.

Walker matched the sheriff stride for stride and wondered what was going on. The first time he'd met Abe Dunleavy—in Josie's diner on his first morning in town—the Santa Clause lookalike had attacked him without provocation. Dunleavy had come off worse for their little contretemps. Pete, the acolyte, had done nothing but watch. He hadn't even cheered Dunleavy on.

At the time, the Three Stooges had worked as lumberjacks for the Geddes clan. What these two were doing this far out of town and driving in the Consortium's SUV was, no doubt, something Walker would learn soon enough.

That Caspar Boyd, one of the most capable men Walker had ever met, was acting so officiously, added more interest to the episode. Everyone in town knew Abe Dunleavy and Pete were mostly harmless.

The next few minutes would prove enlightening.

Dunleavy let loose a theatrical sigh. "As security officers employed full time by the Middle Lake Development Consortium, we are empowered to investigate any malfeasance that takes place on any property owned by the said Consortium."

Dunleavy recited the words as though reading from a script.

"And?" Boyd asked.

"Me and Pete was on patrol. We spotted this here wanton vandalism and took it upon ourselves to investigate. It's our duty, Sheriff. You know that."

Caspar took another pace closer. Dunleavy flinched, and Pete hid behind him, lost in the shadow of the much larger man.

The sheriff, in all his official glory, stood up straight and tall. "Now listen to me and listen good. My deputies and I represent the law in Lucky Shores." He emphasized the words by jabbing a thumb into his own chest. "Your job starts and ends inside the confines of the construction site. You two ain't nothing but night watchmen. Janitors. Get it? Far as I'm concerned, you're now trespassing on private land. And that'll be the case until I see the local ordinance telling me you're now the law in Lucky Shores."

Dunleavy crumbled under Boyd's withering verbal attack.

"Aw Sheriff, there ain't no call to be getting so worked up. Pete and me is only doing our jobs."

"No, you're doing *my* job. And what's more, you're undermining my authority and the authority of the LSPD. I'm happy to support Neighborhood Watch initiatives, but the operative word here is 'Watch.' Get me?"

Pete edged around from behind his protector. "What's 'operative word' mean, Abe?"

"It means," said Caspar, dialing back the aggression and upping the level of patience, "you watch. You don't enter and disturb my crime scene, Pete."

"That right, Abe?" Pete asked, dragging his gaze away from Caspar and looking up, almost in adoration.

"Shut up, Pete," Abe said, elbowing him away. To Caspar, he said, "Sorry, Sheriff. We was just trying to protect our employer's … I mean, we was doing our part as concerned citizens."

"By disturbing my crime scene?"

Dunleavy lowered his head and nodded. "Sorry again, Caspar. But we didn't do nothing wrong."

"What did you find?"

"Looks like someone threw a rock through the window. Didn't get in though, far as we can tell. Prob'ly just kids up to their high jinks."

"Yeah. Prob'ly just kids," Pete echoed, nodding like he was trying to shake water from his left ear.

Dunleavy stood taller. "We were just going to take a look inside to make sure the place was empty and call Manny Micklewhite to board the window up, but you got here first."

"How were you going to gain entry?"

Dunleavy fiddled inside his jacket pocket and came up with a single brass key on a ring. "We got this here master key for the back door of every house on the street. We were gonna let ourselves in and search the inside of the property."

Boyd held out his hand and beckoned with his fingers. "Hand it over."

"What you say?"

"I said, 'hand it over.' You gone deaf all of a sudden, Abe?"

With some reluctance, Dunleavy stretched out a hand and passed the key across. He maintained the distance between him and Boyd as though he were a schoolboy afraid of being clipped around the back of the head.

"How long you had this?"

"Since nine o'clock this morning," Pete said, keen as a butter knife.

Dunleavy shoved him again. "Shut up, Pete. I need that back, Sheriff. It's my responsibility. Had to sign for it, I did."

"When did you learn to write?" Boyd said in a rare display of his acerbic wit. "Or did you mark it with an 'x'."

"Oh, very funny, Caspar. There ain't no call for such an insult."

Behind the big man, Pete hung his head and cast his eyes to the concrete path beneath his feet. For a change, he said nothing.

Walker shivered again and crossed his arms against the cold.

Dunleavy leaned to the side to see around Boyd. "Who's that back there? Damn, look Pete, it's Chet Walker. The new doctor. How you doing, Doc?"

A huge grin stretched the white beard. He shuffled forward, taking a wide berth around the sheriff, and thrust out a hand the size of a small shovel.

Walker didn't move. The last time he'd touched the same hand, he'd nearly removed its thumb, and he doubted Dunleavy had forgotten the incident.

"Bygones, Doc. Bygones," Dunleavy said, still smiling. "Forget our little misunderstanding back in the diner all them years ago. I have. You and me don't have nothing to argue over, and I ain't got no hard feelings. I was in the wrong, and I am a big enough man to admit it." He swept his hand in an expansive arc that took in the whole of the town. "You and Little Joey Donoghue saved this city. Damn it, you saved the whole county. Without you two, we'd still be breaking our backs on the Geddes' farm felling trees and milling lumber for minimum wage. We owe you one hell of a lot. Please, put it there."

He thrust the paw forward again. This time, Walker took it and accepted the enthusiastic handshake. Pete stood where he was and dug his hands deeper into his pockets.

"That's all very heartwarming," Caspar said, "but you need to get out of here. Go on, now. Move along."

"What about my key?" Dunleavy asked.

"I'm confiscating it ahead of confirming that you're entitled to it. For security, I'll be storing it in the safe in my office. You can tell Mr. Steiniger to come get it during normal office hours. He'll need to sign a release, in triplicate. And in person."

"Aw hell, Caspar. That ain't right. Mr. Steiniger don't have time to collect no keys. He's an important man. A busy man."

201

Walker moved alongside Caspar. He relaxed his arms and refused to appear cold although he was the only one not wearing a heavy coat.

Dumb ass.

"Who's this guy, Steiniger?" Walker asked.

Dunleavy puffed out his chest. "He's President of the Middle Lake Development Consortium. I've actually met him in person. More'n once, too."

"Me too," Pete echoed, showing his gap-toothed smile for the first time that evening.

"Run along now, boys," Caspar said, waving a dismissive hand—again giving it the schoolteacher vibe. "Away to your homes." He tipped his hat to Dunleavy and added. "Give my regards to your Izzy."

"Will do, Sheriff," Dunleavy said and shuffled to the Nissan with Pete following close at his side.

Caspar turned and watched them all the way to the car. He waited for the Nissan to make the right turn onto Main Street before coughing out a rasping laugh. Walker smiled through chattering teeth and returned to hugging his chest.

"Hell, Doc," Caspar said, once he'd stilled his raucous bellowing. "Don't get many pleasures in my life, but one of the purest joys of being an officer of the law is rousting those two harmless fools."

"Caspar. You are a bully."

He nodded. "Can't argue with that, but in this case it's justified. When it comes to the MLDC it's doubly so. Steiniger's been trying to undermine my office since the get-go. Aiming to show I'm not up to the job anymore. My guess is he's planning to bankroll a puppet candidate for sheriff in the elections next year. Same way as he's trying to control the mayor." Caspar arched his back and grunted. "Tell you the truth, Doc, not sure I'll stand again. Getting too damned old for all this political bull crap."

"Probably," Walker agreed, adding a cheeky grin. "Seems as though I'm missing some background to this, but before telling me more, can we hurry up? Hypothermia's setting in."

Boyd clapped Walker's shoulder. "Like I keep telling you, Doc. If you don't learn to dress appropriate for the mountains, you ain't going to last through the next winter." He pointed his key fob at the Chevy and pressed the button. The locks disengaged. "You'll find a spare coat in the back. Help yourself while I check out the house. If you do come looking, make sure you announce yourself. I'd hate to shoot the town's new chief medic. All that paperwork? Hell no." His teeth glinted in the backwash of the flashlight.

"Gee, Caspar. You're all heart."

Walker jogged back to the Chevy, found the fleece-lined police coat, and gratefully pulled it on. Despite it being a little tight under the arms, it cut out the knifing wind and improved his situation instantly. The five-pointed sheriff's badge on the breast pocket somehow made him feel taller. Now all he needed was a holster, a nightstick, and a pair of handcuffs dangling from a utility belt, and he'd be set.

Walker grinned at his nonsense. He'd never wanted to be a cop. As a kid, all he'd ever imagined for himself was to be an astronaut, a doctor, and a singer—in that order. Heck, as the classic rock song said, *Two Out of Three Ain't Bad*.

Walker grinned to himself in the rearview mirror and headed along the path leading to the house.

Chapter 21

The Party People

Caspar had moved away, his flashlight producing a sweeping cone of white at the back of the house.

A quick search of the SUV's glove box netted Walker a spare penlight. He twisted the head and a surprisingly powerful beam lit up the inside of the cab. No doubt about it, he really had to learn to be better prepared in the wilds of the Colorado mountains. Not many streetlights thereabouts, and the ones in town turned off early.

Near fully dark, Walker followed the sheriff's lead and made his way around the side of the house. A concrete path led to where the excavations cut into the hill were being held back by large rock walls retained with thick stainless steel mesh cages. The little more than shoulder-width gap between the house's stone foundations and the rock wall crowded in on Walker. He scrunched his shoulders, held his breath, and rushed through to a multi-terraced back yard.

The rear door stood open.

"Caspar," he yelled loud and clear, "I'm coming in. Don't you dare shoot, now. You hear me?"

"It's okay, Doc. The place is clear. Stay right where you are, I'm coming out."

Walker did as he was told, and the sheriff arrived at the open rear door seconds later, following the brilliant white beam of his Maglite which he pointed at the ground to avoid blinding Walker.

"Looks like a bunch of kids used the place for a party. There's all the usual telltale signs. Used condoms. Joints. Empty beer cans. I'll get Lionel to go over the place with his forensics bag in the morning. Bound to find some usable fingerprints, although

204

I've a good idea who organized the party and sent out the invites."

"Anyone I'd know?" Walker asked.

Caspar shook his head in the near dark.

"Doubt it. The usual suspects. High school kids looking for a quiet place out of the cold. This building site's near completion, but the whole block's still empty. Perfect for their purposes. Trouble is, they don't have the sense God gave a possum. So stupid, they broke a front window, and not one at the back. Didn't even bother to clean up after themselves. Left so much evidence lying around, catching 'em is gonna be easy."

"Kids aren't all born to be criminal masterminds, Caspar. Maybe they'll learn the trade with the proper schooling. Make it more of a challenge for you."

Caspar tilted up the brim of his hat with an index finger and snorted. "It'll give Lionel an excuse to play detective, and my kindergarten deputies a chance to learn correct police procedures."

"Darn it, Caspar. When did you turn into a 'glass half full' kind of guy? What happened to the gruff old sheriff I grew to disrespect so much?" Walker smiled through the words.

The not-so-miserable old lawman didn't respond to Walker's taunts.

"Okay, Caspar. Cold shoulder noted. What next?"

Boyd scratched his chin. "I'll get Lionel to call Manny Micklewhite."

"The guy Abe mentioned?"

"That's right. You won't have met him yet, but Manny's the city's chief handyman. He'll secure the scene and send the bill to the MLDC offices." Boyd rubbed his gloved hands together and headed for the door. "C'mon, Doc. I'm itching for some of Joey's coffee and pastries. Assuming the diner's still open."

"It will be. She's waiting for us. Better hurry or I'll be in the doghouse my first weekend back."

"Wouldn't want that to happen, son. I'm kind of looking forward to having you around. Certainly wouldn't want you putting little Joey in one of her moods or the whole town would suffer."

Walker hurried through the constricted alleyway at the side of the house, and waited for the slower-moving lawman to join him in the front yard. He took a couple of deep breaths to clear his head and looked up. Framed by the darkening sky, the mountains with their solidity, permanence, and beauty soothed his racing thoughts. Together with Josie, the mountains acted as his anchor.

Walker turned his back on the Rockies and looked down. The Lucky Shores streetlights twinkled amber in the velvet black. Other lights, hidden behind curtains, added to the color palette and sparkled like jewels over the beautiful but freezing waters of Big Lake. The town certainly had grown since he'd been away. More lights sparkled, and they seemed to stretch further around the lake, although that could have been an illusion brought about by his present height above the inky black water.

Caspar stopped at Walker's side.

"Still not comfortable with closed spaces, Chet?" he asked, keeping his voice down.

Walker ignored the question and kept studying the scene.

"Don't think I'll ever grow tired of that view," Caspar said, picking up on Walker's reluctance to focus on his weaknesses.

"I've missed it these past four years, that's for certain."

They stood in silent awe, enjoying the beauty before Walker's curiosity overcame his sense of the poetic.

"Is George away somewhere? I've never seen Abe or Pete without the Third Musketeer."

Caspar shook his head. "Guess you didn't hear. George passed away two years back. Lung cancer from smoking three packs a day most of his life. He didn't leave any family behind, just Abe and Pete."

The melancholic way Caspar spoke, and the sad look in his eye told Walker he feared the same fate for himself. "Not to worry, Caspar. I'll be there when they plant you. I'm booking the dance on your grave."

The old lawman smirked. "Good. I plan to have them bury me in the middle of Big Lake."

They laughed the whole way to the Chevy—all five paces of the trip. To Walker, Caspar's laugh sounded more than a little forced.

Back in the Chevy, with the engine running and the heater churning out a furnace of hot air for Walker's benefit, Caspar made the first of his two radio calls. As the warmth built inside the car and seeped into his bones, Walker tuned out Caspar's deep voice and allowed his mind to drift.

After four years of frenetic learn-work-learn, he'd finally made it to his new home. He and Josie would be so happy here. Already, he could feel the calmness easing over him. The peace. The warmth. The deep sonorous rumble of Caspar's voice as he continued his call.

He reveled in the sense of being home. Of being with people who cared about him. Of being with Josie.

But he couldn't help himself.

Despite his promise to keep his head down and concentrate on building his new life, there he was, sitting alongside Caspar, neck deep in another crime. At least this one didn't involve guns or personal danger. This time, he had the strong arm of the law at his side. In that, he felt comfort, and he knew Josie would feel the same way.

The temperature inside his borrowed coat became uncomfortable. Sweat formed under his armpits and ran down the middle of his back. He undid the zipper, worked the coat from his shoulders, and draped it across his lap.

Better, but still too hot.

He lowered his window a crack, rested his forehead against the cool glass, and stared up at the cloudless evening sky. The sun's dying glow brightened the sky's western edges and backlit the mountains in a golden halo, but the color darkened as it flowed toward the east. It changed from orange to white, moved from celestial to presidential blue, and finally descended into night black. Later, the starscape would prick the blackness and become a magnificent dotted map of the heavens.

With luck, later that evening he and Josie would sit out on the porch, wrapped up warm inside one of Aunt Jean's fluffy quilts. They'd look up and pick out the easy constellations: Cassiopeia, the big, lop-sided W; Orion, with its three-pointed belt; and Ursa Major, the Big Dipper, the important one for the travelling man. They weren't the only constellations he could find, but they were the easiest to spot. Josie knew them all, too: Perseus, Aquarius, Andromeda, and many of the others in the northern sky.

On their first night together in the open, Walker had played dumb, and made her promise to teach them all to him. She'd started with the Big Dipper, and told him how to use the pointers to locate Polaris.

"Find the north star and you'll always know your way home," she'd said. He'd smiled and thanked her.

Not that he needed her to identify Polaris. He wasn't that ignorant, but at the time, he'd been happy to let her take charge. The way she talked about the mountains—with love and deep respect—had captured his heart, and he'd needed to hear her talk. He'd needed the anchor.

Caspar ended his conversation with Manny Micklewhite and dialed in a different radio frequency. "Sergeant Doge, this is Sheriff Boyd. You there Lionel? Over."

The heat was becoming unbearable. The temperature reading on the dashboard showed eighty-seven degrees and climbing. Hot. Too damned hot. Caspar, still looking cool, repeated his summons to Lionel.

The fresh air through the part-open window brought with it the tang of pine trees, which Walker had finally grown, if not to love, then at least to tolerate. It also brought the fresh cool taste of Big Lake with its promise of fish and employment. Walker smelled something else, too, something sweet and sickly.

Walker sniffed again. Cloying, but not rancid, not horrible. It came from inside the car—his shirt sleeve. He raised his arm, sniffed again. What was that?

208

Baby spit. Yuck.

Although the alcohol wipe had cleaned away some of the stain, it had failed to remove the smell entirely. Walker smiled. The baby girl, a mere six weeks old, had taken offence to his cold stethoscope and his prodding. Her well-aimed projectile vomit had found its target with unerring accuracy. The mischievous glint in the tiny child's eyes had said, "Don't mess with me, buddy!" The little mite had given him fair warning. He should have listened.

Walker smiled again at the memory. He still had so much to learn. Medical school had taught him the basics, but only years of practice would make him a real doctor. Only years of practice would dampen his terror of screwing up, of making a mistake. The Mom & Baby clinic had been a two-pronged attack. Tiring and rewarding in equal measures. Babies. They'd been a joy. Messy and loud, but a joy nonetheless.

What would happen when Josie and he became parents? Would he have to deliver their child?

With the clinic that afternoon and Mary Anne Hatfield's emergency birth outside of Fort Wycombe, he'd been inundated with newborns recently. His clothes had taken a battering, as had his nerves.

The shape of things to come.

Still. Onward and upward, Walker.

Boyd ended his radio call with Lionel.

"Ready, Doc?"

"Always, Caspar. Always."

The old lawman slid the truck into gear and aimed the Chevy toward town.

209

Chapter 22

Chatting and Munching

As usual, the diner was bright, warm, and spotless. The aroma of fresh coffee was as welcome as the sight of Josie, who greeted their arrival with hands planted on hips and a forced scowl.

"I expected you two thirty minutes ago. I was just about to empty the coffee machine and head for home. Where were you?"

Caspar elbowed Walker in the ribs and chuckled.

"Son," he said in a stage whisper out the side of his mouth, "you're in trouble now. She's got a tongue on her that could stun a rattler."

Walker held up his hands and stepped closer to the counter. He'd spent most of the day away from her and wouldn't wait a moment longer. They kissed, keeping it short and sweet for the old lawman's benefit, and Walker took his favorite stool at the bar. Caspar took the one next to it.

Josie skipped round to the kitchen side of the counter and filled two large mugs for them and a glass of water for herself.

Walker eased forward, rested his elbows on the stainless-steel surface, and cradled his coffee in both hands, savoring its aroma before taking his first sip. Holding off the pleasure somehow made it taste better. Like their nearly four years of separation. He settled back and watched the ritual of Josie taking care of the sheriff and Caspar pretending not to enjoy it. He'd seen the dance many times before but still enjoyed the performance.

Josie took a small plate from the refrigerator and set it in front of the sheriff, adding a fork and spoon.

"Been saving this for you, Caspar. Apple pie and Chantilly cream. Your favorite."

Caspar held back. "You shouldn't have, Joey. I'm not really all that hungry. Coffee's all I need."

She slid the plate toward Walker.

"In that case, here you go, Chet. It'd be a real shame to waste it."

Caspar shot out a hand, corralled the dessert, and picked up the silverware.

"But as you held it back for me," he said, using the edge of his fork to cut a slice of pie topped with cream, "it'd be rude of me to refuse now, wouldn't it?"

He stuffed the slice into his mouth and made appreciative sounds as he chewed.

"You make the best darned pie in the state, and I've sampled pies from here to Denver."

The remark drew a happy smile from Josie, and Walker took his first sip.

Heck, it's good to be home.

While Caspar ate his dessert, taking longer than usual, but clearly savoring the delights, Walker explained the reason for their delay. When he reached the part where he and Caspar approached the Nissan, her scowl returned, this one genuine.

"Now wait just one minute," she barked, rounding on Caspar, who'd just popped the last piece of pie into his mouth and couldn't defend himself.

"Caspar, what the heck do you think you're up to? Chet's not one of your deputies and shouldn't be anywhere near a police incident."

Walker smiled at his little protector's bridled defense. "Now, Josie. There's no need for—"

She pulled her focus from Caspar and leveled her sights on him. "Don't you 'Now, Josie' me, Chester Walker. I only just got you back, and after what happened with Fulton Hatfield, I ... I ... Darn it, Caspar, I don't want Chet anywhere near danger ever again. You got me?"

Caspar gave her a sheepish nod. "We weren't in any danger, Joey. It was just old Abe and his idiot sidekick. I knew that, and besides, I told Chet to stay in the car. That right, son?"

Walker gave a quick double-take. He'd never seen the old man back down so quickly. It was out of character, but he didn't want to dig a deeper hole by pressing the point.

"That's right, Josie. Caspar ordered me to stay in the car, but curiosity got the better of me. Sorry."

Josie scoffed. "Curiosity? Darn it, Chet, don't give me that bull. You were playing cops 'n' robbers again. Weren't you?"

Oh dear, she knows me so well.

"Not guilty, darling," he said. "Well, not proven."

Caspar set his fork and spoon on the cleaned plate and pushed it away. "Thanks, Joey. That really did hit the spot."

Still frowning, Josie took the plate and bent to load it into the empty dishwasher that stood next to the grill, giving Walker an enticing view of her backside in tight jeans. Caspar studiously avoided looking, keeping his eyes trained on the contents of his coffee cup.

"So, tell me exactly what happened in Fort Wycombe," the sheriff said, twisting to face Walker. "Who exactly is this Fulton Hatfield character, and what did he do to cause offense to my town's doctor?"

Before Walker could answer, Josie topped off their cups, saying if they didn't empty the carafe the coffee would go to waste. As she finished, Walker started in on the explanation. Josie added her own commentary of events in the hospital and her interpretation of Walker's actions. He hoped she'd think of them as heroic, but she went with "foolhardy and stupid." She did, however, mention how happy she'd been to see a settled Mary Anne and her gorgeous new baby. Josie also managed to give Walker begrudging credit for ensuring the girls' safety.

"And then he spoils it all by complaining about the lack of decent security on the psychiatric ward," she added, shaking her head. "Accused one of the nurses of being a drug addict, too. It was so embarrassing, I wanted the floor to swallow me up."

She slid her hand across the counter and held his tight.

"And I don't mean one word of it. Nothing he did would ever embarrass me. I'm so proud of this man, Caspar. And that's why I'm protective of him. Get me?"

Walker grew hot under the collar, and Caspar dipped his head.

"Message received, Miss Joey. Kid gloves from now on. No dangerous police situations. You have my word as the well-respected chief of the LSPD."

He ended the pledge by placing his right hand over his heart. Josie and Walker groaned at the overelaborate action.

Walker let the moment pass before asking a question he'd been dying to pose since his chat with Gerrie Hoover in the boastful Beth's Eatery.

"So, Gerrie—I mean Sheriff Hoover—said she'd met you a couple of times. That right?"

"Yep." Boyd took another sip, but added nothing else.

"Well?" Josie prompted. "Where did you meet? What's your opinion of her? Nice lady?"

Caspar sighed and lowered his empty cup to the counter.

"Don't know much about her personally other than she's better company than most law officers in the state. Local police is a small community. We first met at a conference down in Denver when I was still chief of detectives. She was giving a lecture on sexual harassment in the workplace. Feisty woman with powerful views." He paused a moment before adding, "Reminded me a little of you, my dear."

"The 'better company' or the 'feisty' part?" Josie asked, and the stern frown reappeared.

The sharp lawman held up a hand. "I'm standing by my fifth amendment right not to implicate myself."

"Good answer, Caspar," Walker said through a chuckle. "Okay, so as far as you're concerned, we can trust Gerrie Hoover to do what she says and look after Billy and his sisters?"

"That you can, Doc. Where d'you leave it with her?"

"She said I'll likely be called as a prosecution witness when Fulton Hatfield goes on trial, but that's likely months away. Apart from that, she'll keep me apprised of the situation with the kids. Maybe I'll pay a flying visit to Laramie one weekend to see Billy on his dude ranch and when Mary Anne and the baby are settled. What d'you reckon, Josie? Fancy joining me on a trip north in a few weeks?"

"Just you try stopping me."

"Wouldn't dream of it."

"Good. I'm glad to hear it."

Walker let the conversation drop. He'd have the last word one day, but not this day.

Caspar eased himself from the stool with all the grace of a man carrying a heavy load. "Well, I'll be on my way. Doc, Joey, it's a pure pleasure seeing you back together." He waved to Josie and dropped a hand on Walker's shoulder as he passed.

When the bell rang and the door closed, Walker looked enquiringly at Josie. "How long's he been like that?"

"Like what?"

"Tired. Lackluster."

She scrunched up her beautiful face. "Hadn't noticed. Are you sure it's not just you noticing things 'cause you've been away?"

"Maybe." Walker stood. "But he was talking about hanging up his badge. I'll make an appointment for him to see me in the clinic. Give him a full-service checkup. Wouldn't want Lucky Shores to be without its police chief any time soon."

Josie scooted around to his side of the counter and stared up at him, concern filling her eyes.

"Are you really worried about him, Chet?"

"Not so much." He pulled her into a close hug, and she folded into him. "I'm probably just being the over-cautious new medic. Let's go home. I need dinner and some alone time with the most wonderful woman in the county."

"Aunt Jean's away for the night. Staying with a friend who's just lost her dog."

"I meant you, girl."

She giggled and tilted her head up for a kiss. "I know."

Chapter 23

Josie Donoghue

Josie couldn't have been happier. She was in heaven and had been since Chet returned some nine days earlier.

Chet sat on his favorite stool with his gaze fixed on her. Just one look from him could still cause ripples of electricity to run up and down her spine. He sat cool and easy, fending off the attentions of the departing patrons, having a smile and a kind word for everyone, even those he didn't know. If she had anything to do with it, he'd make Lucky Shores' best ever doctor. Not that he needed her help, but he'd have it anyway. She'd be with him every single step of the way.

There weren't many customers left, just a few diehards reveling in the warmth before heading home to their TV shows. Chet accepted their good wishes and bade each one a hearty goodnight, but the look in his eye told Josie he was praying for the last one to leave so the two of them could walk home together for supper. They'd take the long way around, walking along the shore, holding hands and chatting about nothing and everything: their future together, where they'd live, how they'd rebuild the cabin on Little Lake and turn it into their special quiet haven. Their getaway.

She still hadn't found the strength to let him into her secret. She yearned to tell him, but feared the repercussions. And the longer she delayed, the more difficult it became. As things stood, their life was perfection itself and she hated the idea of changing it with her news. How would he react?

Dang it. Tonight. I'll tell him tonight. I have to.

Since his return, they'd only managed the stroll home four times. The other five nights had been interrupted by the surprise party and four medical emergencies, one of which had been Mrs.

215

Schuler, an octogenarian, who'd stubbed her big toe on the leg of a table.

The three other so-called emergencies had been equally minor and could have waited until the normal clinic times. They had still eaten into his and Josie's quality time, but Chet claimed not to mind too much. Such were the expected trials and tribulations of a small community's solitary doctor.

Behind Chet's back, she'd spoken to Consuela, asking if she could reduce his burden with some sort of triage or whatever. After all, the Cornhusker and the doctors before him hadn't been at everyone's beck and call. Consuela assured her things would calm down once the novelty of having a new full-time doctor in town had faded. The townsfolk would be more reasonable once they'd tested the boundaries and Chet had settled into his role. For the short term, Chet told Josie he was happy to play the game.

Fortunately, the building work at Middle Lake had produced no injuries since Chet's arrival but, judging by the recent records, the current lull probably wouldn't last long. In fact, that morning at breakfast, Aunt Jean, in her official role of mayor, had told them of an extraordinary meeting of the city council. They were set to discuss MLDC's use of the city's infrastructure and its responsibilities in terms of county taxes and the upkeep of the roads. During the same breakfast, Aunt Jean had extended an invitation for Chet to attend the meeting to add his professional gravitas to the proceedings. To cap it all, she made it perfectly clear that, barring an actual medical Armageddon—like an outbreak of pneumonic plague—his attendance was obligatory. After all, she argued, an increase in corporate taxes would eventually make it possible for the city to hire an assistant to lighten Chet's workload.

No doubt about it, Aunt Jean knew how to work a crowd, even if the crowd consisted, in its entirety, of her future nephew-in-law—assuming there was to be such a relation—and Josie herself.

Small town politics, Josie wanted no part of, no matter how many hints Aunt Jean gave her when she talked about "taking things easier" and "moving aside and allowing new blood to take over." Josie had other issues on her plate. Personal issues.

By the time the final customer left and the setting sun had kissed the western mountaintops, Chet had finished his second coffee and was definitely itching to leave.

"How long will you be, honey?" he asked.

Josie lifted the metal spatula she was using to scrape clean the grill and smiled into the green eyes that could turn her heart into putty.

"Fifteen minutes if those two chatterboxes"—she waved the spatula at Allie and Peg—"get on with their work."

The chatterboxes in question broke apart and carried on clearing the tables. Josie stepped closer to the counter and stood on tiptoes. He stretched forward and they kissed. Their first kiss since breakfast. It was lovely. His scratchy stubble would soon soften into a nice full beard, his hair would grow and flow and wave, and he'd be back to the man she'd met. The handsomest, most wonderful man she'd ever seen. Tall, strong, powerful, honest. What wasn't to love about him?

"No need to stay," she said, snicking a smudge of her lipstick from his lower lip with her thumb. "Why not go home and put your feet up. I can walk back alone. Been doing it without you most of my life."

"Uh-uh, not a chance, honey. I've been looking forward to strolling along the shorefront with my girl all day."

His dark smile made her heart flip.

"Aw, you can be so sweet."

"I know. Renowned for it, I am. Besides, I'm happy here watching you work your firm little butt off. Yummy." He whispered the last part.

She slapped his forearm gently and returned to her cleaning.

"Need any help, ladies?" Chet called to Allie and Peg. "I've been told I'm pretty handy with a mop and bucket."

Peg dipped her shoulders, suggestively flashing her girls at Josie's man. She just couldn't help herself, the tall devil in a short dress. No mind, Chet was immune.

217

"Well, Doc," Peg said, her voice an octave lower and more sultry than usual, "that's the best offer I've had today, but—"

"But," Allie interrupted, "we're paid to do this and you need all your strength for …"

"Doctoring," they said in unison and burst into cackles of laughter.

"Girls!" Josie scolded. "Leave my fiancé alone. Can't you see how embarrassed he is?"

Chet threw a hand up to cover his eyes for a moment. "I sure am. Never more embarrassed than when I'm being hounded by a coven of—"

His cell phone buzzed, interrupting his thread. He grabbed it from the counter and stared at her, eyes apologetic, the edges of his mouth turned down.

"Doctor Walker here."

Darn it, there goes another quiet walk. Another opportunity to tell him.

Would the right time never come?

Chet ended the call. "Sorry, Josie. Medical emergency up at Steiniger's Crescent."

"Another stubbed toe? Someone got a toothache? A hangnail?" She tried not to sound angry or to pout, but it was really difficult.

"No, that was Caspar. He needs me ASAP. Wouldn't give me the details, but it sounded serious."

Chet edged around the end of the counter and entered her kitchen space, the only customer she allowed back there. He picked her up in a gentle bear hug, let her feet dangle, and kissed her, hard enough to curl her toes.

He moved his lips to her ear. "Be back as soon as I can, love. Promise. Keep it warm for me."

After patting her backside, he lowered her gently to the floor, said goodbye to Allie and Peg, and hurried out the door. As usual, he'd parked his Ford in the newly designated and painted "Doctor's Parking Space" outside the diner's front door. He didn't take long to jump in, fire it up, and roll away.

218

No sooner was he out of sight than the two old gossips rushed up to the counter and started singing his praises.

"Lord, he's so sweet, I'd like to eat him up," Peg said, mashing the broom handle into her massive cleavage. The top five inches of the handle disappeared into the folds.

Allie chuckled and took hold of Josie's left hand, staring at the engagement ring. "You've got to be the luckiest girl in the county."

"The state," Peg added.

"The world," Josie contradicted. "Now can we please finish the cleaning so I can close up and we can all get home?"

Giggles erupted from the two and they busied themselves with the business at hand.

Less than a minute after Chet disappeared, the bell over the door dinged. It opened and brought with it a gust of ice cold air. A man, average height, wiry, clean shaven, with dirty clothes and shining eyes, stood in the doorway. He removed his battered black hat, held it by the brim with both hands, and let the door close softly behind him.

"Begging your pardon, ladies," he said in a deep voice of quiet authority, "but am I too late for coffee and victuals?"

Josie examined the man. Judging from his clothes, he'd been on the road for a while, but that was nothing out of the ordinary these days. Since they'd started building the resort, more strangers than ever had drifted into town in the hopes of casual laboring work. These were day rate workers, who often arrived in town with hope but left in disappointment.

"Coffee, we can handle,' she said, "but hot food's out. We're closed for the day."

The stranger's eyes fell to his dirty hat, and the brim crushed under his tightening grip. "Alas, though I prayed to the Lord, I hastened and did not delay, my tardiness has become my undoing."

Josie caught Peg and Allie as they rolled their eyes in unison. The diner had received its fair share of preachers over the years. Old time sermonizing didn't tend to sit well in the high mountains, where the harshness of the weather and unforgiving terrain produced a more tolerant piety in the worshipers.

As usual, Josie took pity on the newcomer. "Although we're closed for hot food, we can rustle you up a sandwich. How does cheese, ham, and salad sound?"

"Like a warming miracle on an ice cold day, child."

The man's smile revealed discolored and uneven teeth. Without expensive dental work, he would certainly struggle to make a living as a TV evangelist. That *would* take a miracle.

She pointed to a table by the window and near the door. "Take a seat over there, and we'll be right with you."

"Thank you most kindly, my dear." He raised the hat in salute and slid into the chair with more fluidity than Josie expected.

"Peg, Allie, carry on with your work. I'll fill the order."

Allie leaned close and whispered, "Take care with the Bible-basher. Seems to me he's wound up a little tight."

Peg nodded and adopted a similar pose as her friend. "You think he's got any money in those rags?"

"It doesn't matter," Josie whispered back. "We can spare a few scraps for a hungry man. Maybe it'll earn us all a prayer. I'll need all the help I can get with what's coming … Well, let's not go there."

Peg rested a hand on Josie's forearm. "You and your soft heart. It's a wonder you've stayed in business all these years."

"Oh stop that."

Josie waved them away and got to work fixing the preacher's supper. She added a side order of cherry pie and cream—left more than enough for Caspar—and served it with a large cup of coffee.

"Enjoy."

"I will, my child. The Lord's bounty is a joy to behold. Each time I partake of his offerings, my soul it does fill with the spirit and the light of Heaven."

Preacher closed his eyes and prayed in silence before lifting the cup to his chapped lips and slurping the coffee. After swallowing, he sighed. "This here is a drink straight from the challis of the Lord God Himself."

Josie smiled behind her hand. If believing in a god helped Preacher get through his day, who was she to complain? As long as the man did his sermonizing outside the diner, it was okay by her. She returned to the kitchen, her domain, and cleared her small mess.

Josie watched the man in black through the mirror above the sink. Preacher took a huge bite out of his sandwich and chewed.

"This," he said to himself, eyes closed, sunken cheeks bulging with the packed food, "is pure Manna straight from the golden shores of Paradise."

Allie, who had made her way to the table next to Preacher, said, "Amen to that," to the man's obvious delight. She cleared away the cutlery and flatware, sprayed and wiped the surface, stacked the chairs on top, and moved on to the next table in line. Having finished cleaning the kitchen, Josie ducked into the storeroom and completed her stock count.

By the time she'd emailed her order to her suppliers and returned to the dining area, the place was empty save for the girls and Preacher.

He'd scraped his plate clean and sat, cup to his lips, staring through the window, taking in the view. If the man's god did exist, his work was on full display for the world to see right outside the diner's window.

Josie smiled sadly. She'd lost her faith when Mom died and the townsfolk ran Daddy out of town. Even when Chet arrived and things started looking up, she hadn't felt the need to return to a church that had turned its back on her and hers. Where was their Christian charity when she needed it? If not for Aunt Jean, she'd have been packed off to a children's home in Douglas Ferry at aged fifteen.

The old preacher finally lowered his cup and turned to face her. "Is there a hospital in this town?"

"We have a medical center. Are you unwell? Do you need an ambulance?" Josie asked.

"No, child. It's nothing urgent," he said, smiling and exposing his yellowed teeth once again. "I am in need of a repeat prescription. My meds are coming to an end."

Josie pointed toward the turning where West Boulevard became East Lane. "Take a right turn onto Main Street and keep walking uphill for a couple of miles. Keep tight to the rocky side to avoid the traffic."

"Thank you kindly, my child."

He stood and the feet of his chair scraped on the floor tiles. Josie winced at the noise and steeled herself against the expected begging bowl.

"How much do I owe you for those excellent victuals, my child?"

Josie couldn't quite manage to keep the look of surprise from her face, but before she could let the pitiful soul off the charge, Peg called from beside the till. "Eight dollars will cover it."

Preacher smiled benignly and started patting his pockets as though searching for his billfold.

Josie sighed. She'd been waiting for the excuse and he wasn't about to disappoint her.

"Oh my word," he said, still patting his pockets, "I'm afraid I have nothing smaller than a fifty. Are you able to make the change?"

"Sure, no problem," Peg answered quickly, with an arched eyebrow and a wry curl to her upper lip.

"You can?"

The relief on his face couldn't have been more forced. The guy couldn't act his way into a pulpit to save his, or anyone else's, soul.

"Yes. We can indeed."

Allie had finished bussing all the tables and joined Peg behind the counter.

Preacher patted his pockets some more.

"Um, I am most dreadfully sorry," he said, mortification itself. "It seems I have … left home without the wherewithal to—"

"That's okay," Josie said, waving a hand in a dismissive motion. "Bring it with you next time."

A big smile broke across the man's pale and wizened face. "Bless you, my child. Your trust and charity will bring joy to the Lord and riches to you in another realm. I shall return tomorrow with your payment when my finances are fully restored. On that you can surely rely."

Yeah, sure I can.

"Tomorrow's good, sir."

Side-stepping the preacher man, Josie walked to the door and held it open for him, braving the bitter early-evening wind that gathered moisture and lost heat as it ripped over the surface of Big Lake.

"Have a Blessed evening, my child."

Josie maintained her forced smile. The "my child" nonsense could grow old very quickly.

He pushed his hat firmly down on his head and tipped it to each of them in turn. Leaving Josie until last, he added a deep bow to her before passing through the door and wandering along West Boulevard, heading toward Main Street.

Josie pushed the door closed and turned to face her staff.

As usual, Peg was the first to react.

"Joey Donoghue," she said, frowning and adding a disappointed head shake, "Little Bobby and me rely on this job to pay our rent and buy our groceries. How are we going to survive if you run your business into the ground by giving away so much free food?"

Allie crossed her arms and nodded her considered agreement. "You know it's Sunday tomorrow and we're closed? He ain't coming back."

Josie joined them by the counter. "He's nothing but a harmless old preacher. I couldn't turn him away hungry."

"Harmless?" Peg scoffed. "Did you see the way he was looking at my girls?"

She pushed out her enormous breasts, which strained to free themselves from a bra two cup sizes smaller than required and

223

stretched her polo shirt to near breaking point. Her cleavage, admired by all the heterosexual men in the county, was guaranteed to fill the tip jar twice as fast as when she was on vacation.

"Land sakes, Peg," Allie said, "the poor man could hardly avoid noticing them darned things, the way you flash them all the time. You don't even know you're doing it half the time."

"Doing what?"

Allie flicked her painted fingernails at the offending articles. "There. That's what I mean. You could put someone's eye out with those puppies."

"What? These little old things?"

Peg waggled her shoulders, her "girls" jiggled, and the women giggled.

No longer embarrassed by her inability to fill a hammock-sized bra, Josie allowed Peg and Allie to continue their friendly bickering. Chet seemed to enjoy her own average-sized "girls" well enough. What else mattered?

Nothing, that's what.

Peg stopped moving her shoulders, but it took a while for her assets to settle down.

"Seriously though," she said. "That man creeped me out. I don't mind people catching an eyeful. 'Course I don't. But him? Ew!" She shuddered. "I mean, spouting all that God-speak, you'd think his mind would be on higher things."

"Honey," Allie said, "he's a man. There ain't nothing else on their tiny little minds."

"Hey," Josie said, "not all men."

Peg pouted. "No, of course not. Your Chet only has eyes for you."

"I hope so," Josie said, half to herself. "I really hope so."

Chapter 24

A New Crime Scene

With medical bag in hand and dressed nice and warmly for the conditions, Walker climbed out of his Ford and pushed through a small but mumbling crowd of onlookers. The police cars' red and blue lights rolled around the houses, bathing the circle of homes in an intermittent and surreal glow.

The tubby and white-faced Deputy Jordan stood in charge of the yellow police tape they'd tied between two spindly aspens. The youngster smiled nervously.

"Hi, Doctor Walker."

"Evening, Deputy. Caspar … Sheriff Boyd called me. Didn't tell me why, but guessing from all the activity, it's serious?"

Deputy Jordan dipped his head. "I haven't been inside yet, but from what I hear, you won't be needing your medical bag."

He lifted the tape and Walker strode up a familiar-looking path—the new houses in town were all from the same school of architecture. Variable in size, but stamped out using the same cookie-cutter template and not particularly inspiring. He followed the path around the side of the house to a well-lit rear entrance.

Another deputy, whose name Walker hadn't caught, tipped his hat and pushed open the back door. Walker nodded his thanks and entered a house with an internal temperature cold enough to store frozen meat. Despite every one of his thermal layers, Walker shivered, but it had precious little to do with the cold.

Having seen plenty of TV crime scenes, Walker set his medical bag on the floor and tugged on a pair of surgical gloves. A box on the floor by the door contained disposable, one-size-fits-all overshoes, and he pulled a pair of them on, balancing on one foot at a time.

"Caspar?" he called.

"Up here, Doc. Work your way through the kitchen and up the stairs, but hug the walls. We don't want you contaminating any evidence. You got your gloves and overshoes on?"

"Sure have."

Walker followed Caspar's muffled instructions and hurried past a laundry room and through into an open plan kitchen-dining area. A full-specification kitchen complete with granite-topped surfaces and real wood cabinets filled the left side. The dining area spread out to the center and the right. White walls, plenty of glass—probably triple glazed and thermally efficient—including sliding double-doors that looked out over a multi-terraced back yard and the western mountains.

The landing at the top of the stairs showed him five doors, all slightly open. Bright light shone through the gap around one of the doorways. He knocked and entered a frigid bedroom. Despite the outside chill, the double windows stood wide open. The unmistakable stench of death hit him first, and he took a moment to adjust his thinking.

Caspar stood over a king-sized bed, his breath hanging in a cloud of condensation around his head. Hands stuffed into his jacket pockets, he studied the fully clothed corpse. Someone, maybe the sheriff himself, had pulled back the covers to expose the body. A dark stain on the pillow and the dead man's misshapen head showed the obvious cause of death—blunt force trauma to the cranium. Multiple blows. Mercifully, death would have been more or less instantaneous.

Slowly, Caspar turned to face Walker.

"Hi, Chet. Sorry to call you out this late, but I need the pronouncement. Emergency helicopter's on its way from the Douglas Ferry Coroner's Office, but it won't be here for another hour, and I can't let them move the body without an ME's say so. And that just happens to be you."

"I'm the town's Medical Examiner, too?" Walker asked, working his fingers to keep the blood circulating.

"Didn't you know?"

Walker raised an eyebrow and added a sigh for emphasis.

"Keep learning all the time. Although we were given a cursory introduction to autopsy procedures at med school, looks like I'll have to find time for extra study. YouTube might have a course or two."

Caspar guffawed and Walker took a step closer and read the time from his watch for the death certificate. 7:52, p.m.

"Poor fellow's dead, sure enough."

Walker jotted the time in his recently acquired notebook and leaned forward to press an index finger to the wrist of the corpse.

"You ain't likely to find a pulse, Doc," Caspar said, sounding incredulous.

Walker sighed again. "Testing for rigor, which has completely passed. The man's been dead at least thirty-six hours, maybe as long as sixty, but that's as close as I can estimate. With the open window, and the temperature in here, there's no point taking the liver temperature. There won't be one."

"Two to three days." Boyd nodded. "That's what I figured. Blood pooling"—he waved a finger at dark patches caused by lividity—"suggests he was killed close by and dumped in the bed soon afterward."

"Any idea who he is?"

"Wallet was still in his pocket. No money left in it, but according to his driver's permit, his name is"—Caspar pulled his notepad from his breast pocket and flipped to the most recent page—"Miguel Garcia. Business card has him as Vice President of Architecture for the MLDC. Normally lives in Phoenix. The wallet holds a picture of a woman and three young kids. I'm guessing it's Mr. Garcia's family. Goddammit. At least I won't be making the notification. The Phoenix PD will have that particular pleasure. Hate that part of the job. Always have."

"What happened?" Walker asked.

"Huh?" Boyd frowned at him.

"I mean, who raised the alarm? How'd you find the body?"

"Oh, right. Abe Dunleavy and Pete noticed the open windows during their 'rounds.'" Boyd shook his head when using the word "rounds," making it clear what he thought of Abe and Pete still playing at security guards. "This time, they called it in rather than enter the house themselves. Seems that even someone as dumb as old Abe can learn."

"I'm as surprised as you are, Caspar," Walker said, through another long sigh.

"Might have something to do with the verbal ass kicking I gave Steiniger and his minions the last time his hired hands screwed up a crime scene."

Despite the grim contents of the room, Walker smiled at the memory of Boyd regaling him and Josie with the story of his meeting with the head of the Consortium when he'd been forced to collect the master key in person. When primed with a free slice of cherry pie and a mug of coffee, the old man could tell a decent tale. He had them both in stitches.

"Any obvious suspects?"

Boyd shook his head. "Not a one, but we ain't hardly started the investigation yet."

Light footsteps padded up the stairs, made the landing, and approached the bedroom. Lionel poked his head around the part-open door. His face, although devoid of color, showed excitement.

"Hi, Doc. Sorry to call you out so late, but ..." He shot a pained glance at the bed before looking at his boss. "Sheriff, you'll want to come take a look at this. You too, Doc. If you please. I can't make head nor tail of it."

Walker followed the lawmen downstairs and into the living room. It faced the southeast and windows the whole width of one wall framed a spectacular view of the lake and the mountains. Sparsely furnished, the room boasted polished hardwood floors, a love seat and sofa, a huge widescreen TV, two small coffee tables, and fitted bookshelves, all empty.

"What d'you make of this?" Lionel asked, pointing to the far corner, where a mess of blankets had been spread out on the floor in the shape of a bed. It ran diagonally out from the corner, with the feet end pointing into the center of the room, slightly away from the feature windows.

"Interesting," Caspar said. "Probably explains the open windows upstairs. Killer wanted to air the room and disperse the smell of decomp."

Lionel slowly nodded his agreement. "That's what I thought. Seems like the killer made himself comfortable. Doesn't look like he feels the cold too much since there's no heating on. He'd have been pretty cold without a fire, but he'd at least be out of the weather."

"Anything in the stuff to identify the owner of this crud?" Walker asked.

"Nothing much, 'cept this." Lionel pointed to a dark rectangle on the nearest coffee table.

"What you got there?" Caspar asked.

"A notebook." Lionel knelt on the floor, opened his forensics case, and removed an evidence bag large enough to hold the item. "I've flicked through the pages, but can't make anything out. Nothing but scribbled nonsense and crude sketches."

Caspar held out his gloved hand and Lionel passed him the notebook and the empty bag. The sheriff tucked the Maglite into the crook between his neck and shoulder, and flicked through the pages. "Words and numbers scribbled on most of the pages. And all these drawings. Crosses, grave markers, and ... what are these things? Five pointed stars?"

"Pentagrams?" Walker offered, craning to see over Caspar's shoulder.

"Yeah, that's right. Pentagrams. Weird," Caspar mumbled, half to himself.

"Why would he leave it here?"

"Who knows. Abe and Pete might have disturbed him."

Boyd angled the pages to shine the flashlight at an oblique angle to one sheet and held it at arm's length, squinting to bring the scribbling into focus. After a couple of seconds he shook his head. "Damn it. Can't make out many of the words. You try. You've got better eyes than me."

229

He handed the notepad to Walker, who tried the same treatment with his penlight, but held the paper closer. "*Deut: 18:13/15. Matt: 13:42. Ps: 106:48.*' Bible verses? 'Deut' could be Deuteronomy, and 'Ps' could be Psalms, right?"

Caspar curled his upper lip. "Suppose so. Been a while since I attended a Bible study group. Any idea what those verses are?"

"Heck, Sheriff. You're asking the wrong man. What I know about the Bible wouldn't fill the back of a postage stamp. Hang on. I'll try an online search." Walker reached for his cell phone. No bars. "No signal up here?"

Lionel shook his head. "Sorry, Doc. There's a dead spot in this part of town on account of the hills and the fact this block is still under construction. Phone and internet facilities are just about the last things installed. We'll have to drive back to the sheriff's office for the nearest internet service."

Walker selected the camera app on his cell and turned to Boyd. "Mind if I take a picture, Sheriff?"

The old man shrugged. "Sure, why not. Knock yourself out."

Walker took a couple of shots of the more lucid pages.

"You have any preachers in town?" Walker asked, checking the pictures for quality and finding them acceptable.

"A few. Father O'Driscoll and Pastor Robbins. There's a rabbi, but I doubt he'll have a Bible to hand." Caspar checked his watch. "Ten after six. I'll run a search when I get back to the office and maybe call Father O'Driscoll for an interpretation, if we need one."

Walker turned another page and found more hieroglyphics and scribbled designs, and the occasional, barely legible word and phrase. *Lord. Almighty. Doom. Purgatory. Hell and Damnation.* The writer had used a blunt pencil and pressed hard enough for some of the lines to tear through to the page beneath. Walker saw rage and a limited education in the ill-formed lettering.

Hell and Damnation.

He'd heard the words recently—in a broken-down pig farm— but Miguel Garcia's murder couldn't have anything to do with Fulton Hatfield. That particular religious zealot was safely tucked away in a padded cell in Laramie. This particular killer had to be a different disturbed individual. One who now roamed the outskirts of his beautiful and peaceful new home.

While Lionel did his forensics thing with camera, fingerprint dust, and measuring tape, Walker turned his attention to the bedding, more a crumpled nest than a proper bed. The head end, indicated by the throw cushion used as a pillow, was tucked tight into the corner, with the feet end sticking out into the room, rather than running along one of the walls.

Interesting.

In the morning, the killer would have been able to sit up, lean back against the wall, and take in the panorama through the floor-to-ceiling windows. The view included pretty near the whole of the town, Big Lake, and the western mountains.

But why didn't the killer put any distance between himself and his victim? Why stay in a house with a rotting corpse upstairs? And why stay in a room overlooking the front garden and not hide away at the back of the house, where he'd run a lower risk of being seen by a passing construction worker?

Walker shook his head. Was there any point in trying to double-guess the mindset of a person he'd never met? He pulled back the top cover of the makeshift bed. The blankets underneath were soiled with dirt and bodily fluids. He didn't want to hazard a guess as to the constituents of the fluids.

"You've searched the rest of the house?"

Caspar nodded. "Nothing unusual upstairs but the body. The other bedrooms and the master bathroom are untouched, but we found something interesting in the downstairs toilet."

"Yeah?"

"Hair in the sink. And lots of it. Looks like our guy took to barbering. Tried to tidy himself up."

"How'd he do that without running water?"

"Used bottled water, but not enough. He blocked the plughole. Made a real mess of the place."

"Hair color?"

231

"Black with heavy streaks of gray. A wild guess, puts him in his forties or fifties."

Walker sniffed. "Not necessarily. I started going gray in my early twenties, but you're probably in the right ballpark, for the average."

"Okay," Lionel said, staring at the bedding, frowning in concentration, "so we've got a partial description. Middle-aged scruffy man with salt and pepper hair and a pale face."

"A pale face from shaving?"

"Yep. His beard was long. Had to use scissors before he could attack it with a razor. Means he's been wearing it a while. He'll likely look like a ghost until the sun gets to work on him. Judging by spots of blood in the wash basin, he's probably sporting some fresh shaving cuts, too."

"You can add that he's poorly educated."

"You can tell that by the penmanship?" Lionel asked.

Walker nodded.

"Find anything else in there?" Caspar asked, indicating the notebook with a dip of his head.

"Nothing of value, but I'm a simple medic, not a detective. What exactly am I looking for?"

"Clues, Doc. Clues. And don't give me that innocent medic routine. You're sharper than most detectives I've worked with— Lionel excluded." He nodded to his deputy, who, down on one knee taking pictures of the makeshift bed, didn't seem to notice the compliment.

"If you hadn't already taken up doctoring," Caspar continued, "I'd have invited you to join the LSPD. Maybe tried to groom you into taking over from me when the time came for me to hang up my star. The townsfolk love you. You'd have walked the election. Pardon the pun." He ended with a barked laugh.

"You and I both know that's pure bull, Sheriff, but thanks for the commendation."

"You're welcome." Boyd arched his back and groaned. "Strange thing, though ..." His voice trailed off as though he was talking to himself.

"What's that, Sheriff?" Lionel asked.

"Why'd the killer stay in a house with the corpse? Don't make much sense to me. There's plenty of other empty houses on this plot he could have broken into."

Still kneeling close to the bedding, Lionel shook his head. "Funny enough, that's exactly what I was thinking, Sheriff. But judging from those scribblings and the dead man's injuries, I reckon we're looking for a man not in full control of all his faculties. A total nut job. Right, Doc?"

Walker shook his head and handed the notebook over. "Not necessarily. The murderer might struggle with his letters, but I can't tell any more than that. If you'd seen my song and lyric notes when I was on the road, you'd have questioned the state of my mind, too."

"If you remember, I did, Doc."

Wearing a crooked smile, Caspar pushed the notebook into a plastic evidence bag, signed it across the seal, and placed it on top of Lionel's evidence case.

"I haven't forgotten anything about that night, Sheriff Boyd. You were a total ass-hat." Walker kept a straight face, only half-joking this time.

Caspar turned on his heel. "Yeah, well, I already explained and apologized for what I did. Water under the bridge."

"Yep, sure is."

Walker turned his back on the elderly lawman and took in the bedding and its relationship to the rest of the room. The layout of the room still rankled. What was it? The seed of an idea tickled his mind but he couldn't make the it germinate. Probably too close to the problem.

"What's next, Sheriff?" Walker asked.

"In the absence of an internet connection or a landline here, I'm going to leave Lionel in charge and head back to the office. I need to notify the state police and raise a BOLO. It's about all we can do tonight. I'll have the deputies guard the scene and increase the patrols, but don't plan to send out search parties until daylight. Scrambling around in the dark's too dangerous. Now, I reckon you can head back to the diner. Little Joey's probably pining for you about now."

"Oh no, not a chance," Walker said, shaking his head vehemently. "I'm coming with you. I want to check out these Bible verses and the sheriff's office is closer. I'll call Josie from there."

"What's wrong, Doc?" Caspar asked. "Afraid she's gonna chew you a new one for keeping her waiting yet again?"

Walker grinned. The Ghost of Lucky Shores knew Josie almost as well as he did. "She won't mind if I tell her I'm helping the LSPD. But any more of those snide remarks and I'll let her know you called her 'Little Joey.'"

Caspar winced and held up his hands before marching to the back door. He stood to one side, letting Walker through first.

Chapter 25

The Wrath of God

Walker took his time driving the Old Lumber Road, allowing Boyd's Chevy to disappear into the distance. After the straight urban roads in Baltimore, it would take him a while to get used to driving the mountain switchbacks in the dark. The last thing he wanted was to crash and burn in a road accident so soon after arriving in town. If nothing else, Josie would kill him.

Walker smiled at the thought, hung a right onto the spur road leading to the sheriff's office and home, and parked alongside Caspar's Chevy.

He bounded up the concrete steps and entered the bright and steaming hot office, blinking under the harsh fluorescent lights. Deputy Maxine Burrows, in what must have been one of her last duties before leaving town, was covering the dispatcher's console. She smiled at his approach.

"Evening, Doc."

She wore a loose-fitting uniform shirt which blatantly failed to hide the bump of a woman deep into her third trimester. The bump was so large, she had to sit sideways to the desk in order to reach the radio setup.

"Hi there, Maxine. How's it going?"

She winced and rubbed the left side of her belly. "Baby's impatient to see her sister. Keeps kicking and struggling to get out."

"She'll have to wait a few weeks yet, I'm afraid. Will I see you at the clinic before you go? I'd like to check all's well with you both."

A sadness fed into her eyes. She took a tissue from a box on her desk and blew her nose. "I made an appointment for next week, Dr. Walker. Wanted to say goodbye ... before we left. Gonna miss this old town, but ... you know."

"Shame you have to leave. What if I organized a crèche or a preschool? Would it convince you to stay?"

"Sorry, Doc. My mind's made up. Memories, you understand?"

He nodded and looked up, unable to take the sadness in her demeanor. Behind her on the wall, a large-scale map of the region sported different colored pins: yellow, green, and red. A single large black pin was stuck in an area of green, indicating a forest.

"What are they?" he asked, pointing to the map.

Maxine swiveled her chair to face the wall. "What?"

"The pins."

"Oh. They show different crime scenes. The colors indicate the state of the investigation. Red for active, yellow for pending trial, and green for closed."

"And the black one in the middle of the forest?"

"That's tonight's murder scene. All the recent construction's made the map obsolete. The city plans to hire a cartography service, but they're holding off until the major building work's done."

Walker studied the map again, trying to reconcile the two dimensional map with the topography of the area he'd just driven. At the crime scene in the dark, he'd had no idea how far around the eastern side of the lake they'd been. With his eyes, he followed an imaginary line from the black pin, heading west until he reached the center of town, and ...

Oh hell, no!

An impending sense of doom pulled the walls close around his head.

"Maxine," he shouted, unable to control his raging emotions, "can you get hold of Sheriff Hoover from Fort Wycombe? You have her number, right?"

"Why?"

"Don't ask, just do it. Please."

236

The urgency in his voice must have worked its way through her natural reluctance to take instructions from a civilian. Maxine turned to face her PC and started tapping on her keyboard. An official-looking directory search screen grew on her monitor. Maxine took note of the numbers and picked up her desk phone.

The door to Caspar's inner sanctum opened and the man himself appeared in the doorway.

"Took you long enough, Doc. Night driving's not your—"

"The killer," Walker said, rushing to close the gap between them, "I've got a horrible feeling I know who he is."

Maxine stopped talking and replaced the phone.

"Get hold of her?" Walker demanded.

Maxine shook her head. "She's out of the office on a call. I talked to one of her deputies. They're trying to patch her through now. What's going on?"

She addressed the question to Caspar, but the old lawman shrugged. "Hell if I know."

Walker started pacing. What should he do? He couldn't launch a full scale search on the strength of a hunch. People might get hurt stumbling around in the dark. He needed confirmation before risking lives.

"Care to tell us what's on your mind, Doc?" Caspar asked, a calm voice in the center of Walker's storm.

He stopped pacing. "That stuff back at the house. I think it belonged to Fulton Hatfield."

"The fruitcake from Fort Wycombe?"

"Yeah, that's right."

"Last we heard, Hatfield was bouncing around in a rubber room, safe and secure, right?"

Walker tried to calm his rapid breathing enough to gather his thoughts and speak clearly. "It wasn't that secure. Took me less than five minutes to identify the flaws in Dr. Lannister's so-called High Security Ward, and Fulton Hatfield's had more than a week. He might be a raving nutcase, but he's also cunning and dangerous."

The phone on Maxine's desk clattered into life. Walker jumped and reached for the handset, but Maxine beat him to it.

"Lucky Shores Police Department." Maxine listened for a moment before nodding to Walker. "Hi, Sheriff Hoover, thanks for calling back. I have Dr. Walker with me. He'd like a word."

She offered the phone across and Walker snatched it from her hand. "Gerrie?"

"Doc," she replied, and with the single syllable, Walker knew his instincts had been correct. "I was going to call you tomorr—"

"Fulton Hatfield escaped didn't he?"

"How in the hell—"

"I think he's here in Lucky Shores."

"No, no, he can't be. Hatfield died three days ago. That's why I held off calling you. I've been busy writing reports and handling the media. It's a damned circus around here. TV cameras, press, the works."

"He's dead?"

"Yep."

Thank God.

"Are you certain?"

"Yep." She sounded tired and a little breathless.

Relief hit and the tension exploded from Walker's body as though someone had stabbed a football with a hunting knife. He slumped on the edge of the nearest desk and sucked in a huge breath. "What happened?"

"Long story, Doc," Gerrie continued. "Been a hell of a week."

"You don't say. Tell me about it, but hold off a minute. I'm here with Sheriff Boyd. Mind if I transfer you to his office number and put you on speaker?"

Before she could refuse, he hit the "mute" button and turned to the sheriff. "That okay with you, Caspar?"

The older man shrugged. "*Mi casa es su casa.*"

Walker took his cell and found the photos he'd taken of the notebook pages. He passed the cell to Maxine. "Can you find these Bible references for me?"

The pregnant deputy shot a questioning look at Caspar, who nodded through a frown. "Do as the Doc says. No doubt he'll tell us what's on his mind, *when he's good and ready.*"

Walker snapped to his feet. "Will do, Caspar, but let's hear what Gerrie has to tell us first. Can we go to your office?"

The sheriff let out a brief sigh. "Can't see why not. Maxine, transfer the call like the *boss* here told you."

Chapter 26

Umiak Falls

Caspar's inner sanctum gave its usual winter impression of the inside of a blast furnace. Walker removed his jacket and found it bearable—just. A log fire roared in the fireplace, throwing out heat and flickering orange light. He stood aside and Caspar led the way deeper into the room.

The PC on Caspar's desk emitted an old-school telephone double ring, and the monitor flickered into life. A gray and white funnel of light bathed the sheriff's chair and illuminated the poster-bedecked wall behind it.

Maxine called from the office. "I've hooked the call up to the video link on Sheriff Hoover's satellite phone."

"The wonders of modern technology," Caspar mumbled as he dropped into his squeaky swivel chair and waved Walker into the chair on the other side of his desk. Caspar turned the monitor so he and Walker could both see the screen, and he hit a button on the keyboard.

"Sheriff Hoover?"

"Hey, Sheriff Boyd. Call me Gerrie." She smiled, breathing every couple of words. "Hey, Doc. Good to see you. How you doing?"

The picture shook and lines of interference crackled. She talked on the move, looking down at her cell phone. In the jerky, fast-moving background behind her head, clouds filled a dark gray sky. Her eyes kept flicking up to check her route and her heavy breathing suggested she was climbing a steep hill. She'd aged in the days since Walker had left Fort Wycombe. Dark worry lines showed beneath dull eyes, and her mouth drooped. Her optimistic smile had gone. Tension built at the base of Walker's neck and across his shoulders. He tried to fight it off.

"Hi again, Gerrie. What happened with Hatfield?"

"Straight down to business, hey Doc? No howdy dos?"

"Gerrie, please."

She paused to catch her breath. The picture stopped shaking so much. Tree branches and leaves swirling in a gusting wind framed Gerrie's head. The woodland crowded in around her, but something in her eyes, the way she avoided looking at the screen sent out shafts of warning.

"What's wrong, Gerrie? There's something you're not telling me."

Her head dropped and she stared at the phone's camera. "It's bad, Doc. Billy's dead."

"What!"

"Billy's dead. Hatfield killed him four hours after he escaped the psych ward."

"How?"

"Someone must have told him where we'd put Billy."

"Chambers!"

"Who?" Caspar asked.

"The psychiatric nurse with the 'roid rage issues! The evil, slimy asshole."

Gerrie nodded. "Sheriff Dubois, chief of the Laramie PD, is questioning him now, but the man ain't saying squat."

"How did Billy die?"

Gerrie took another breath. "We have the murder on CCTV. Hatfield walked right up to him, at the dude ranch, shouted something, and then stabbed him in the neck with a pair of garden shears. Billy just stood there, terrified. Didn't even raise a hand to protect himself."

Walker closed his eyes for a second. The poor damaged kid. After a hellish start in life, he'd done the right thing by his sister and had made it through only to die at his father's hand. What sort of a world could allow that to happen?

Fear clenched Walker's stomach.

"What about Mary Anne?"

241

Gerrie's lips stretched into a thin smile. "It's okay. They're safe. The Laramie police found the car Hatfield stole from the hospital parking lot before he could get to her. He crashed a road block and the police gave chase."

"Is that how he died? A car crash?"

"No, he evaded the pursuit and made it all the way to Fort Wycombe. Me and Horace ran him to ground in the city park."

"What happened? Suicide by cop?"

"Nope, just plain old suicide. The mad SOB took a swan dive into Umiak Falls."

The muscle tension returned, this time stronger, threatening to overwhelm Walker. "Did you find the body?"

Please say you did!

"Not yet. That's one of the reasons I didn't call you earlier. I wanted to have everything wrapped up neat and tidy for you. You've seen the falls, Doc. The body would have been crushed on the rocks at the bottom of the plunge pool. Umiak River runs fast for thirty miles. It might take weeks before the body washes up, if it ever does. This is hunting country. Pretty rough and isolated."

Walker couldn't fight his anger any longer.

"Damn it, Gerrie. I told you the psych ward was a sieve. I told you all, and you let Hatfield walk right out the door, free as a bird! And Billy died as a result."

Gerrie frowned and looked hurt. "That's harsh, Doc. I don't have any say in how Laramie Mercy handles its security systems. I talked to Dr. Lannister and Sheriff Dubois, and voiced your concerns about their security measures. They both gave me a load of guff about how their protocols met the highest standards required by state health and penal codes. Yada, yada. In effect, they told me to shove it. What else could I do?"

"I don't know, Gerrie. Go over there and knock some heads together? Fulton Hatfield was *your* prisoner. Your responsibility."

Gerrie's jaw jutted as she gritted her teeth. "You think I don't know that?"

Caspar leaned forward and grabbed Walker's forearm. "Pull your horns in, Doc. Recriminations ain't helping. We can hash over who did what and when another time."

Walker knew he was being unfair to her, but Gerrie was three hundred miles away and could take his tongue-lashing.

"I should have forced the issue, but I was too keen to start my new life."

"Come on, Doc," Gerrie said, passing over his accusation. "You can't blame yourself. This is the hospital's fault, not yours."

"I'm not blaming myself, I'm blaming Dr. Lannister and your Sheriff Dubois." Walker took another settling breath. He needed to regain some control, but it had already slipped away. "Hatfield was delusional. Psychotic. Suffered a complete break from reality. Last I heard from him, he was calling down seven demons from hell to smite the world and flay the heathens. And you know he included me in that group. He was a danger to anyone he came into contact with."

"Is that why the notebook spooked you so much back at the house?" Caspar asked.

Walker ground his teeth and took another moment to think things through. Losing control would get him nowhere. Maybe he *was* overreacting.

"Yep, but I guess I panicked over nothing. Our house-breaker must be a different guy."

"Notebook?" Gerrie asked.

Caspar cut in. "It's nothing, Gerrie. Something we found at a … crime scene."

Gerrie wiped the sweat from her lips with the tips of her fingers and cast a glance at the sky. The picture flipped to show a fractured shot of Gerrie's booted feet and then returned to her face. "Sorry, I'm on the trail to the river. We had a call. Somebody spotted something in the water. I'm hoping it's Hatfield's body. Then I'll be able to draw a line under this sorry case."

"Tell that to Billy and Mary Anne, Gerrie."

243

Walker regretted his remark the moment it left his mouth, but he was too angry to retract it. Although Billy had died as a result of police and medical negligence, no amount of deflection could absolve his responsibility. His reluctance to stick around and finish the job he'd started played a massive part in the boy's death, and the guilt weighed heavily.

Caspar eyed Walker and turned the monitor toward himself. "Will you let us know what you find at the river?"

"Sure thing, Sheriff Boyd. Tell the Doc I'm sorry for ... everything."

"He knows, Gerrie."

Caspar hit a key, and the light from the monitor dimmed. Walker scrubbed his face with in his hands. Something still irritated the back of his mind, but he couldn't put words to the feelings.

Maxine knocked and entered the inner sanctum. She held up a book-sized computer tablet. "I found some of those references for you. Mainly Old Testament fire and brimstone. This one's kind of interesting, though." Maxine slid a finger across the screen and started reading. "Matthew 13:42, '... *there will be weeping and gnashing of teeth.*'" She touched the screen again. "And this one, Numbers 14:12 says, '*I will smite them with pestilence and dispossess them.*' Hell, Doc, whoever wrote this is seriously upset."

"What about that one from Deuteronomy?" Walker asked, an ominous feeling flooding over him.

Caspar frowned. "Why that one in particular?"

"It had those upside-down crosses all around it. Stood out a little more than the others."

Maxine worked the internet. "There are two verses. The first reads, '*You shall be blameless before the Lord your God,*' and the other one says, '*The Lord your God will raise up for you a prophet like me from among you, from your countrymen, you shall listen to him.*'" Maxine curled her upper lip. "That's nothing. I've heard worse from Pastor Robbins, and his sermons have them packing the aisles."

244

Dread worked its way into Walker's bones. It twisted and ground its way through his defenses.

Caspar stared hard at Walker. "Doc, what's wrong? You look worried."

"Last time I heard him, Hatfield was spouting those same words. Claiming to be a prophet bringing the word of the Lord to the heathen multitudes. Blaming his kids, and me, for all the world's woes."

"And?" Caspar asked.

"Gerrie still hasn't found a body."

"You think Hatfield's still alive?"

"Yes. I do. Someone—it had to be that Nurse Chambers—told him where to find Billy and the girls. Chambers is Dr. Lannister's pet Rottweiler. He had my details and he met Josie and me. Oh hell, Josie!" He leaped up, snatched the phone from Caspar's desk, and dialed a number from memory.

"What's that about Josie?" Caspar asked.

She answered on the second ring.

"Caspar?"

Walker closed his eyes.

Thank God.

"No, Josie, it's me, Chet."

"About time you called. I was going to send out search parties."

Walker smiled and gave Caspar a relieved thumbs-up. "You haven't had any strangers in the diner this afternoon?"

"Funny you should say that. We did have one guy come in. Strange fellow. We called him the Preacher."

Walker's world stopped.

"What? What was that?" He almost shouted the question.

"Chet? What's wrong?"

"Who was this Preacher? What did he look like?"

"Average height. Skinny. A little stooped. Cuts on his neck, like he'd shaved with a blunt razor."

"Oh God. How long ago, Josie?"

245

"I don't know. Maybe ninety minutes. I gave him a sandwich. Poor guy looked half starved."

"Is he there now?"

"No. He left about an hour ago."

"Which direction was he headed?"

"He asked the way to the medical center. Said he needed a doctor for a prescription. Oh!"

"What's wrong?"

"He's out there on the street right now. Heading this way. Looks weird—"

"Josie, it's Fulton Hatfield! Get out of there. Lock the door."

The sound of shattering glass and Josie's scream tore down the phone line and sliced through Walker's heart.

Walker dropped the phone and ran.

Chapter 27

Josie Donoghue

The watery autumn sun fell toward Tooth Mountain and foretold the onset of evening. The pine needles remained dark green, as they would throughout winter, but the sporadic clumps of oak and aspen had already started to change color. In a couple of weeks, a month at most, the glorious patchwork of orange, yellow, green, and brown would give the view through the diner windows an even more spectacular backdrop than it did right then.

Of all the seasons, Josie loved the bitter-sweet romance of fall—or as Chet sometimes called it, autumn—best of all. The fresh air, the high winds, and the last few intermittent warm days made preparation for the long winters almost bearable.

Josie had finished mopping the floors and put away the cleaning stuff before cashing up the till and locking the day's takings in the safe. She should have walked the money around the corner to the night depository at the bank, but that could wait until morning. She didn't want to miss Chet's return—if Caspar Boyd ever let him go. What on Earth did the LSPD want with him now? An accident at one of the construction sites? A brawl where the combatants needed stitches and bandaging?

She smiled at the idea of her Chet ministering to the sick and the infirm.

Four years ago, if anyone had told her she'd fall hopelessly in love with a long-haired, sweet-voiced stranger, and that he'd give up the traveling life for her and become the town's medic, she'd have laughed in their faces. Yet here she was, the strong, self-contained, cool-headed Joey Donoghue—Chet's Josie—waiting for him and wondering how she'd ever lived without the gorgeous man.

Times change. She'd changed. He'd sworn to return to her as a doctor and, he'd made good on his promise.

A darkly shining SUV rolled past the front window, headlights blazing, picking up the glittering grains of glass embedded into the asphalt. She couldn't make out the driver in the dark, but whoever it was tooted the horn and Josie waved back in acknowledgement. Lucky Shores, the name now reflecting the good fortune she and Chet had brought back, was a good place to live. A good place to work. A good place to bring up a family.

She'd give him five more minutes. If he didn't call by then, she'd head to the house and wait for him there. Darn it, he'd have to learn to say no once in a while, or she'd have to learn more patience. She could do that. She'd been patient for eight years, waiting for Daddy to return, and four more waiting for Chet. So much wasted time, but … heck no use crying over the sadness any more. She'd cried enough in sorrow, now she'd maybe shed a few tears of joy.

Her Chet was back!

While waiting, she tidied storage units beneath the counter and found the old wooden baseball bat she'd used for defense in the days when she worked the diner alone. The bad days when the town nearly went under after they'd robbed the *Savings & Loan* and Daddy took the blame.

She smiled at the memory of Chet's arrival in town. Abe Dunleavy, the one-time bully, had picked a fight and Chet had made short work of him, forcing him to his knees. She'd raced around to help with the bat in her sweaty hands, and Chet had recoiled, thinking she was about to hit him with it. As if she'd ever do such a thing. They'd laughed about it afterward, but at the time, the hurt in his eyes when he thought she'd mistrusted him upset her even then. She'd known him less than an hour, and already they'd built a connection. They'd both felt it even though it had taken her three more days to admit it, even to herself.

Dang, here she was, sounding like the dizzy heroine in a romantic movie. She patted the light brown bat and left it where it was—on top of a pack of paper napkins.

She turned and set the water to boil. The first thing Chet would ask for after greeting her with a tight hug and a warm kiss would be a large cup of coffee. Lord, the man could knock back the coffee. The first time he'd set foot in the diner he'd drained five large cups—black, no sugar.

Not that she'd make a habit of waiting on him hand and foot. Oh no, that would never do—theirs was a partnership of equals—but for his first few days home, she'd make a special allowance.

Five minutes passed without sign of her errant doctor.

"That's it, buster," she told the cooling kettle, "you'll have to make your own darned coffee."

As she always did, Josie cast a final glance around the diner before locking up. Front of house looked good. Chairs on tables, floor washed, spotless and dry. The serving counter, too, met her exacting standards. Stainless steel surface polished to a high sheen, food cleared away, food display cleaned and ready for the breakfast setting.

She collected her coat from the back room and headed for the front door, cinching the belt tight around her waist.

The phone rang.

"About time."

She rushed to answer it, but the number of the display showed the LSPD, not the medical center. She picked up the handset.

"Caspar?"

"No, Josie, it's me, Chet."

Josie saw her smiling face in the mirror above the sink. Did she really look that dopey every time they spoke? If so, what did he see in her?

"About time you called. I was going to send out search parties."

"You haven't have any strangers in the diner this afternoon?"

He sounded serious. What had he gotten himself tangled up in this time, and why was he asking about strangers all of a sudden? Her mind wound back to the soft-spoken, glassy-eyed man spouting Bible verses.

249

"Funny you should say that. We did have one guy come in. Strange fellow. We called him the Preacher."

"What? What was that?" He shouted across her words.

"Chet? What's wrong?"

"Who was this Preacher? What did he look like?"

She described him and he asked for more details. She told him that Preacher had left about an hour ago, heading for the medical center. "Said he needed a doctor for a prescription. Oh!"

Movement through the front window caught her attention. A dark figure, white-faced, wild eyes, lips bared to expose stained and crooked teeth.

"What's wrong?"

"He's out there on the street. Heading this way. Looks really weird—"

"Josie, it's Fulton Hatfield! Get out of there."

The man's arms raised above his head as he rushed forward. The door smashed open. Glass shattered and fell in a starburst to the floor.

Josie screamed.

Chapter 28

The Shattered Diner

The three-mile drive into town in Caspar's Chevrolet Tahoe was the longest in Walker's life. Caspar had refused to let him drive and sat behind the steering wheel staring hard, looking grim and determined. Walker screamed at him to hurry, but the lawman kept the speed just the right side of suicidal.

The Chevy—warning lights flashing—bounced and slid down the road, flying around hairpin corners, sometimes on two wheels. Still too slow for Walker's needs, he kept shouting for Caspar to, "Pull your finger out of your Goddamned ass." His mind brought up images of his brave little Josie trying to fight off the bony fists and swirling arms of a murdering madman.

Even before his meltdown, the wiry Fulton Hatfield had spelled danger, but he'd been no match in a fist fight with a strong man. Back at the rundown pig farm, Walker had made short work of the man, but Walker was an experienced fighter. Josie wasn't. Although feisty and brave, she barely tipped the scales at ninety pounds. A flyweight up against Hatfield's middleweight.

It would be no contest.

His Josie. God. What would he do without her?

The Chevy's tires lost grip, they slid and clipped the safety rail on the outside of a curve. The road dropped sheer away, ending in the boulder-strewn valley floor two hundred feet below. It bounced back, four wheels settled on the asphalt, and the Chevy lurched forward once more.

"Come on, Caspar. Floor it, man!"

He tried ringing the diner again but picked up nothing but a busy signal. Sweat slicked hands turned the cell phone into a bar of wet soap, but it still creaked under his crushing grip. Walker's heart rate climbed to the mountains. He wanted to scream, but that way led to madness.

What was happening down there?

He'd only just arrived in town and already Josie was in danger, fighting for her life. Why did this keep happening to them? Damn it. All he wanted was to settle down and live in peace with Josie as his wife, and … and …

If he lost her now that everything had fallen into place, what would he do? How could he survive? Josie needed him and he'd left her alone to face that monster.

Hell.

Salt tears stung his eyes. He wiped them away. He had to hang tough, hold himself together. Tears could come later, if Josie …

He twisted in his seat and glanced behind. The blue flashing lights of Maxine's Ford filled the rear window, more than two hundred yards behind them. Caspar had made good time, but Walker needed more.

"Hurry, Caspar. That madman's got Josie."

"I know, Doc. I'm flat out here. Try Jean Hallibone. She's got a hunting rifle."

Walker dialed the guest house. No signal.

Useless Goddamned cell phone!

An array of red brake lights flashed below them. A truck! Slow moving. Taking up the full width of the narrow road.

Caspar's right hand shot out long enough to activate the sirens, and then returned to its fight with the steering wheel. The howling wails cut through the night, screaming out their wild ululating warning.

They reached the eighteen-wheeler in seconds, but with no room to overtake, Caspar had to jam his foot hard down on the brake. They slowed to a painful crawl.

Walker lowered his window and stretched his body half out of the car. "Move, damn it," he screamed. "For God's sake move over!"

The Chevy's sirens wailed. The red and blue lights flashed, picking out the oval MLDC decal on the trailer's tailgate. Canvas covering the load flapped in its slipstream. Caspar flashed the Chevy's headlights and pulled the mic from its hook. He flipped a switch on the dashboard, and hit the talk button.

"This is the LSPD. Pull into the next passing spot!"

Caspar's words boomed louder than the sirens and echoed off the cliff face. The truck edged into the middle of the road but ignored the first emergency passing place.

"Goddammit! Pull over!"

The truck's brake lights flared. Caspar's foot hit the pedal, the Chevy slowed, but the truck crawled on. Their speed fell to an excruciating fifteen miles per hour. Caspar allowed a gap to form.

A left-hand curve gave Walker a side view of the truck's cab. The driver stuck a fist out of his window and gave them the finger. Walker lowered his window, leaned out as far as he dared, and screamed, "You asshole. Move the hell over!"

Walker had never felt so helpless.

Caspar threw the mic into a cup holder in the central console and hit a button on the dash. A red "Sport Mode" badge lit up. "I'm gonna have that guy's license," he growled, jaw set. "Give me a distance countdown to the next safety cutout."

Still hanging halfway out of the window, one hand gripping the grab strap, the other clutching the spotlight anchor, cold wind whipping his hair and stinging his eyes, Walker watched for the countdown markers.

"Five hundred yards," he yelled. "Just after the next left-hander."

Caspar silenced the sirens. Allowed the gap between the Chevy and the truck to widen slightly, giving himself a run-up.

"Three hundred yards!"

They eased around a left-hand hairpin. The centrifugal force forced Walker against the doorframe, and he nearly lost his hold on the spotlight anchor. The cold numbed his hand, but he refused to let go.

"One fifty!"

253

They reached the left-hand curve.

"Go. Go. Go!"

Caspar floored the throttle. The Chevy shot forward to the right—edged closer to the rock wall. Walker ducked back into the cab. A fraction of a second after he let go, the spotlight hit rock, the anchor strut snapped, and the unit shattered on the road behind them. Glass flew and metal clanged.

Walker braced his hands against the dashboard once again and clenched his jaw.

"Fifty yards!"

The gap between the cliff face and the eighteen-wheeler was less than four feet. The Chevy needed six and a half, maybe more.

They weren't going to make it!

Caspar feathered the throttle. Timing was key.

"Now!" Chet screamed.

The trailer passed the emergency cutout. The cliff face receded. The gap widened.

Five feet …

Six feet …

Seven …

The Chevy slipped between rock and canvas, nothing to spare. Another wing mirror disappeared. Caspar stamped on the throttle, shot past the truck, and made it back onto the road mere yards before the cutout became a sheer granite wall.

The eighteen-wheeler fell behind, Maxine's lights forming a red and blue halo at its back. Walker studied the driver. Shaggy dark hair, bushy beard, glasses, lips peeled back in a snarl, missing front tooth.

I'll remember you, buddy. God help you if we don't reach Josie in time.

Caspar activated the sirens again.

"Maxine's got a good memory for license numbers. We'll impound it tomorrow and tear it apart. Asshole," he growled.

"Thanks, Caspar. That was tight."

Way to go with the understatement, Walker.

254

Caspar pushed the Chevy around the final turn. Orange streetlights glowed and Big Lake stretched out in its silver majesty. They'd reached the outskirts of town. The road straightened and flattened out as they reached the valley floor. Caspar pushed on, and their speed increased. Eighty miles per hour in a thirty zone, lights and sirens clearing the way for them.

Main Street ended in the T-junction. Cars and pickups yielded at their approach. Caspar yanked on the emergency brake, screamed the Chevy into the ninety-degree, left-hand turn, and squealed onto West Boulevard. The engine roared as the Chevy picked up speed out of the corner.

Fifty yards. That's all. Please be safe. Please be safe.

People. A handful of them. Standing outside the diner. Staring at each other, talking. Walker slammed his fists on the top of the dashboard.

"Why aren't they helping? Where's Josie?"

Caspar jammed on the brakes and the Chevy juddered sideways, blocking the road. Blue smoke billowed out behind them and the cloying stench of burning rubber reached Walker's nostrils. He jumped from the Chevy before it stopped.

"Move," he called, barging his way thought the crown. "Get out the bloody way."

A big man scowled. "Watch it, buddy!"

"Move!"

Walker jabbed him, stiff-fingered, in the kidney. The man grunted and doubled over. Walker side-stepped past him before he could recover.

The diner's fluorescent lights—so bright they dazzled after the gloom of the race—shone on a scene of destruction. Glass pellets hung from the metal door frame. Gravel-sized nuggets lay piled in a glittering heap on the welcome mat.

Oh God!

A body, dressed in black, sat on the floor, its back scrunched against the counter, right arm cradled tight to a narrow chest, its left leg stretched out straight, and its right knee bent into an inverse "K" angle. Walker grimaced. Although there was nothing

255

wrong with a knee forming a normal "K" angle, when it bent the wrong way, it presented a serious problem for the orthopedist tasked with rebuilding the joint. The patient undergoing the surgery and the subsequent rehab wouldn't exactly be having too much fun, either. Then again, Walker didn't give two hoots for Fulton Hatfield's discomfort as he sat, bloodshot eyes creased in pure agony, tears flowing, mumbling a stream of curses bald enough to make a sailor blush.

Such a crying shame.

Josie stood over the crumpled figure, tapping the head of a baseball bat in her cupped right hand. She glared at the newly crippled man, as though daring him to move so she could take another swing.

"Josie!"

Walker rushed toward her. She turned, raised the bat.

He raised his hands. "Easy there, girl. One home run is enough for tonight."

"'Bout time you got here," she said, a beaming smile stretching out on her beautiful face, "I was starting to get bored."

The dam holding back Walker's tears broke and he pulled her into an almighty hug. "Jeez, girl. You had me worried for a moment."

She felt so tiny in his arms, he eased off for fear of crushing her, but she squeezed back. The bat handle pressed into his spine.

"I tried calling, but you—"

"Sorry, honey," she said, talking into his chest. "I didn't have time to answer. Kind of had my hands full here, and the sirens told me you were on your way."

He eased a finger under her chin and lifted her head. Her dark brown eyes shone bright. So beautiful, so delicate. He leaned in for a kiss. She responded, and he tasted the salt of their mingled tears.

"I've never been so scared in all my life. If I'd lost you ... God."

"Don't be silly. That coward"—she loosened their embrace and turned to look at the broken killer—"is used to terrorizing scared kids, not grown women. He collapsed like a wet tissue after the first swing."

"The first swing? How many did you get in?"

She scrunched up her beautiful face. "Two good ones. After I smashed his elbow, I had to make sure he wouldn't get away. You can't run with a busted kneecap."

He sucked air in through his teeth and shook his head slowly.

"Heck, girl. Remind me never to annoy you."

"I will."

He kissed her teary eyes.

"Doc?" Caspar called. "This man needs medical attention."

"Call an ambulance and the Douglas Ferry emergency unit. We'll need a helicopter evacuation."

"Chet," Josie said, "are you going to leave him like that?"

"Of course not, but I can't move him without help. If I did that, I could do more damage. When the paramedics arrive, we'll stabilize his injuries and restrain him until the air ambulance gets here. He'll be better off at the Douglas Ferry Trauma Unit. That knee's going to require serious surgery and that's something I can't provide here." Walker leaned closer and whispered in Josie's ear. "Besides, after what he did to Billy and what he tried to do to you, a little suffering will be good for his immortal soul."

Hippocratic oath or not, Hatfield could wait. Walker wasn't about to rush to help a man who'd intended to kill his beautiful wife-to-be.

"What do you mean, 'after what he did to Billy?'"

"I'll tell you later," he answered and bent to kiss her again—the only way to shut her up. "Caspar, when you're done calling Douglas Ferry, the diner door needs fixing. You maybe want to contact that guy to board up the door? What's his name, Franny?"

"Manny. Manny Micklewhite," Caspar answered, reaching for his cell phone.

"That's right and perhaps you can send the bill to Laramie Mercy Hospital. I don't see why Josie should pay to make good after their screw-up."

"Ha! Good luck trying to get any joy out of that bunch of—"

257

"After I get finished with them they'll be begging me to take their money, just to shut me up. I mean, Billy's dead, Mary Anne's alone, and this sorry asshole tried to hurt Josie. Someone's got to pay, right?"

Josie tugged on his arm. "Chet, don't worry. The diner's insurance will cover it and I'm okay. Billy's dead?"

He nodded and gave her the shortened story, ending with, "I could have lost you, Josie. I don't know what I'd have—"

She stood on tiptoes and took her turn to shut him up with a kiss that almost drowned out Fulton Hatfield's ranting, but the words, "*He that commits fornication, sins against his own body,*" all but ruined the moment.

Walker broke the kiss first and looked straight at the old lawman.

"Caspar, if you can't keep him quiet, I'll straighten his leg and I'll forget all about the need for anesthetic."

"*Marriage is honorable ... the bed undefiled, but whoremongers and adulterers, God will judge, ye!*"

Caspar tapped Hatfield's bad leg with the toe of his boot. The injured man screamed.

"Darn it," Caspar said. "I'm terribly sorry, sir. Didn't see you down there. You'd best be quiet. Wouldn't want to jog your leg again, now would you?"

Maxine arrived, but stayed in the doorway.

"Everything okay, Sheriff?" she asked, staring at the stricken man on the floor.

"No problem here, Deputy. Ms. Donoghue made a citizen's arrest and clearly used reasonable force to defend herself."

Maxine pursed her lips and nodded her considered agreement. "Looks that way to me, Sheriff."

"Did you see the cretin in the eighteen-wheeler?"

"Sure did, Sheriff. Captured the whole episode on my dashcam, too. Pulled him over at the bottom of the hill and took his details. I figured you and the Doc had it covered and wouldn't want me near any violence." She rested a hand on her bulge. "Driver's an out-of-towner working for the Consortium. Right

258

now, he's sitting in the back of my prowl car. I arrested him for dangerous driving and impeding a law officer in the performance of his duty. He's kicking up a storm, demanding his phone call. Said he's gonna set Bruce Steiniger on our asses."

"Steiniger?" Walker said. "Again? My list of people to 'talk to' is growing. I just hope some of them will need my professional services one day."

Josie leaned closer. "You've got a hit list already?"

"Sure have, and it's growing, too. Let's see now, there's, Steiniger, the driver of that eighteen-wheeler, Dr. Lannister and Nurse Chambers over at Laramie Mercy, and maybe the Laramie Police Chief, too." He shot Josie a grim smile.

"All that after less than two weeks in town?"

"I could always add Dr. Cornhusker. He didn't help any." Her grin cooled his anger and made him feel a million times better. "I'm sorry. This isn't the start I wanted for us."

"Me neither, but it's never dull, is it?"

She wrapped her arms around his waist, rested her head on his chest, and fit as perfectly as if they'd been designed for the interlocking position. In that brief moment, life was good again.

Maxine coughed. "Want me to move these people back, Sheriff?"

"Yeah. Clear a path for the paramedics."

Maxine turned to the onlookers in the street, arms spread wide. "Run along now, folks. Nothing to see here. We'll make a statement in the morning, and you'll hear it on the news."

The crowd shuffled a few paces away, but hung around, searching for morsels of gossip to spread over their breakfast cereal.

Caspar sidled closer to Walker and edged him to one side. "Doc, answer me one thing, will you?"

"If I can."

"Apart from the religious mumbo jumbo in the notebook, what made you so sure it was Hatfield who murdered Miguel Garcia?"

"Couple of things, Caspar. Remember the questions we had over his bedding? We wondered why he stayed so close to the

259

body and slept downstairs, in the front of the house. I didn't make the connection until I saw the map on the wall behind Maxine. The one with the black pin."

"What about it?"

"At the crime scene, it was pretty dark and I got turned around by the location, but the map showed me the house had a perfect bird's eye view of the diner. In fact, it's just about the *only* place in Lucky Shores you can see the diner from without being noticed."

"You mean—"

"Yeah, Hatfield was spying on Josie and me. Biding his time. I'm betting when you look into Miguel Garcia's activities immediately before his death, you'll find he was inspecting the houses on that development. Maybe that's how he ran afoul of Hatfield."

Boyd nodded slowly. "Okay, makes sense. As I said earlier, Doc. You'd have made a damn fine detective."

Two paramedics appeared from nowhere. One, a young man, carried a collapsible metal stretcher, the other, a middle-aged woman who struggled with the huge medical bag dangling from her shoulder. They pushed through the crowd and entered the diner.

"Bernie Radley!" Walker said.

The woman looked up at him while her partner closed on the patient. "Dr. Walker! As I live and breathe. I've been on vacation since before you returned. This is my first night back. Been looking forward to seeing you again, but"—she glanced at the pile of glass chippings on the floor—"maybe not like this. How you doing?"

"Better than this creature," he said, nodding to Hatfield and adding a sneer. "Where'd you come from?"

"We're based at the Fire Station these days. The town needs full-time paramedics since the construction started. What happened?"

"He complained about the coffee and Josie took offense."

Josie stepped away, but Walker took her hand. He wasn't going to let her out of his sight. Not for a while.

Bernie's bright smile lit the room. "It figures. Joey Donoghue always did have a fierce temper."

Josie stretched taller. "Now just you wait a minute—"

Bernie let the medical bag slide from her shoulder. "Take it easy, darlin'. We're joking. The sheriff already told us what happened."

Caspar added his voice to the discussion. "I'm surprised you rushed over. I did say we weren't in any hurry and you could finish your coffee and donuts."

Bernie winced as she rolled her shoulders. "Unlike you cops, we don't spend our lives cramming junk food and sodas into our faces. Now, let's see what we have here." She cleared some broken glass with her boot and knelt beside Hatfield, on the opposite side to her partner. "That Louisville Slugger of yours sure packs a wallop, hey Joey?"

"Way I hear it, Ms. Donoghue could have played Varsity Ball, if she'd had a mind," Maxine said, grinning proudly from the doorway.

"And made pro, if I'd been a boy," Josie said, levering her hand free of Walker's. She stood on tiptoes and pulled his head closer to whisper in his ear. "Your phone call gave me enough time to reach the bat. You saved me again. I love you, Chet Walker."

He wrapped his arms around Josie's waist and hugged her gently, pulling her off her feet and planting a wet kiss on her neck.

"Glad to be of assistance, fiancée of mine."

She scrunched her head and shoulder together and wriggled away. "That tickles. Put me down this minute!" she squealed, pushing against his chest.

Suitably abashed, he lowered her gently to her feet and tried to release her completely, but she took hold of his hand and held it firmly—her signal for him to stay close. Not that there was a need. Walker had no intention of straying far.

Josie tugged out the wrinkles he'd made in her polo shirt and turned to face Caspar and Maxine. "And talking of coffee. How about it?"

"Yes please," they both said, with feeling.

"Decaf for me," Maxine added, rubbing her bump.

"Coming right up."

"Hey, Doc," Bernie said, looking up from the floor, smirking. "Are you planning on canoodling all night, or can we expect you to do some doctoring while you're in town?"

Walker peeled off his sweater and tugged up his shirtsleeves. "Both. I don't have my med kit with me. What analgesics do you carry?"

"Demerol and morphine sulfate."

"In that case, give him an intra-muscular injection of Demerol. Fifty milligrams will do. Give it a couple minutes to take effect and then we'll straighten that leg and immobilize it in an air cast."

Bernie nodded. "Sounds good to me. You'll sign the papers?"

"Will do," Walker and turned to Bernie's partner. "Did you find anything else?"

"No, sir. Some swelling at the elbow and upper arm, but no open wounds. The femur looks intact, but that knee ..." The young man sucked air between his teeth and tilted his head. "He's in shock, rambling."

Hatfield's glazed eyes rolled back into his head and his mumbling continued, but lower in volume.

"Vitals?"

"Heart rate's one twenty-three. Blood pressure's one forty over ninety-five. Slight tachycardia and hypertension, but nothing unexpected for a man with these injuries. What do you want us to do first?"

"Lean him forward and strap his arm tight to his chest. After that, we move him onto the stretcher, hold him in place, and then—pop and crunch!"

The color drained from Caspar's face. He swallowed hard and strode to the doorway. "Maxine, find out what's happening to that helicopter and clear these people right away. This ain't no TV game show."

Josie made herself busy with the coffee-maker. Maxine shooed away the crowd. Caspar stood in the doorway, facing into the diner, not taking his eyes from his prisoner, but avoiding looking at the treatment.

Walker looked at each paramedic in turn. "Ready?"

They both nodded. Walker took a deep breath and leaned in close.

Again, Fulton Hatfield screamed.

Chapter 29

A Beautiful Evening

Walker nodded into the cellphone.

"Sure thing, Gerrie. I'll be there."

He returned the handset to its cradle. Three copies of the *Lucky Shores Times* sat on the hall table ready for collection by Aunt Jean's paying guests. Above the fold, the headlines screamed:

> ***"Joey Donoghue Survives Murderous Attack.***
> *Doc Walker Sheds Tears of Joy.*
> *By Anton Poulson, your eyes on crime."*

Walker grinned. He'd already read the story. Two days after the event, he'd had time to process the information and come to terms with the facts. He couldn't have done anything different. Poulson, the cub reporter, had hyped up the tale into a half-hour deadly chase followed by a ten-minute fight worthy of a Hollywood blockbuster. He'd included phrases like, "baseball-bat-wielding terrier," and "in a life and death struggle for survival." For Walker's part, Poulson had turned out, "mad dash down Main Street," a "near death battle with a runaway truck," and, "screams of rage and agony."

Poulson would have to wait a little longer for his Pulitzer, but he'd at least gotten the basic facts right. Names, dates, times, locations, all accurate, all verifiable.

The journalist had even tried a doorstep interview with the two of them, but Josie had claimed traumatic amnesia, and Walker had cried off as being a witness for the prosecution. As a result, Poulson had followed the path laid down by investigative reporters over the centuries—he invented details that made for good copy and sought out eyewitness accounts. The power of the press knew no limits.

Walker pushed through the front door and joined Josie on the veranda. She sat on the swing, feet tucked under her pert backside, wrapped up tight in one of Aunt Jean's luxurious Native American quilts, staring out over the lake. She'd refused his offer of wine and sipped from a glass of iced tea instead. The starlight on the water shimmered and danced, with barely a breath of wind to ripple its surface.

"Who was that on the phone?"

"Gerrie Hoover over at Fort Wycombe."

Josie frowned. "What did she want?"

"They've set a date for the inquest into Billy's death. Next Thursday."

"And you've been called to testify?"

"Of course."

"Have I?"

"Nope. They're happy to accept your written statement. You weren't really involved in Laramie. Your time will come during Hatfield's trial."

She shuffled across to give him room. He slid beside her and draped an arm around her shoulders.

"Have Dr. Lannister and Nurse Chambers been called?"

"Yep, along with Sheriff Dubois, and the chief administrator of Mercy Hospital."

"I'll come with you."

"You really want to?"

"Sure do. I'm looking forward to watching them try to squirm out of their responsibility for Billy's death."

"Gerrie's expecting a full-blown media circus. Fox News is promising to send a crew and all the local media outlets will be represented, TV and press. This story is made for the gutter press. Incest, murder, a mad Bible-thumper. It'll be a feeding frenzy."

"Save your breath, Chet. You don't have a chance in heck of talking me out of it."

"Fair enough. We'll make a long weekend out of the trip. I'll have Marcy rearrange my clinics and call in a locum from Douglas Ferry." He squeezed her shoulder. "I never could refuse you anything."

She sat up and held his gaze, her expression serious.

"Is that true?"

"True as I'm sitting here looking at my future wife."

He leaned close for a kiss but she held him off. Was she finally going to tell him her secret?

"C'mon, honey. Out with it. What's on your mind?"

"What makes you think—"

"My darling girl. You've been putting off telling me something since you showed up at Fort Wycombe."

"You noticed?"

He gave her an old-fashioned stare. "Well? What's the problem?"

"I ... I don't know how to tell you." She broke eye contact and tucked in her chin. "I'm worried you're going to hate me."

"That's never going to happen. You might exasperate me at times, but I'll never hate you. Come on. Tell me what's wrong."

She looked up through tear-filled eyes. "I've been trying to pick the right time to tell you, but what with everything that's happened ... and then Hatfield arrived and you had to spend the night in Douglas Ferry. And then there were the statements and cleaning up the diner. We've barely had a moment's peace since your return. There's no easy way to tell you ..."

"For goodness sake, girl. Tell me. Please."

Her lower lip trembled and the tears fell. "I ... I'm pregnant."

He smiled. "Yes, I know."

"You ... you know?"

"Of course. I suspected the first moment I saw you in Gerrie's office, but I've been certain since the night in the cabin."

"How?"

He shook his head slowly. "I'm a doctor, you silly thing. If I can't spot the early signs of pregnancy, I'd have to go straight back to med school."

Walker wanted nothing more than to laugh and shout and howl at the moon, but he held himself in check for Josie's sake.

"Why didn't you say anything?" she whispered.

"Why didn't you?"

"I've been terrified. Didn't know how you'd react. I hated the idea of you thinking I'd done it on purpose, just to trap you."

"You silly, silly girl." Tenderly, he cupped her cheek in his hand. "How do you feel about it?"

"Me? I'm terrified and … ecstatic. For heaven's sake I'm carrying our baby. What … what about you?"

"Josie, I've never been more delighted about anything in my life." He jumped up, leaned out over the veranda railings, and screamed, "We're having a baby! I'm going to be a dad!"

A couple he didn't recognize, out for an evening stroll, waved and shouted their congratulations.

"Thanks," Walker said, still beaming. "Wonderful night for a walk."

"It is, Doc. It surely is."

Walker turned, picked Josie up, and spun her around and around. They both laughed hysterically. Millie barked in confusion and danced around their feet. Walker only stopped spinning when he started feeling giddy. Carefully, he returned Josie to the swing and wrapped her back up in the quilt.

"Does anyone else know?" he asked.

Josie, flushed and breathing heavily from the laughter, shook her head. "Only the girls in the diner, but the whole town probably knows after that ridiculous demonstration."

"I mean, have you told your Aunt Jean?"

"Of course not. I wanted you to be the first to know, after Nurse Cortez, of course. She'll be my midwife. The girls in the diner guessed, but I swore them to secre—"

"Are you and the baby healthy?"

"We're fine, Chet. Blooming."

"I can see that. You've never looked more beautiful. So, let me work it out. Last time you visited me in Baltimore was early

August. So you're due in early May. Fantastic. If it's a girl we can call her Frances, after your mother."

"And if he's a boy?"

"Michael, of course, in honor of your dad. After all, if not for him, you and I would never have met."

"Love you, Chet Walker."

"Love you too, Josie Donoghue." Walker rested his hand on her slightly rounded belly. "And this little one, of course."

The End.